Cover design: Jeffrey Brett

For more information, please contact:

Jeffrey Brett at magic79.jb@outlook.com

ISBN: 9781549552984

Leave No Loose Ends

Introduction

Jason Phillip Chancery sat grinning smugly to himself at the rear of the classroom occupying what was considered by his peers as the privileged corner desk where he felt exuberantly jubilant at the sudden change in his personal circumstances. Changes which had taken him by surprise and not yet settled the adrenalin flowing through his veins. Not in the remotest of dreams could he have envisaged such a transformation of fortune where Jason had gone from being the low-life of the class to an unexpected hero and esteemed individual.

He neither cared who liked him and who didn't. The mood of opinion had altered so swiftly that it had not only affected Jason, but all those around him. What had started with the usual harassment, bubbling to boiling point and expanding with intimidation had ended in confrontation and a violent skirmish. A coming together of opposites during the mid-morning break which had been battled out before the clouds above had time to pass on by or the events below reach the attention of the lone teacher on duty in the school yard. Most significant however, in the few minutes that had seen the change, had been the presence of so many witnesses, leaving them astounded and stunned.

The unfortunate victim, a renowned bully both in and out of school had finally met his match. When the brief confrontation was over, it wasn't just the loser's pride that had been dented, but the boy's body as well. Victory on the other hand had left Jason Chancery confident that there would be no return match or future retribution.

Scouring the faces that peeked back at the corner desk Jason gave the occasional nod and acknowledged their apprehension. Even one or two of the girls dared to look. Physical altercations, scuffles and fights were part and parcel in these parts and a way of life, but none in the class had ever witnessed such a cool, calm underlying intention. Jason's defence had been executed with precision, the stealth of his hands, clenched with arms extended had landed each blow with unwavering dexterity. Finally the years of bullying, torment and derision had come to an end. It was unfortunate that only Alex Machin suffered that morning as others skulking, hiding in the crowd were equally as guilty and should have been likewise punished.

Continuing to smile Jason suddenly realised that the verbal taunts regarding his masculinity had also ceased. The girls dared not look below his beltline, warily maintaining eye-to-eye contact where they felt they had safety in numbers, yet none wanted to be alone with him. As the chalk scratched the surface of the blackboard, the atmosphere inside the classroom felt charged, almost alive. For the first time in his life Jason had the upper hand, it was a moment that would mould his future.

The teachers mouth continued to open and shut as the lesson progressed with the ever present second hand circumnavigating the clock face as Jason began recalling the events of the past two hours starting with his customary walk from home, taking him through the dirt ridden

3

tenements, long winding alleyways and crossing over barren patches of grassy wasteland that the authorities prided themselves upon, inappropriately calling them the green expressions of the community. In stark reality however, they were the battlegrounds where the local gangs lay in wait for unsuspecting victims, pouncing when the opportunity presented itself, relying upon their reputation to strike a chord of fear through the heart of the victim before they assaulted and robbed, safe in the knowledge that none would dare go to the police.

For more years than he could remember Jason had run the gauntlet every morning and afternoon with Alex Machin and his gang targeting the loner as their main element of fun, persecution and taunts. On many an occasion his stomach had gone without food where they had stolen the few coins lining his pocket, until today. Wisely he had left a few minutes earlier than usual and managed to avoid the daily ritual, although convinced that come the first lesson break they would be waiting for the opportunity to make up for lost ground.

Holding back the build-up of pressure in his bladder he had squirmed in his seat until the bell had sounded and ended the lesson. Jason was first out of the class and across the school yard to the outside toilet block where unzipping the front of his trousers he sighed loudly as the thin veil of steam began to drift upward, using his free had to steady himself on the white tiled surface. He looked down and watched the flow continue as it burst from his body with the force of a fireman's hose feeling the pressure ease from his shoulders. It was only when he heard the tell-tale scrapping of rubber soles on the toilet block floor that he suddenly tensed again. A stiffened finger jabbed emphatically through the fabric of Jason's blazer and stabbed him between the shoulder blades, causing him to turn and see to whom it belonged.

'We missed you today Chancery. In fact if I didn't know better, I'd say that you were trying to avoid us!' Several grunts of support came from the doorway, where the escape route was blocked.

Swinging around and away from the wall, going to his right Jason held onto his penis taking with it the expulsion of urine. Like a spray caught by a sudden breeze the fluid arched and landed on Alex Machin's trousers, turning the fabric a much darker colour. Machin and Jason opened their mouths in unison as they looked at one another, whilst shrills of laughter and taunts exploded from the doorway. Jason saw Machin's fist ball and turn white as the grip intensified.

'You fucking ignorant under developed spawn... you've just pissed all over my trousers Chancery. For that... I'm gonna bust you up real bad!'

Jason Chancery however was no slouch, for years he had been ducking and diving out of the way of his father's fists. Tucking his penis inside his trousers he suddenly kicked out straight and caught the underside of Alex Machin's knee taking the bully screaming down onto the wet floor as the cartilage gave way. Jason was the first to react recognising that he had the advantage as he charged at the boys blocking the doorway, where to his surprise they stepped aside too shocked that their leader had been put down so easily. Before leaving the entrance he stopped only to zip up his fly before casually walking back out into the school yard.

The blood curdling shout from Alex Machin instantly attracted all nearby as he ordered Jason Chancery to stop walking and remain where

5

he was. Somebody yelled out 'fight' and a crowd started to swarm across the yard. Amazed that Chancery had complied, Alex Machin was even more astonished when the boy that had just pissed all over his trousers, turned and faced him out. The gauntlet had been laid down. Forming a circle the spectators jostled for the best view.

The teacher on duty that morning and there to prevent such encounters saw the gathering of pupils as they swelled the circle, but above the melee of heads he found it impossible to see through to the centre. It was only when Alex Machin handed his blazer to another boy that he recognised the premeditated signs. Taking a sports whistle from his pocket he put it to his mouth and sent a series of short sharp shrill signals to the staff room above, sending mugs of coffee and half-drunk tea clattering down onto convenient tables and stools as adults ran from the room to offer their assistance where trying to forge a path through the crowd stood firm.

Those closet could see the determined look in Jason Chancery's eyes. They were set low and menacing like that of a bull about to be slaughtered, only the nose wasn't flared nor did it emit any snorts of anger. When Alex Machin baited the onlookers, revelling in his own importance they watched and waited for a reaction, surprised, but not disappointed when it came, only from whom it was delivered.

'I'm gonna fucking kill you Chancery... you ugly little bastard. You struck lucky twice back there in the bog, but it won't happen again. This time I'm gonna take you down real fast and make sure that you don't get

up. When the school nurse finds what's left of you, she'll call for an undertaker, rather than an ambulance.'

Alex Machin drew back his fist and launched himself at Jason Chancery, but Jason neatly side-stepped the onslaught and caught the side of Machin's ribcage with a skilful low punch. The older boy gasped as the breath exploded from his lungs. He instantly rounded on Jason trying to save face, but the loner was ready. Leading with his left hand he smashed it down centre of Alex Machin's face feeling gristle and bone give way beneath his clenched fist. Immediately Machin cupped his nose as blood seeped through his fingers. Her tried to talk, but couldn't. A loud cheer erupted just as a solitary face came to the window two floors above where the headmaster who despised either boy, observed the altercation. His only emotion, the surprise as to who was winning the battle.

Suddenly the tide of power had changed. With one final strike Jason kicked the injured bully in the groin putting him down onto the cold and hard surface of the yard, where he would stay until attended to by the nurse. Whistles coming in from all directions began parting the crowd as pupils bunched and drifted away. There was a rule, however that all observed, albeit inside or beyond the school gate. It mattered not who had taken part, it was always the pupils against the teachers. None that day would give up the name of the victor, only the loser would face the consequences and the wrath of the headmaster watching from his office.

When Scruffy Jones the Maths teacher reached Alex Machin, he felt no sympathy despite kneeling down by the injured boy. Justice as far as he was concerned had at last been served. The math's teacher saw the face

7

watching from the upper level before it disappeared, but he neither shook his head nor indicated that it was serious, Machin could suffer until the nurse arrived.

Looking absently at the blackboard Jason Chancery rubbed gingerly his knuckles below the desk feeling the tenderness beneath the skin where he had hit Alex Machin. He felt different, not exactly elated, not even victorious just different. He smirked to himself accepting that he now had the will to answer back, to challenge the opinions of the many child specialists and juvenile psychiatrists that he had been forced to visit. Some might have even patted him on the back and called the moment in the toilet block and the school yard a defining moment of real progress, but others would see it differently, as a turning point, not good, but seemingly bad.

One day Jason Phillip Chancery would banish the demons that had persistently haunted him. One day he would show the world that he had the strength of both body and mind to fight all that opposed him. Alex Machin had been the first victim, but there would undoubtedly be others, of that Jason was resolutely sure. From this day forward the misery that he had endured throughout his childhood would be reversed. From now on the tables had started to spin the other way and many would come to experience the true reality of fear.

Chapter One

Lucetta Tate sat resting her elbows on the desk top tracing the crease of her lips with the tip of her finger as she mused over the photographs lying before her. The image of the main feature bore a grainy resemblance to the man she believed to be her prime suspect. From what she could determine, his build and stature both lean and wiry, almost begrudgingly athletic had hardly altered with age, but without a full facial recognition making a positive match was never going to be easy. Jason Chancery was shrewd, astute enough to conceal his face whenever a camera came lurking above a shop doorway, a lamppost or concealed behind an opaque dome of glass. It infuriated Lucetta, even annoyed her that Chancery smiled knowing that at some time she would end up with an image taken from the recording.

She leaned back on her chair and instead drummed the desk top. Like always Jason Chancery was toying with her. Sitting opposite Charlie Bright, an inept weatherman with a very inept surname looked across seemingly bemused by her preoccupation.

'Anything worth my expert eye cogitating over? He asked.

Lucetta or Lucy as she was more commonly known throughout the office shook her head.

'Nothing of interest that would warrant your time Charlie.'

She picked up the image that she considered had the best definition of pixel enhancement, noticing that Charlie was still watching.

'At least, nothing that a storm front could help predict.'

Suddenly disinterested and reminded that his job was to scan the meteorological charts Charlie averted his gaze back to the screen in front of where he sat. He sniffed, then replied as always getting in the last word.

'If my predictions were that creditable, I wouldn't be sitting here in this dingy office, but as you ask I foresee black clouds looming around four this afternoon with rain imminent soon after.'

A voice from the other side of the office shouted over.

'Yeah right... and if the Pulitzer Prize should suddenly land on my desk Charlie, I'd believe in the tooth fairy too!'

The comments, grunts all around showed their support for the reporter sitting in the corner. Charlie didn't respond.

Lucy however peered over the top of the photograph. Charlie was never down, always smiling and normally had an answer for everything. Some believed that he'd been born on a cloud that had a silver lining, although envy ran high throughout the office where a good scoop could carve a decent notch on the side of your desk and do your career wonders.

She rubbed the underside of her nose and wondered about her own position. Long hours and thankless pursuit, chasing down leads that often hit a brick wall was all part and parcel of being a journalist. In a way she envied Charlie. He made his predictions, calculated from what he saw materialising on the screen then told the public what they wanted to hear. If he got it wrong the only rumblings of dissension that he'd encounter would be at the bar in the local pub. When the sun shone next, all would be forgotten and forgiven, whereas if Lucy or any of the other slipped up it could be costly. An undisclosed amount on a cheque, a public apology and one of Charlie's dark clouds that could linger over your career for some time. The scales tipped heavily in Charlies favour. Life was black and white in journalism, without any recriminatory or forgiving grey bits. Charlie scrapped his chair back and got up.

'Would a coffee help?'

Lucy smiled and shook her head, she had already consumed too much caffeine that morning. Charlie made his way between the desks jovially ignoring the banter as he made his way over to the small kitchenette.

Taking a magnifying glass from her desk Lucy swept the lens up and down trying to make the image come alive, but Jason Chancery refused to look up at her. Down the years she had gathered as much on him as she could by whatever means, sometimes not always quite above legal. When she put down the glass disc the one thing that had always shouted back at her from anything she received on Jason Phillip Chancery was that he covered his tracks, leaving nothing to chance.

Chancery was a strange individual, unpredictable and yet very much like a panther. Meticulous as to his habits and the way he stalked his victims, rarely seen as he emerged from cover, coming fast and with stealth, unaffected by anything legal.

She watched Charlie spoon in three heaps of sugar, concerned about his diabetes when she noticed the dark mark showing through the cotton back of a shirt belonging to the reporter nearest to where she sat. Grabbing the magnifying glass Lucy scanned the image once again, only this time she knew what she was looking for. This time she saw the small dark line on the back of his hand, knowing that the tattoo went up his arm and ended on the bicep. It was the tail of a serpent where the head was hardly ever seen. Lucy reached for the receiver and tapped in the number. Waiting for the call to be answered at the other end she continued to drum her fingertips on the images recalling certain facts that she attributed to the family.

Born to parents, Mary and Phillip Chancery, Jason had survived a long and arduous birth that had presented both mother and the nurse certain complications. Without the intervention of others the infant would not have made it through the night. The experience had left Mary Chancery barren, internally damaged although very happy to have a son at last. The problems however, did not end there. The difficulties had affected Jason physically, disturbing the natural balance of his growth pattern and some professionals made comment, part of his brain, although it was never diagnosed exactly which part. In later years the growth of certain parts of his anatomy would become the butt of many jokes, jibes and torment. Emotional torture that would make him a recluse and shunned by both boys and girls.

Like Charlie's forecast a dark black cloud hung over the boy well into his teenage years. Lucy had read a good many official and some unofficial reports on Jason Chancery, but she had never known about the fight with Alex Machin in the schoolyard or what changes had been brought about that day because the headmaster had not documented the event. Had it been recorded, it would have helped a great many, not least the psychologists, the police and Lucy. Not that they would have been sympathetic, but they might have at least understood. However much

Lucy knew or continued to learn, one discerning fact bore true and that was that Jason Chancery was part of her life whether she liked it or not. At night she would sometimes see his eyes watching her from somewhere in the bedroom, his dry pock marked skin moulded around a pair of hauntingly black irises that did nothing but stare back. She was trying to ignore his stare when the receiver at the other end was picked up.

'Hello... Crusader Newspaper. Penny Schuchel speaking.'

It had always puzzled Lucy why Penny had never escaped the cobbled coastline and ventured further inland to the much brighter lights of the metropolis, where journalist opportunities were greater and the pay substantially better. The Crusader was small in comparison and stifling. Penny had once lamely argued that it was because of her loyalty to the people of the south coast and to her overweight editor that she had stayed.

'Hi Pen... it's me. I got your package, thanks!'

'It was the best I could manage, was it any use?

'I have been going over the photos and I am almost certain that it is Chancery, although he always manages to avoid looking up at the camera. It's like he has an inbuilt radar that detects anything technical which will record his image. If I didn't know better, I'd say that the devil looks out for him.'

A muffled chuckle crackled down the line. 'I am really sorry Lucy. I know that they're probably not the best quality and I would have got in closer,' she hesitated 'only there's something about Jason Chancery that makes my skin crawl.'

Lucy shook her head. 'You did right Pen. Chancery is so unpredictable and has an agenda all of his own, especially towards females. Without back-up it would have been foolhardy to have got that close.'

Lucy hadn't let anybody know, colleagues, family or friends that on more than one occasion she had been very close, either watching or stalking. In Brighton Penny Schuchel felt the goose bumps creep up her arms.

'I would hate to be that close to him!' she said.

'Since our last call, have you given thought as to why he was down your neck of the woods?' Lucy asked.

Like she was flicking through her notepad Penny Schuchel gathered together her thoughts.

'Nothing absolutely concrete, only Brighton rocks at the best of time with locals and grockles filling the streets, clubs, bars and shops. There's always something splashed across the billboards to highlight the attraction. Ordinarily Brighton's the place to be unless of course you encounter a monster like Chancery.'

She looked at her arms where the pimples had laid root under her skin.

'I don't suppose that he's here for his health or the fresh taste of our salty sea air.'

Sitting himself back down Charlie nodded and resumed looking at the screen, occasionally peering up at the sky outside. Optimism or pessimism, it was hard to determine which.

'It might help if you could send me a list of all the events that have taken place during the past week or are going ahead during the next seven days. We might see something jump out that would take his fancy. Whatever has drawn Chancery to the area, one thing's for sure and that it that he never stays long.' Lucy ended the request, not wishing to add, unless it's long enough to inflict some kind of havoc.

'There is one event that stands out,' Penny added 'Sienna's managed to get herself through the prelim heats of the beauty contest and she's representing this area in the regional heat.'

'Hey, that's great, be sure to give Sienna my love and best wishes. It will be like a walk in the park and she'll win.'

'I'll pass it on, although she's still a bit nervous in front of an audience. It's the leering men she can't stand, but most of the proceeds go to charity and she's always up for a worthy cause. I have to say that I couldn't bear parading around half naked in front of a lot of men that I didn't know listening to their whistles, explicit remarks and drooling tongues.'

As they talked Lucy typed in the details of the pageant, waiting only seconds for the results to start popping up. It was the magnet that would certainly draw Chancery down south.

'I don't suppose that it's enough to go to the police with?' Penny asked.

'No.' It was a reluctant reply, although Lucy's mind was already going into overdrive. 'Their gut might tell them in which direction they need to go occasionally, but acting on a hunch from a reporter is hardly likely to have them jumping through hoops. Chasing imaginary shadows won't do much for the interaction between the police and the press.' Lucy changed the direction of her conversation.

'I'm pretty busy just at the moment, but what say that the three of us get together the week after next. I'll hop on a train down and we could sample some of that good food that you're always going on about before hitting a club. It's about time that I dressed up in my glad rags and let my hair down?'

She saw Charlie look up as he raised his eyebrows, but Lucy had worked around men long enough to know how they should be handled. She blew him a kiss then averted her attention back to Penny.

'Cool. I'll let Sienna know. She'll be thrilled to see you again, me too of course!'

They ended the call exchanging customary goodbyes as good friends do, before replacing the receivers.

'If that was a male at the other end, then I'd say he was a lucky fella.'

Lucy grinned. 'Girlfriend actually from Brighton way.' She licked the tip of her tongue across her lips and looked up at the sky. 'Don't look like rain today Charlie.' Picking up her mobile she walked over to the kitchenette to make a private call.

'Henry Hurst.'

The respondent was official and seemingly abrupt, but it was what Lucy was used too.

'Henry, its Lucetta Tate. Can you do lunch today?' She didn't wait for the reply, but instead added a prompt 'ordinarily you know that I wouldn't be so demanding, only today I've a hunch that what I bring to the table could be of interest to you!'

Henry Hurst, Head of Criminal Intelligence at Snowdown Hill Police Station tapped his fingertips as he checked the calendar on his screen. She heard him suck in the exhale.

'Lunch is good. Normal place?' he asked.

'Normal place. Shall we say twelve thirty and like the times before I'll pick up the tab?'

Henry confirmed that he would be there, then replaced the receiver. Lucy checked her purse before going to visit the cashier's office, for once the petty cash tin could take the strain.

It wasn't customary to give away a valuable lead, but Jason Chancery was no ordinary lead, Lucy had seen the havoc that he could leave behind and it wasn't pleasant nor unforgettable. She grabbed her coat and left the office knowing that she could be letting the chance of a good story go begging, but knowing that she had a duty to protect the public as well.

High above the rooftops of the office blocks the sun continued to shine casting long shadows down over the road, pedestrians and pavement. Whether Charlie was proved right or wrong a storm was almost certainly brewing, only it would come in the form of a human cyclone, wreak death and destruction then leave as though it had never been there at all.

Chapter Two

Jason Chancery sat unaccompanied on the wooden bench almost directly opposite the main entrance to the Grand Emperor Hotel watching as the possession of taxi's regularly despatched their fare before heading back to the station concourse where others were waiting.

Adjusting his line of vision he made sure that his eyes were barely visible beneath the overhanging peak of the baseball cap. The peak served to diminish the glare of the sun and helped disguise his interest in the arrivals, although there was one in particular that caught his attention more than any of the other woman.

The beauty pageant wasn't the main reason why he had come south and found himself in Brighton, but the draw of the advertising dotted about the front of shops windows and billboards had invited his presence. He watched her climb the stone carved steps then disappear under the safety of the hotel entrance.

When the moment felt right Jason casually crossed the road falling in step with a cute freckle faced auburn blonde that had momentarily averted his attention away from the previous attendee. Neither she nor the hotel employee manning the door took much notice as Jason followed her up the steps. He smiled to himself, he knew her, had seen her the previous day, only as yet he didn't know her name. Locating a quiet spot in the crowded foyer he removed the cap and ruffled his hair as he watched the freckled face approach the reception desk.

It had been strange although entertaining how the woman had engaged unwittingly in the game of cat and mouse as they had dodged one another, diving down the maze of alleyways, ducking into shop doorways and hiding in between the odd market stall, trying to outwit one another. Whenever she thought that he had not been looking she had raised a pocket camera and snapped off a shot, and with each photograph daring to get that much closer. He wondered if she was a plain clothes police officer, but there something about the way she operated that allayed his concerns. The young woman didn't possess the confidence of a stalking operative, she instead seemed apprehensively hesitant, almost jittery as though as any moment she would skulk into a doorway then never emerge again, using a rear exit that she knew. It had been an interesting interlude to an otherwise boring day, although he was keen to establish her identity.

The game had ended abruptly when she had virtually leapt in front of an approaching taxi, hailed it down, jumped into the rear compartment and ducked out of sight as the vehicle went on by. If she had been the police she would have fronted him rather than scurry away like a frightened rabbit. He watched her walk away from the reception desk and go down a descending corridor to the rear of the hotel. Jason was about to follow when his way was suddenly blocked by a young female in a uniform. She had a name badge pinned to her waistcoat.

'Are you a paying guest Sir, or a member of the press?' she asked.

Jason flashed a quick smile, grabbing the opportunity that had been so easily presented to him.

'Press. Although my garb might suggest otherwise,' quickly excusing the way he looked 'I was enroute to another assignment when I got diverted to cover the pageant.'

He expected her to ask for some identification, but she went back to the reception returning seconds later with a badge.

'Use this...' she suggested 'it will prevent any awkward questions down in the conference room.'

Jason smiled longer this time as she helped pin the badge onto the fabric of his jacket. This was as easy as taking candy from a baby. He thanked her as she went away to mingle amongst the crowd, asking their intentions. Near to where he was standing a stuffy faced woman in her mid-fifties remarked to the man standing with her that the standards of the press were plummeting beyond any acceptable level of personal pride. He remembered her face in case their paths should cross again in the future. Arriving at the pavement outside a highly polished limousine came to a halt as the mayor embracing his gold chain stepped out to be greeted by the hotel manager. All eyes turned towards the dignity as Jason slipped down the corridor to the conference room.

Cautiously pushing open the door he noticed that the atmosphere in the room had already been set with the lights dimmed and the set dressed. At the back of the room a small bar was open and swerving drinks to members of the press that had arrived earlier. The barmaid gestured that Jason approach where she offered him a complimentary refreshment.'

'I would take it if I was you sir... the management of the Grand Emperor don't give away much, so grab it whilst it's free!' Jason took a wine and helped himself to a handful of salted peanuts.

'What time does the pageant begin?' he asked.

She looked at clock on the far wall. 'In about twenty minutes or once our mayor, Jack Thorpe has seated himself. I doubt that the old bugger would miss the offer of a free drink.' She topped up the bowl of peanuts. 'Thorpe has a prime seat in the front row so that he gets to be in all the photos and where his press secretary believes he can endorse his support of the pageant, unofficially it's because our mayor is a lecherous old git.'

Almost on cue the door opened and in walked the mayor accompanied by the hotel manager and an entourage of hangers-on. Jason found a seat at the back where it was dark and less conspicuous. Scanning the seats ahead he easily spotted the cute auburn blonde, she was nestled amongst a group of men with cameras and notepads. As the room began to fill he wasn't surprised to see that nobody chose to occupy the row where he sat. There was something silently intimidating about the man at the back.

When the lights dimmed completely a solitary spotlight illuminated the centre of the stage moments before the compere, a man in black tie and tails took up his position behind the microphone. He slickly rolled off a greeting to the mayor, dignified guests and the audience, nominating the various charities that stood to benefit from the pageant proceeds. When it was complete a drum roll introduced the first contestant to a boisterous cheer from the males in the audience. Jason saw the compere whisper to the woman telling her to ignore the whistles and remarks, as hotel employees issued warnings to any large numbers of men.

One by one the women paraded over to the microphone, did their bit then stepped back to wait in line as the next contestant appeared. When the woman that Jason had watched get out of the taxi and climb the stone stones stepped onto the stage he instantly saw a likeness between her and the auburn blonde sitting amongst the reporters. He saw her give an acknowledging wave at the contestant. The cheer and applause for Sienna Schuchel was much louder than any of the previous contestants, although none showed their disappointment.

Standing beneath the spotlight the difference between the two women was almost identical. They had the same freckles, nose, eyes and figure. Either one could have been in the pageant, but each had chosen a different career path. Jason now understood why the reporter had been following him around Brighton the day before, the only consideration that went through his mind was why. He had never encountered her before, but she seemingly knew him, or was is the case, that she knew of him. Perhaps there was another source that had tipped her off. It was something that he needed to know. Whatever the reason Brighton was turning out to be much more interesting than he had given it credit.

The compere obliged by telling the audience her name and that she lived not two miles from the grand emperor in a small hamlet known as Amerton Wick. It received a substantial cheer. Nobody noticed the man sitting alone smile. The naivety of people never failed to amaze Jason, they always failed to recognise the importance of privacy, risking all by giving out personal details, information that they normally kept secret and guarded with their lives. Like his mother had once warned him, always be on your guard with what you say, do and leave behind because you never know when it can come back to haunt you. Sound advice only there was no telling just how many nutters roamed the streets of the mainland.

As Sienna Schuchel lined up with the other women Jason decided that he had seen enough, he grabbed a handful of peanuts, winked at the barmaid then slipped away from the conference room unseen. Standing at the bottom of the stone steps he breathed in hard, filling his lungs with the salt air coming in off the English Channel. He asked a passing stranger the direction of Amerton Wick then promptly ambled off in that direction. It was a pleasant temperature, not too hot nor too sticky for the two kilometre walk and just right for taking in the sights along the way.

Chapter Three

Waking suddenly from a bad experience can be deduced as like being ejected without warning from something, some strange place or from persons that you know or have never met, where you desperately seek to uncover the outcome, only infuriatingly the finale disappears like an unresolved mystery. Dreams without an ending can seriously affect the brain too making us suffer punitively as we pitifully battle to thwart the apparent time warp that separates reality from our thoughts, dumping our bodies in a sluggish, catatonic trance, drained of all energy and desperate for additional oxygen to starve off the ever present yawning.

As I took myself over to the window for that extra mouthful I remembered through the haze going to bed sometime between ten and quarter past, conceding that both body and mind needed the resurgence of rest. At what point I actually closed my eyes and fell asleep was irrelevant, what however was significant was the time when I looked at the clock beside the bed which boomed back through a stark red illumination that after the counter changed from three twenty seven there would still be a good three hours left in which to sleep. Looking beyond the bedroom window the stars were still out and the hum of the traffic from the inner city limits was just audible.

I recall dousing the back of my throat with water from the bottle that I kept beside the clock, then being annoyed that I had to visit the bathroom having added even more to my bladder. I was too young to be concerned about interruptions during the night, but once awake it seemed a natural expectation. With the sound of the flush dying away in the background I watched a barge make its way towards Tower Bridge as I tried to fit together the pieces of my dream. Accepting that I could neither sense or reason for the scant bits that I could recall I went instead to the kitchen and switched on the kettle, there was little chance of sleeping whilst my mind was working overtime, maybe caffeine would help.

On the side were the bundle of papers that I had used that previous afternoon officiating in court number one, before the presiding judge Matthew Tiverton QC. I don't know I undid the string holding together the bundle, but I did. The case had been reluctantly won and whereas I should have rejoiced at the victory, I felt somewhat bitter. Had the result left my subconscious still battling between common decency and deceit, it was a possibility. To that end I hoped that my client was also suffering, although I very much doubted it.

Tiverton was good at his job, scrutinising every detail of a case, but his weakness was that he had a roving eye for a good looking lady. My client soon latched onto this flaw in his armour and skilfully made sure that the facts dented the wallet and pride of her ex-husband standing opposite her in the dock. Damage limitation was all she sought and the poor man knew it. For my part I could offer no help although I had wanted to give it. Soon after the clock hand struck four fifteen her bank balance had suddenly multiplied substantially and a defeated, broken man sat with his head in hands wondering at which point in his life he had been so foolish to have been involved with such a scheming siren.

Alison Forsythe-Trent's pouting red rouge lips and hip wriggle had throughout done nothing to raise my blood pressure nor accept her invitation to dinner where she intended celebrating her victory. My one and only rule was never to get involved with a client. I smiled as the additional oxygen blew in through the kitchen window and recalled as she had turned away rejected, but undented and undeterred unashamedly making her way across the carpark where she knew the judge had his car parked. I watched as she and Tiverton left the carpark scoffing to myself that another sucker had just been caught in the net. It was one case that I would not be fighting, whichever came beating at my door first.

Stirring in sugar for extra energy I took myself out onto the balcony, a haven in the centre of London where the view was amazing, the breeze refreshing and the peace priceless. I don't know why, but as I sipped the coffee I thought of Lucy, then my experience.

I suppose that somewhere around midnight I had been aware first of a light flashing over my eyelids, then the sensation that I was being touched. The lights I could account for living next the river, but the fingertips on my skin that was different. When I had opened my eyes it had discounted the scene that had presented itself before me. Like a spinning carousel the bedroom was full of light and moving figures, it was too easy to describe them as ghosts, but their spectral form was life-like except that for the occasional transparent limb. Ridiculously my first thought took me back to when I had read Peter Pan, but when the face came in close, either the boy had rapidly grown old or Captain Hook had come in his place.

Ignoring that I was naked beneath the sheets I had without resisting stepped forward, mesmerised by his presence and able to read his thoughts as he begged me follow him. How I ended up in a Victorian street attired, suited and booted in the dress of that era was hard to explain. What I did know was that I somewhere along the journey lost my travelling companion. The first thing that I noticed was the smell, which wasn't just grime, but a mix of stale, urine and excrement. From the buildings that I recognised I was near the old bailey, only I didn't recall the residential lodgings being in the area. I mingled with the crowd that seemed to have a purpose to their stride as they marched towards the end of the road.

Acutely aware of a buxom woman leaning out of a second floor window I stopped and watched as she launched the contents of a metal bucket down into the street ahead instantly receiving the threats and remonstrations of those below as they danced an awkward jig to avoid the sewage as it hit the cobbles. It accounted for the smell, the ale was obvious. In the gutter a part eaten dog was swarmed upon by a mass of swirling flies.

At the junction the march ceased as the crowd filtered left, right and centre where they jostled for the best view. Above their heads I noticed a wooden gallows. It looked fresh although from the many notches burnt into the top brace, it had been used many times before. I took my place alongside an elderly woman holding onto a young female child. In the crook of her free arm she held onto a woven basket of unripe fruit. The child who had saucer like eyes and gold coloured hair smiled up at me, her toothy grin appealing and full of mischief. I wondered who in their right mind would bring a child to such a horrific gathering.

When the door of the prison opened it was met by a tumultuous cheer as the prisoner was pushed forward and made to climb the steps. The guard helped embrace the cheering as he jabbed his baton into the condemned man's spine. Next came the priest, the warder and the executor, the latter masked in a black hood. I looked around and wondered if I could escape, but all around faces seemed to be watching me. Handing the young girl fruit from the basket the old woman asked if I wanted some as well. I respectfully declined to which she shrugged her shoulders and listened twisting her head to one side so that she could hear better with her good ear. I was amazed to see the attention that the young girl afforded the warder as he spoke, considering that this was not her first hanging.

'Behold the condemned...' he began, again receiving applause and cheers. It was worse than being at the theatre *'I give you Reginald Benjamin Pike.'* Although it wasn't necessary, he pointed at the face of the terrified as pieces of fruit flew through the air and hit the body of the man with the noose about his neck. The warder continued.

'Found guilty by a jury of twelve good and honest men Pike is hereby guilty of treason and theft against Her Majesty the Queen – our good and gracious Victoria. He is hereby sentenced to death by hanging and we trust in god to show mercy and spare his soul.'

As the priest crossed himself so did a good many in the audience. Although clearly disturbed by the gallows and what lie ahead I was surprised when the condemned man refused the hood to cover his face. I was even more surprised when he looked directly at me. It was the face that had been standing alongside my bed. No wonder I had lost his companionship enroute here. I called out to help, hoping that the warder would hear my cries, but the baying of the crowd was too intense and loud. I read his thoughts which were repeating themselves, constantly reciting the words *'I am innocent, I am innocent... I am innocent.'* I felt a hand grip my heart as the executioner made the gallows ready.

Between the wooden slats ahead I saw a heavy sack hanging to which a short length of rope was tied. Following the weave upward I noticed that the other end was tightly wound around Reginald Pike's ankles. It was blatantly obvious that if the fall didn't break the poor man's neck, the sack was there to bring about a successful conclusion.

A deathly hush descended throughout the crowd as the warder nodded and the executioner placed his strong hand around the release lever, then on the first chime of Big Ben as it struck eleven he let yanked it once and sent Pike down to hell. Rotten matter of all shapes and sizes clattered about the wooden hitting anything alive or dead. I felt a segment of fruit hit my cheek as I saw the priest shield himself with his bible putting himself before god as the warder ran for the steps. When the rope stopped twitching a loud and rapturous cheer went skyward. I saw the young girl clapping and wondered if her young mind had actually absorbed the full extent of what had just taken place. Almost as quickly as the crowd had gathered they dispersed like a football crowd returning home.

I kicked something as I too turned away and reached down to retrieve a newspaper, I folded the sheets and put it in my pocket. I was about to walk off when I felt a sharp tug on my arm. When I looked down the saucer eyed child was standing at my side. She tugged again getting me to bend down so that she could whisper in my ear.

'He was innocent mister!'

That said she ran after the old woman with the basket. The next that I knew was when I looked at the clock and it registered three twenty seven and I was back in my bed. The bedroom was as it had been when I went to bed and the only witnesses around to substantiate my weird dream, experience or whatever it was, were the stars beyond the window and even they could not justify my sanity.

Chapter Four

I had always mistrusted the meaning of *surreal* accepting that what concurred had appeared as part of a strange, unexplained dream, but the more I tried to break down the rationale of the experience and solve the missing link, the more inexplicable it all seemed. It wasn't until I discovered the folded newspaper on the hall table that I thought about doubting the truth.

Top right of the front page the date was clear, Friday the 21st day of February 1868. To make sure, I checked it out on the iPad although instinctively knowing before I tapped in the details that it would come back as genuine. Putting the newspaper back down on the hall table I took myself back out to the balcony where the open space helped me think clearly.

Mystics around the world, who knows perhaps the universe, concur that most unexplained events happen during the hours when one half of the world is without light and the shadows bear witness to what mysteries creep from beneath the rocks, the mainstay of our imagination. As a practising lawyer I dealt with fact only, solid proof that had been derived from what somebody saw, heard, smelt, touched or tasted. The five senses that we each possess from the day of our birth. Anything else was pure speculation and unless somebody could prove otherwise I was as sceptical as the next human being.

Resting on the metal balustrade I watched a police launch go by its searchlight undulating left and right which had me wondering what it was that they were looking for as I hoped that it wasn't another body. Just recently it had become trendy to participate in a ridiculously dangerous game of dare to challenge the unseen forces of the Thames swimming from one side to the other, in blatant disregard of the warnings notices and unforgiving undercurrents. Despite the tragic consequences of three drownings in the past six months the temptation to pit one's wits against the forces of nature still avidly persisted.

The media had been quick to label the challenge as the *'changing tide of adventure'* where I on the other hand looked upon it as a senseless waste of young life. So far the toll was three too many and a needless loss of life, losing out to the vice-like grip of the Thames which had been happy to end their futures and heap suffering on those left behind. The river was at the best of times mercilessly cold, but when the temperatures plummeted it would became deadly and should an unfortunate soul be caught between the banks they would only survive three to four minutes before hypothermia set in and sent them down to a watery grave.

Looking above the rooftops I wondered what it was about the current generation that they were so desperate to risk all and seek out such dangerous adrenalin rushes. If they weren't climbing ridiculously high structures and hanging perilously over the edge, they were surfing electrified trains or standing on top of the roof of a speeding car, like a crazed drugged up junkie, the sole purpose to obtain a decent 'selfie' to help soar their social credit rating up another million or more.

What happened to pushing the limits, only safely, getting the buzz from pot-holing, surfing the ocean and jumping from a plane with a parachute? There were times when I envied the young their energy and enthusiasm, but as I watched the launch stop and pan the searchlight to the starboard side I suddenly pitied them. I turned away not wanting to know what it was that they had found, one death during the night was already enough. Peer pressure had nothing with being surreal, death was real and weren't we supposed to be the masters of our own destiny, but how often did the force of others drive a lesser mortal to their death. Nothing short of stark madness.

I heard the toilet flush in the next door neighbour's apartment and realised that I didn't even know their names. A married couple, apparently professional like myself and yet all we ever did was nod in passing. I reflected that life was falteringly fragile and forever changing. The launch below turned off the revolving blue light as it turned back, its quest complete.

A light breeze from the east whipped up from the street below and touched me across the face as I gyrated my jaw feeling that my right cheek felt sticky. Placing the tips of two fingers on the skin I swept them down, then held them under my nose where I detected the essence of orange juice. It was only then that I remembered being hit by the segment as the trapdoor of the gallows fell apart and swallowed up Reginald Pike.

The dawn came creeping up over the rooftops opposite soon after five slowly rising as though an invisible hand was drawing back the sheets of the night. It was a welcome sight as I heard a car draw up below, stop and moments later a driver's door close. I was tempted to look, but knew before I did that it would be Giovanni arriving early to open the delicatessen-cum-coffee shop. A haven with a memorable aroma that none could compete with this side of the river. I heard the shutter concertina back heading for the shower. The coffee pot in the kitchen was now cold and the contents looked like deep sea oil. My stomach positively begged for an injection of fresh baked croissants and Italy's best roasted coffee beans.

By the time I hit the lobby on the ground floor I could already detect the aroma infusing the air outside having permeated from the caked vanes of the extractor fan set into the side wall of the deli. I had once asked Giovanni why he had never had the fan serviced or cleaned, but he'd responded defensively that the build-up of coffee particles added to the charisma of the coffee shop which helped draw in the punters from the four corners of the city believing that the aroma mingled with the bouquet of London and was an attraction to be explored. In my opinion he had lost touch with reality a long way back, London did not smell like an expensive perfume, but as long as he continued to arrive early every Saturday and start my weekend with croissants and coffee, he could believe what he liked. I sat myself down at the customary corner table where I could see the river in all its murky glory.

'Ciao Riccardo, how is work...?' he peered over the counter as I settled myself 'only you look lika shit!'

It was meant as a compliment, although laced with a hint of concern. Despite the shower I couldn't shake off the haggard look that masked the end of the week. As a partner in the firm Wilkinson, Quinn & Hemp the workload never eased, even though I now had on board Jonathon. We were a firm that prided ourselves on providing a twenty four seven service and with a wealthy client listing they regularly used it to its full provision.

'It pays the bill Riccardo!' I replied.

He scoffed as he checked around my cup to ensure that it was the best.

'You work too hard... sometimes you should leave time to play.'

It was richly disparaging coming from a man who hit the streets around five to quarter past, opened daily soon after and did a full day, sometimes going through until the same time in the afternoon with only Sunday's off so that he could spend time with his beloved wife Anna and take his family to church.

'As always my friend the baking smells of home which proves that the fan still works its magic!' I knew that Giovanni would cast an eye over to the wall where the aroma of the coffee machine below was coming to the boil.

'Si...si, it is like my Anna, it reminds me of my homeland and rounded with love.'

It was a parody to suggest that Anna was anything like big. She was in fact beautiful, slim and the complete mother. Giovanni was the envy of many men as the priest often reminded him. He switched on the radio in time to catch the half past news. It was still three hours till I met up with Jonathon and we took ourselves to the Grove Side Hotel to meet our client who had flown in especially for the meeting. Ordinarily we tried to avoid business meetings at the weekend, but this was important and the client had been insistent, so duty called as the fee would reflect.

Having filled my stomach and quenched my palate I took the newspaper from my pocket and carefully flattened the pages. Surprisingly it was in good condition for its age and having travelled forward in time. Like the deli and coffee shop it too had a distinctive smell, only the paper was laced what seemed like stale ale. Over time paper would age, become brittle and the print fade, but this copy had yet to suffer such fate.

The front page was about the forthcoming execution of Reginald Benjamin Pike and I could tell from the enthusiasm with which the reporter had documented the story that the public hanging was no ordinary punishment. Treason hit the headlines as much as a latter day celebrity being caught where they shouldn't. Scanning the page I noticed that certain bits were missing, information concerning the trial, which I assumed to have been a forgone conclusion, the opinion of the treasury to whom the paper mentioned as being the innocent party and most importantly what evidence the guilty had presented in his defence. Like most journalists they went straight for the jugular and gave the public the juicy bits ignoring the more mundane detail. An artist of the era had sketched the gallows and added some ghostly figures, a fitting touch to add more emphasis to the story. I had to admit that it worked.

Although I had shaved I could still feel the roots of new growth on my chin as I rubbed my fingers back and forth contemplating my next move. Investigation was a large part of our business, digging and delving, our efforts being conducted mostly legally, although occasionally we had to use other unorthodox methods by which to obtain evidence. I didn't need proof that I had been to Cheapside during the night, I had that in the paper and my sticky cheek, but moreover what I needed was some sort of spiritual help, something that could help identify why me.

I had never believed in things that went bump in the night and fictional hocus-pocus was the stuff of a writer's imagination where they introduced into a story a magical world of wizards, fire-breathing dragons and masculine heroes who rescued inept maidens from ghouls, ghosts and demons. Chortling at the sketch on the front page I reached for my mobile phone and scrolled down the listing, dialling the number of the only person to whom I thought could help. Waiting for a response I remembered the young girl with the old woman. How had she known that Pike was innocent, the finding out intrigued me. The call was answered just before it went to voicemail. The voice at the other end was low and husky, driven by sleep.

'This had better be worth it, whoever you are… otherwise I will come visiting and ram something blunt up your…' at this point I thought it best that I introduce myself.

'Really Lucetta Tate, presumably you was going to say where the sun never shines and yet if you peer above the covers you'd notice that the sun is already in evidence and promising to be a glorious day!' I heard her groan as her head thumped the middle of the pillow.

'If it was anybody, but you Quinn they would already be dead!'

Inept I know, but I couldn't stifle the chuckle that burst from my lips. I apologised, feeling envious that she was still between the sheets. I sipped my coffee to concentrate on the task in hand and not let my imagination wander. Thoughts that I had about Lucy could seriously affect one's health. She heard me replace the cup on the saucer.

'Have you called to invite me out for breakfast?' she asked.

I wanted to reply and say that the suggestion had merit, was temptingly suggestive and I could have kicked myself for keeping to the reason why I had phoned. I would store breakfast for another occasion.

'Unfortunately, I've a business meeting with Jonathon latter this morning otherwise I be seriously tempted to say yes. I've called because I need your help.'

She thumped air into the pillow and I wasn't sure whether out of frustration or she just needed a punch bag. Her response answered the question.

'You know sometimes Quinn, pleasure comes before business. As a top London lawyer, you have been known to miss the most fundamental of human needs.'

We had known one another since primary school when the teaching assistant had sat us beside one another during the mid-morning break, where from that moment in time we had formed a long and lasting friendship. If I was honest it was a special bond that neither wanted to break and we had always been there for one another, just not under the same roof. If I took time out to reflect, I would have to admit that there was just one final hurdle left to clear. It meant starting with a breakfast date and ending with breakfast the following morning. Before I could reply she continued, her tone less inviting.

'Go on Casanova, tell me how I can help, although I warn you that my rates are still the same, somethings don't change Quinn!'

The rates included a lavish meal, good wine and at my expense. It came cheap in comparison to what I charged my clients and the company was decidedly much more engaging, better looking and much more fun to be with. Lucy knew that I would agree whatever the terms. As a well-respected reporter for a large paper Lucy had earned her spurs through hard work and giving long hours to the profession. Success didn't come overnight.

'Do I need to add a disclaimer?' I asked.

'Only if you welch on the deal and remember that I know Matthew Tiverton professionally.' This time it was her turn to laugh as she rolled over. I had never thought to ask if she was alone, but I'd hoped that she was. 'So why the early call Quinn?'

I didn't elaborate, pan out the experience, but told it just as it had happened, when I had finished Lucy was silent for a few seconds and I was sure that I could hear the cog-wheels turning inside her thoughts. I wasn't surprised when she did speak.

'You know, experiences such that you have just described rarely occur. Nobody is picked at random and transported forward or back through time. There has to be a reason and a connection!'

Giovanni came overt topped up my cup then left silently seeing that I was engrossed in a deep and meaningful conversation.

'A connection, how exactly?' I probed.

'That's something that I can't tell unless we go through the encounter piece by piece and even then the connection might not be glaringly obvious.'

'So who makes the choice?' As soon as I had asked the question I realised just how ridiculous it sounded, but Lucy didn't knock me back.

'Now that's a question that's way beyond my scope Quinn, maybe beyond many others as well including Mama Maria, Lucy's grandmother, who it was reputed could communicate at a higher level than her grand-daughter. Perhaps you come off this time around with a better deal,' she reverted back the conversation to the meal, adding 'maybe just this once we should dine at yours rather than a restaurant. Diners might object to the topic of our discussion and bringing along the crystal ball is bound to freak them out!'

Of course I knew that Lucy making light of the suggestion, although in reality she part meant what she was saying. The use of clairvoyance was taboo in certain circles and amongst most religious denominations. Dining at my apartment overlooking the river sounded cheaper.

'It would suit me.' I agreed.

There was another pause as she thought through her agenda.

'I can't tonight as I'm working Quinn. Would tomorrow evening be good?'

As I'd already explained Lucy's professional dedication sometimes involved long hours, blood, sweat and tears. The long hours I could cope with, just not the rest.

'Tomorrows good, I've promised Alison and Stephen that I'd pop over for lunch, but I'll be back around four to four thirty.' Whenever the conversation with Lucy involved my parents I always addressed them by their Christian names rather than use their maternal titles. It was more habit than anything secretive or guarded, although I had known for a long time that my mother had designs on helping Lucy arrange our wedding.

'I'll get a taxi over so that I can drink only by then I'll be needing one. I should be there by five thirty, but until then do me a favour Quinn and bugger off as a girl needs her beauty sleep. I didn't hit the sack till the early hours this morning and I be out till late tonight. We'll delve into your dreams and the like tomorrow, who knows maybe we'll unearth your missing millions.'

We were almost done, but for some weird and uncharacteristic intention I hastily added. 'Be careful tonight Lucy, whatever it is that you're up too!'

Lucy almost cooed down the other end of the line. 'That was nice Quinn somewhat unusual, but nice.'

I heard what I thought was a kiss then the line went dead, which wasn't unusual, only that was how we always ended our conversations not believing in mawkish farewells. We had both agreed a long time ago that saying goodbye had a level of risk attached, a sudden finality that seemed misplaced and inappropriate. Friends however close needed to hear the comforting tones of that voice the next time that they rang or went visiting.

I raised my cup to proffer my thanks to Giovanni, wondering at the same time why I had mentioned that she should be cautious, especially as I had never done it before so it was a mystery as to why today should be any different. It was hard to say whether it was my heart or my head controlling my emotions. I watched the various boats going up and down the river, riding the tide. Like the mix of swirling undercurrents I felt that being at Newgate had changed a number of things in my life, not least my thoughts for Lucy, but that the experience had also served as a warning. To what extent and how relevant was yet to be unravelled.

Chapter Five

The walk to Amerton Wick was pleasant taking in the coastal path as it meandered in and out from the beach as the warmth of the afternoon sun overhead beat down on his back. The village, moderately sized for the area was easy to find and more rewarding for Jason at least was the unsuspecting generosity of the elderly lady that he came across who freely offered information with liberal ease. At the mention of Sienna Schuchel, the retired shop assistant, deemed the young woman as a local celebrity, her watery eyes awash with a distant memory of when she'd had a figure to equal the beauty queen.

When he left her dead-heading the flowers that were annoyingly poking through the hedgerow he smiled to himself, adding purpose to his stride armed with the fact that professionally the older of the twins worked as a veterinary nurse in a practice the other side of Brighton and domestically she shared a rented house with her sister, confirmed by the resident as a local journalist. Jason looked back before he turned the corner and observed the old woman kick the cut flowers under the hedgerow where they would mulch down and save her from bending. He doubted that she would even remember that he had stopped to talk to her. Sometimes age could be a bonus when the vulnerability of the elderly was brought into question.

There was every possibility that Sienna Schuchel wouldn't arrive home till later so Jason killed time by going to the local park where he could relax before paying the house that the young woman shared a visit. Lying on the grass the only sounds around were the birds twittering in the trees and a toddler playing in the fenced off area set aside for children her age. The mother who had her back to him watched her daughter from the bench where she was seated. He followed the exploits of the little girl as she flitted from the swings, to the slide and then the roundabout, going around and around using the amenities in a circulatory source of giggling entertainment. In a way Jason envied her happiness wondering where exactly his own childhood had escaped his younger years. It was like he had never enjoyed the freedom of innocence, but had instead endured the harsh reality of a brutal and dark upbringing, where his drunken father had dominated every minute of every day.

Lying with his hands supporting the back of his head he turned his attention away from the girl and her mother to the clouds overhead, where they drifted across the vast expanse of blue like a lost ice-cream in a sea of ultramarine oil paint. He liked the sky whether it was during the day or the night as it offered so many different mysterious possibilities, where the magic of what lie beyond would fascinate his imagination. As a boy he had dreamt of being an astronaut and zooming away from earth in a rocket, forever leaving behind the tiny house which he shared with his family and never coming back. Jason would have been content to transverse the universe exploring and discovering rather than cowering away from the constant threat of abuse.

The sudden presence of a dog, a black and white collie brought his thoughts tumbling back to earth as it playfully ran around where he lay, Jason sat up so that he could stroke its head. As a boy he had always wanted a dog as a pet, but his father had denied him the idea, stating that flea-ridden canines only ever passed the time eating, shitting and wrecking the house. At the time the argument could very well have mirrored the input that he himself injected into the home. He smiled as the collie continued snucking left and right licking the back of his hand. The owner a middle-aged man came over, puffing hard and desperate to regain control of his dog.

'Rory heel,' he ordered as the dog saw his approach. 'I am really sorry mate,' he excused 'the dog's only just turned a year and still hasn't mastered the art of obedience.' To evidence that his master was right, the dog wagged its tail and nudged low into Jason's arm once again.

'No problem,' Jason replied 'he's a lovely dog and really friendly, I would have liked one like him!'

Without being asked the owner sat himself down on the grass.

'Unfortunately, the local rescue centre is full of dogs like Rory. Seems that the Christmas spirit soon loses its appeal come the end of January and that when the kennels start to fill-up.'

'Just like some foster homes.' Replied Jason, although the actual meaning was lost on the other man. Jason recalling when he had been farmed from one place to another at the whim of the foster parents and social services. The man threw a ball for the dog to chase as he delved into his jacket pocket and produced a hipflask.

'Damn dog loves this place, is good around kids and it gives me some time to myself.' He took a swig of the contents, wiped the rim then offered the flask to Jason. 'Be my guest lad, it'll help put hairs on your chest!'

Jason laughed as he took the flask.

'You sound like you was in the navy?'

The man nodded as he watched the little girl come down the slide.

'Boy and man, I did twenty six years and loved every minute. Saw the world, said hello to a few ladies, but the good thing was that I only ever saw them the once.' He took another swig then passed the flask over again. 'Best thing about the navy was the adventure. You never knew what was going to happen next.'

Jason swilled the rum and felt it drop down his gullet warming his chest as it passed on by. He and the man had something in common, he normally only ever met any woman the once before he moved on. From seemingly nowhere another dog, a golden Labrador came bounding over to be greeted by Rory, within seconds the pair were chasing one another around the park like demented idiots. The man waved at a woman about his own age as she entered the playground enclosure to sit with the young mother.

'Daft bugger comes here around the same time every day to play with Rory, although he's a lot older so can't always keep up.' He kept watching the dog's antics as he asked. 'I've not seen you here around here before lad, you're not from these parts are you?'

Jason felt the hackles of caution rising on the back of his neck. He contemplated, had the ex-mariner left the navy to join the police, as he felt his left hand slide down the side of the rucksack where he kept his knife.

'No… that's right.' He responded. 'I'm from the north and a reporter. I came down early this morning to cover the beauty pageant. The editor wanted me to studying the competition as we've a local girl that's made it through to the big one in London.' It seemed a sound and plausible reason and had the man rocking his head as the old sailor considered the talent that was on show.

'Certainly beats anything interesting that I've been doing today,' he replied 'normally the closest that I get to a woman these days is giving one a wave from about fifty metres away.'

'I'd have thought that you'd have a wife around?' inquired Jason, but again the man rocked his head.

'I did, but the old girl passed away last year to the ravages of that damn cancer.' For a moment he seemed lost in some other place, he re-opened the flask and offered it to Jason. 'We should have one more lad, in honour of her memory!' Jason raised the flask and thought of his mother and instead he saluted her memory.

That done the older man struggled back up his feet, shook himself down and rolled his shoulders. 'Enjoy life and play it out to the full extent lad, only don't abuse it otherwise the bugger will come back and bite you on the bum. Rheumatism is a damn awful condition. So far it's got hold of ninety percent of my body, come first thing in the morning I can just about take a leak before I need to sit back down. It was nice meeting you and I hope that your editor is pleased with what you've seen.'

The collie owner wished Jason a good day then whistled for Rory to come to his side. He was about to leave when he suddenly turned having had a sudden thought.

'You could of course bolster your luck and get an upfront interview with the lass. She only lives around the corner from the park. It's a Georgian house with red painted eaves and a blue door. Patriotic looking place what with the white pebble dashed walls. Shefford Drive, you can't miss it as it stands out amongst all the others.'

Rory came bounding over as the lady exited the playground enclosure and called to her side the Labrador. Jason watched as the man and the woman walked towards the entrance together. He smiled to himself, the old sailor had narrowed the distance that he got close to any other woman. Like an old sea salt some habits never died, but were carried long on the crest of the next wave.

He watched them leave then turned his attention to the mother who was dressing her daughter in a small jacket. She produced a drink from her bag and knelt down until the little girl had regained her breathe. He couldn't remember his mother doing the same.

Chapter Six

Sienna Schuchel used the heel of her shoe to close the front door as she off-loaded her bag containing her outfits and make-up dropping them down beside the stairs. She should have come back to the house immediately from the pageant, but Penny had invited her out to lunch to celebrate her success. Fortunately, the ride home in the back of the cab had been a quieter affair and given her time to reflect upon the day so far. In three weeks she would be travelling to London to go through the whole process again, only next time on a much bigger stage and with a larger audience. Next time the television cameras would be there.

Coming out of the telephone box sited on the corner Jason watched the cab draw away and the young woman close the front door before he made his way down the cul-de-sac. The collie owner had been right in his description of the house, it did resemble a patriotic advertisement of red, white and blue, standing out amidst all the others. Of all the other drives there was only one vehicle parked out front, a general indication that most of the residents were still at work.

When Sienna Schuchel opened the door she smiled, but her expression changed almost instantly when she noticed the knife in Jason's hand. He barged his way in pushing her back into the hallway before she had time to call out and attract anybody's attention. Keeping the knife arched under her chin Jason kicked shut the door as he escorted the pageant winner through to the kitchen at the rear of the property. Taking the mobile that she had been holding he placed it down on the side and ordered her to sit on one of the stools. He came in close, real close.

'You're even prettier than when I saw you last.' He indicated, as he toyed with the tip of the knife, stroking it up and down her neck. 'Providing you keep quiet, we can have ourselves some fun before your sister comes home. What time should we expect her?' he asked.

Sienna gulped down the excess saliva. 'Whenever... it's hard to determine!'

'Depending upon what?'

'Whether, the editor asks for a re-run or a last minute scoop hits the news desk.'

'Or she needs to go snooping around the town, playing cat and mouse!'

Sienna looked bemused. 'I don't know what you mean?'

Jason shook his head as he undid the top button of her blouse then traced the line down. He ordered her to strip down to her underwear threatening to destroy her chances at the next pageant if she didn't comply. In no time at all Sienna was clutching her chest wearing nothing but her underwear as Jason licked his lips.

'What do you want?' she inanely asked, expecting the assault to begin any minute.

With his free hand he removed his jacket as he dragged her over to the fridge freezer, taking a bottle of wine from the shelf where it had been recorked the night before. He collected two clean glasses from the dishwasher and poured out the wine.

'To pass the time pleasantly together till your sister gets home.'

Despite the uncertainty of her own predicament Sienna's thoughts turned to that of her sister.

'And what happens when she gets home?' she asked.

Jason wiped his lips dry, the wine tasted bland in comparison to the old sailor's rum.

'That all depends on the answers she gives to some questions that I need asking!'

Sienna wondered what the man needed to know, but was shrewd enough to realise that pressing him further might only antagonise her own situation. What disturbed her more was the cool manner in which he seemed to float her around the kitchen selecting items of food from the cupboards, fridge and all the time keeping her close by his side, not quite touching her, but letting his eyes absorb every part of her body. He reminded her of a black panther where having selected its prey kept the intended victim waiting for the inevitable. Drinking the wine as ordered, she felt her senses numbing wishing that she had consumed more for lunch.

When the bottle was drunk Jason began fondling her, starting with her breasts then kissing and tasting the curves of her body as he savoured his lust upon her. Sienna looked up at the ceiling wishing and praying for it to end, wanting Penny to put the key in the door, but at the same time hoping that she didn't come home that night.

'I don't know how you endure the scum that whistle and stare at you?' he implied as he continued mauling her finding her lips where he clamped himself upon her mouth. When he let go she coughed and spluttered, feeling the trickle of blood where his teeth had caught the side of her mouth.

'Please...' she begged. 'Let me get dressed, I'll give you money, anything as long as you don't hurt me!'

Jason chuckled as he cut through the strap of her brassiere and tugged it from her body.

'Do the men in the audience excite you?' he asked, as he pulled her arms clear exposing her chest. He didn't wait for an answer as he buried his mouth over her nipple. When she didn't answer he looked up and demanded that she reply. Sienna shook her head through her tears. He was about to remove her knickers when the key at the door found the latch. He spun her around in front of him and placed the tip of the knife under her heart.

When Penny Schuchel saw her near naked sister pinned against a man that she instantly recognised as Jason Chancery she felt her heart sag down to the soles of her feet. She wanted to reach out for Sienna, but the knife was placed perilously close to her sternum. The terrified expression in her sister's eyes concerned her as much as Chancery did being in their house. Sienna wanted to shout out 'run' and protect her twin, but the sound wouldn't materialise in her throat.

'Please... don't hurt her!' begged Penny Schuchel as she put her handbag down on the worktop to show that she meant no threat. 'What is it that you want, only you can take whatever we have in the house?'

Jason whispered into Sienna's right ear.

'Very perceptive isn't she. Already she's pleading and offering in the same breathe. I wonder though if she's as accommodating as you Sienna!'

Sienna Schuchel hated him using her name so informally as though they'd known one another for years. She wanted to respond, but her resolve had abandoned her the minute the intruder had burst through the front door. She knew that Penny was the stronger, but hoped that she didn't hold out and make the situation worse. Jason made Penny Schuchel strip down to her underwear as he marched them upstairs to the bedrooms above.

With both tied to the bedhead and the footboard, stretched like they were on a medieval rack Jason had them exactly where he wanted them. Like the time before he warned Penny Schuchel that if she dared to call out, he would instantly end her sister's valuable trade mark. She nodded that she understood. Removing his jeans and sweatshirt he knelt between them.

'You followed me through the lanes yesterday... why?' He placed the edge of the knife between her breasts.

'I'd heard of you through journalist circles. I wanted to be sure that it was you.'

Jason cut through the strapping of her brassiere as Penny waited for a response. Unlike Sienna she saw no sense in trying to conceal herself.

'It's the truth... I swear!'

He pondered. 'Perhaps, although I have a deep mistrust of journalists as much as I have for police officers. You each have a knack of delving into matters that don't concern you.'

She might have fooled Jason had he not seen Sienna look sideways at her sister. A look that he had seen previously, laced with hidden values. As he toyed the tip of the knife over Penny Schuchel naked torso he sensed that she had not told all.

'And who was it that told you about me?' the question was always going to be asked.

Penny looked at Jason Chancery boldly staring back at him. Suddenly she wasn't afraid, he was after all just another human being, a man who other than a reputation and possessing a knife had been born with the same opportunities as she. The journey to the blue door downstairs might have taken different roads, but in the end life lasted as long as was destined. Penny believed that it went on somewhere else, perhaps different, but who really knew.

'A fleet street journalist.' She replied.

'A female journalist?'

She shook her head avidly. 'No... a male colleague.'

Jason ran his tongue up from her navel to her left breast as Penny Schuchel held her breathe desperately holding back the emotion to cry out.

'Whose name happens to be?' in one swift action he sliced through the thin fabric of her knickers and threw them to the floor beside the bed.

'Simon Harrison. He was employed by a paper called *The Outreach Chronicle*, only he left and took his trade across to South Africa where he became an editor.' Penny knew that if Chancery was to check out Simon, he would find a reporter going by that name, as they had studied journalism together at university along with Lucetta Tate. There was no way that she was however that she was going to give up Lucy, whatever the price, she just hoped that Sienna had not already done so and that Chancery wasn't playing them against one another.

Jason disappeared coming back into the bedroom with an iPad that he had found in the next room. He put in the details that she had given him and waited anxiously as the enquiry filtered through the search database. Moments later what she had said had been confirmed as the truth, but Jason was a suspicious man who had lived by his wits for longer than he cared remember. Her reply had been too glib as though rehearsed. He still had his doubts. Taking the knife over to where Sienna was laying, waiting, he sliced through her knickers and nestled himself between her splayed legs.

'So this Simon Harrison, who told him, because I've never come across him or any Outreach Chronicle.' He leant forward and ran the blade along the underside of Sienna's breasts.

'I don't know, maybe the police.'

'Nice try, but Harrison's forte was political journalism, not crime. Shall we have another stab at the truth?' To show that he meant to get to the truth Jason ran the edge of the blade down over the shoulder where it would leave a scar, despite the best surgeon's efforts, but wouldn't necessarily affect Sienna's chances in London.

'I can't tell you what I don't know... please don't hurt my sister. Hurt me if you have too!'

It was a brave and bold ploy. Jason admired somebody that showed pluck and courage under extreme stress. As a young boy he'd had to grow up fast and become a man much sooner than he should have, missing out on so much as it passed him by, the fun of his teenage years disappearing faster than the moon moving behind a dark cloud. Like the panther he instinctively knew that there was more meat on the bone. After raping Sienna he turned his attention to Penny Schuchel. Before he had finished with her she finally gave up the truth, her tears burning through to her soul as she gave him the name of Lucetta Tate and the name of the paper that she worked on.

The only fortunate escape, if it could be termed as such, was that she had always kept her address book at work in her desk rather than at home. Before he ended their lives the last thing that Penny Schuchel saw was the dress hanging on the wardrobe door, where she had left it after talking to Lucy. She had intended taking it to the cleaners, but realised that it would never be worn ever again, certainly not by her. When

Chancery cut their throats Sienna looked sideways and blinked once, just like when they had as they lie beside one another in the cot.

Using the shower he washed away any trace of their blood from his hands and body, knowing that the police forensic team would still find his DNA in the kitchen and bedroom. When he left the house much later that evening the first signs of smoke didn't start to permeate from the kitchen until he had turned the corner and could see the entrance to the park in the distance.

Some considerable distance away Mama Maria heard the silent screams of the departing souls as Sienna and Penny Schuchel ascended from the ashes. She felt a psychic connection, but could only think of her grand-daughter as she reached for the phone wanting to make sure that she was safe. When Lucy made the call to Amerton Wick she found that the line was already dead.

Chapter Seven

We spent an hour or perhaps a few minutes over with Angus McLeod discussing a company merger trying to make it not seem like a compelling takeover, but more a profitable union to keep all parties concerned happy. With a car waiting to drive him back to the city airport McLeod hastily expressed his thanks then left.

The agreement left us both feeling exuberantly jubilant so I offered to buy Jonathon lunch, but to my surprise he declined defending the denial by stating that his live-in partner was taking him out later to the theatre and treating them both to a lavish meal, therefore lunch might spoil the occasion. I sensed that he was reluctant to offer more information so didn't pursue the matter, but instead insisted that he join for me for at least one pint. It was a poignant moment to reflect as well that he had a partner where at the drop of a hat or in the whim of an idea they could just take themselves off to the theatre and enjoy a meal after. Jonathon's consideration for his partner's expectation's made me realise how much I was missing Lucy. I was tempted to call, but resisted the idea, not wanting to disturb her a second time.

As soon as we walked into the real ale house the connection with the old newspaper hit my nose. I breathed in hard smelling, tasting the air trapped inside the listed establishment. The plaque over the door was dated sixteen eighty nine.

'You got a cold coming?' Jonathon asked cautiously, taking a step back clear of any potential germs.

I shook my head. 'No, I was just making a link that's all.'

'With what?'

I took the newspaper from my pocket and carefully unfolded the creases. As usual Jonathon's enquiring mind lit up his eyes as he scanned the document.

'Is this genuine and can I touch it?' he asked.

I pushed the newspaper closer to where he was sitting, as he put aside his glass. When he held it up to the light I asked what he was looking at.

'A watermark signature. The print shop would invariably have incorporated a hidden design into the paper so that it could be identified as the real deal and not a copy. You'd be surprised at how unscrupulous printing houses could be as far back as a hundred years ago, maybe much longer and forgery, by whatever means has been around longer than that, ask the Egyptians only I'm sure that if they were alive, they'd back me up.

It was a good moment to tell Jonathon about my weird experience and how I came to be in possession of the newspaper. He listened without interruption until I signalled that I have finished.

'If I didn't know you Richard, I'd say that a trip to the funny farm wasn't out of place, but I do know you and that's what makes the difference. Have you told Lucy?'

I nodded and told him that we were dining together Sunday evening to go through the facts. He seemed relieved, remembering that Lucy had helped us recently in a rather bizarre case where some of the evidence was missing, not stolen or lost, just missing. In an unprecedented and unethical approach which we kept tightly under wraps we had asked for Lucy's help in resolving the missing link. Using her *'gift'* she had come up with the mislaid proof, although she wouldn't say exactly how it was obtained and we didn't ask. Sometimes ignorance in law was better than knowing.

Having heard my story Jonathon mused over the front page absorbing everything with his quick, calculating mind. For a man that liked rugby and West Country ales, his mind was neither dented nor befuddled and in the year that we had shared an office we had become well acquainted with one another'd odd quirks and practices. The other aspect about Jonathon was that he was non-judgemental.

'I agree with Lucy in that there has to be a connection and not just with how the paper smells. For all we know the newspaper could have been sitting on a beer keg all morning before being taken by the owner to the execution. How often have we dissected evidence that has been brought to a crime scene, but factored in other interests having originated from a different location?'

Jonathon had a distinct grounding way of putting things as well. He was right of course, not that I hadn't already considered the possibility. Maybe I was too close to see the link.

'What would you have done, if you had been in my shoes?' I asked.

'Nothing different to what you did. I would have observed, listened and taken in as much as I could have absorbed. You should write down everything that you can recall as it might help fill in some of the gaps later.'

When Jonathon excused himself and left that's precisely what I did for the next couple of hours, ordering another pint and a packet of crisps. Surprisingly, I remembered much more than I thought I would. Around a quarter to three I joined the living again walking down Charing Cross Road where a group of Chinese tourists were happily snapping away with digital cameras at anything that moved or was fixed to the ground. I could never see the attraction of what they recorded on their cameras, but perhaps I had become another cynical Londoner, who could tell. Diving into a convenience store which happened to have a corner location I came back minutes later with a bag containing a long seeded loaf, a tub of soft cheese and a good portion of a fresh Norfolk ham quiche with black olives, the quick and easy alternative to switching on the cooker and wasting my evening putting together a real meal. That could wait twenty four hours.

By the time that I arrived home I changed clothes, rinsed the dust from my face and hands then prepared my early supper adding a bottle of wine taking myself to the settee where I could enjoy the rugby international. When I opened my eyes again the sporting event had been played out and was replaced by a children's cartoon, although the level of aggression by the animated characters was equal to that displayed by the guerrillas on the pitch.

To the west over Fulham way the sun was hiding behind the treetops, I looked at the clock on the side and wondered where exactly Lucy was pitching herself on her latest assignment. Since I had asked her to be careful earlier in the day, I had thought about her often and with each thought the feeling had grown stronger. I felt the change even if I couldn't accept why. We had known one another for over thirty years and always used professional commitment as an excuse. As far as I was concerned nothing had changed to alter that arrangement and yet I felt responsible for her, needing to know that she was safe and needing to know where our future was heading.

My thoughts were abruptly put to one side as I ran through to the hall to retrieve my mobile which was ringing as though it need to be answered. Jonathon apologised for the interruption, but said that he had to call before going out, to tell me what he had uncovered, only it would have played on his mind all evening and ruined the show. I agreed mentally visualising Arabella placing her hands around my neck. Whatever she had planned for them both didn't warrant being interrupted by anything that was troubling me.

'When I left you at the *Rod and Trout* I spent the rest of the afternoon researching into what I had read on the front page of the London Gazette. With the help of a friend this is what I found out.'

'Reginald Benjamin Pike, the condemned man, had been a wealthy landowner originating from Surrey, a rich and diverse region where many business men lived having prospered from the spoils of their commercial investments in the city. It would be inept not to mention that within the county there sits the legendary coronation stone where it was recorded that seven Anglo-Saxon kings were crowned.

'Pike had his fingers in a number of commercial ventures, undertakings that saw his investment and energy contracted out both at home and abroad, stretching as far as America, traversing across to the middle-east and down under to where we once sent our unwanted convicts. Whatever else was printed about Pike he had to be admired for his gusto and vision. Commercial exploits in the eighteen hundreds was always going to be a risky business unless of course it involved her majesty's treasury.'

I didn't interrupt, the same as I didn't ask Jonathon's source.

'Pike had a commercial partner, a man who went by the name of Samuel Joseph Byrne. From what I uncovered about Byrne, he had an unsavoury reputation, with a dodgy past and crooked business record. It was an unusual match, but it seemed to flourish for a while until one night when the customs and treasury men came knocking at their warehouse.

'For several years and at least three times in any one given year, the Kinston Trading Company were contracted to undertake the safe passage of her majesty's gold which had been extracted from the Brisbane mines. To keep the valuable safe, it was disguised being transported in beer kegs and hidden under grain, buried deep in the heart of the ship.

'I can only assume that Pike was ignorant of the fact that for some time Byrne who had help from another source been extracting the gold and replacing it with a lesser graded metal, which weighed and looked the same. My guess is that it was the captain and crew.

'The fated shipment that ended the contract and sealed Pike's fate arrived at the warehouse around midnight where under the cover of darkness it was delivered to the treasury vaults only before it could be *loaded for the last stage of the undertaking the warehouse was raided by customs and treasury officials acting on an anonymous tip-off. The only occupant being Reginald Benjamin Pike. Mysteriously Samuel Joseph Byrne was never seen or heard of ever again. It didn't take an official long to determine the deception and theft. Pike was arrested for treason although her majesty was never mentioned in any of the official records.*

'Naturally Pike pleaded that he was innocent, but the irrefutable evidence was stacked heavily against him and without the materialisation of his commercial partner to help prove otherwise, Pike was found guilty on all counts and sentenced to hang. As you'd expect with so many sailings it was difficult to say exactly how much had actually been stolen in gold and no official record was ever recorded on the matter, although the British economy of the time did suffer as a result.

'Pike's fate was sealed watertight also by the jury, a tightly packed rostrum accommodated by twelve, good and honest men, no doubt all city businessmen who saw an opportunity to take over the shipping contract. All they had to do was be rid of Pike. The rest you know!'

I wished Jonathon and Arabella an enjoyable evening as I laid the mobile back down on the hall table. Looking at the sketched image I could almost see the anguish set deep in Pike's eyes. With the noose about his neck his soul was crying out for me to help, only I didn't know where to begin.

When I eventually went to bed I turned my head to the place where Newgate Prison had stood and wondered if the architect George Dancer the younger, would ever have put pen to parchment had he known what horrors and misery would prevail within the dark and dank walls.

I turned over to the other side, sent Lucy a text message telling her to be safe and that I was looking forward to seeing her the next day. I wanted to say how much, but something held my emotions in check. Love and despair, could so easily affect the heart and leave the thoughts psychologically scrambled, without reason or pity. Eventually I closed my eyes and entered the nightmare that had been waiting for my return.

Chapter Eight

Passing through the electronic gates I parked up next to my father's car where through the windscreen I saw my mother waiting expectantly at the kitchen window. She waved before tilting her head forward thinking that I wouldn't see the expression of disappointment masking her face begrudgingly accepting that I had come alone. Pushing the driver's door shut I held up my hands and shrugged knowing that it would have made her day to have seen Lucy get out of the passenger seat.

Like me my father was a lawyer and had been practicing for as long as I could remember my first childhood memory. We were the last remaining relatives of our particular dynasty to be carrying on the family name and upholding the law, on both sides of the, but I was yet to reach the echelons of privilege that afforded a high court judge. Horatio Quinn had successfully flourished just like his father and my great-grandfather before him. Mother had appreciated the call of the bench and not stood in the way of progress, keeping silent her views on our dedication although subconsciously I believed that there were times where she wished for a normal routine and after lunch discussion. Occasionally I felt that we both stifled her and failed to recognise her worth.

Standing beneath the imposing porch with its carved columns they had always reminded me of an ancient ruin that would have been better suited to a Greek temple rather than adorn the entrance of a Georgian house on the edge of the Hertfordshire, Suffolk border. Waiting for the door to open I remembered my last year at school where at my career interview I had enthusiastically stated that it was my intention to pursue a career path digging the earth's crust and uncovering the past as an archaeologist hoping that my father would support a gap year allowing me to broaden my horizons, travelling the province of China and Japan. I got as far as Oxford and my trowel and brush never saw the light of day, in fact if I looked they were probably still in the rucksack where I had left them. The mask had changed once again as mother pulled open wide the door. I stepped up, hugged her and kissed her cheek feeling her breathe a sigh of relief that I had made it.

'When are you going to invite Lucetta as well?' she asked, allowing me to pass.

'She would have come, but she had to work late into the night.' I raised my eyebrows as if to make the reason excusable for Lucy's absence.

'There are times when I wonder if pursuing a professional career dominates the entire control of your lives. At this rate Richard I will never hear the patter of tiny feet on the landing!' It was as much a wish as a dignified admonishment, only as usual in Lucy's absence I felt the full force of her resentment. And as usual from the lounge came my corner of support.

'Leave the boy alone Alison, I've told you that it will all happen when the time is right!'

I smiled at my mother and entered the lounge when I shook my father's hand.

'Although, I'll be mighty glad when you do bring the lass home Richard, only then will I too get some peace.'

My mother shook her head at us both as she left in disgust to busy herself in the kitchen. Neither of us heard what it was that she muttered under her breathe as the lounge door shut on its own weight, but I had a good idea that it was about men not understanding women and their needs. I hoped that Lucy didn't think the same about me. To prove her utter contempt of our male dominance and ignorance she turned on the mixer and added the finishing touches to the cake that she had been making before seeing me arrive.

'Have you been engaged in anything interesting of late?' my father inquired. I was tempted to tell him about Pike and Newgate, but felt that I needed to know more before divulging all. As a judge he was not used to being fed half-baked ideas or evidence.

When mother came back armed with sandwiches and tea we generalised, avoiding anything legal or mystical. I saw her eyes positively light up when I slipped into the conversation that I was having dinner that evening with Lucy. At the same time my father's head drooped despondently, knowing that after I had left the rest of the evening would be set aside to sifting through knitting patterns and going over decorating ideas for the spare room.

When the time came for me to say goodbye and wave before I turned left out of the gate it struck me just how significant Lucy and her aurora had influenced my family and myself. Despite pursing her dream at the newspaper she had somehow managed to leave her mark etched into the fabric of our lives. None of us would rest easy until she was wholly part of it. I engaged second gear, then third and fourth slipping into the traffic going south west eager to be back home.

*****

Turning the generous pieces of steak in the pan I teased the meat with the juices that they were cooking in, rather than add any artificially produced spices, before introducing the chopped mushrooms and cream, mildly pleased with my culinary achievement having pinched the menu from across the channel where French chef's up and down the country from Nice to Normandy thought nothing of producing similar. Long ago I had identified that steak was Lucy's favourite as I made the edge of the pan sear in a wave of blue flame as the added cognac dance with the flame from the burner underneath.

I had already set the patio table deciding that the weather was mild enough to dine al fresco rather than eat inside and everything was going to plan when I heard the taxi pull up downstairs in the courtyard. I wanted to look over the balcony, but the meal was coming together and demanded that I stay in the kitchen. It wasn't until a hand slid around my waist and she planted a kiss on the back of my neck that I realised Lucy was standing behind me.

'Smells divine Quinn and I'm ravenous.' She opened the fridge and placed a bottle of red inside. 'I thought you'd do steak so I brought us a cabernet sauvignon.

I removed the mittens where I had checked the vegetables basting in the oven, turned and made sure that she was in one piece.

'I'm pleased you're here and safe.'

She pulled out her mobile and touched the screen highlighting my text. 'I got your message, but unfortunately I wasn't in a position to send a reply...sorry! It was nice Quinn, although I have to admit unexpected. Is there anything wrong?' she asked taking a step backwards as though waiting for a reaction.

'No. nothing's wrong... I just wanted to send you a message before I went to sleep that was all.'

We had known one another long enough to identify each other's mood changes, think through one another's next move and know when something was troubling the other. Relieved she stepped forward again.

'That's good, because I thought you might be building up to tell me that you've been keeping a big secret from me and that you're secretly engaged, or that the foreign legion has accepted your application or worse still you're emigrating!'

To show that her concerns were unfounded I poured two glasses of wine and handed her one.

'Firstly Lucetta Tate, I would never get engaged without giving you prior notice, secondly my French is somewhat limited, so *la legion etrangere ne m'aurait pas* and thirdly...' I hesitated for a second before ending the sentence 'I am not going anywhere without you!'

There, it was said, it was done. It had taken me almost thirty two years to express what I felt about Lucy and I waited tentatively for her response, wondering if she would open the fridge retrieve her wine and leave.

Instead she came in real close put down her wine, took mine then kissed me passionately. When a plume of smoke rose from the cooker top, we parted.

'I take it that we eating outside?' she asked as she took our glasses through to the balcony.

A few minutes later I served up our supper noticing that she had lit the candle, which flickered gently in the breeze.

'I was beginning to wonder if you had any romantic bones in you Quinn.' She began as we forked the food into our mouths. She placed a finger over my lips before I could reply. 'But, I like what I see. I like that you care and send me text in the middle of an assignment. What took you so long and please don't say work?'

I stopped chewing, swallowed and cleared my palate with a swill of the wine.

'Feebly I would have replied work, but for some time now I have been trying to summon up the courage to tell you how I really felt. The truth is that there is no such thing as a battle between the head and the heart because both dominate as much as the other and every time that I took stock of my life, my future or considered that I had reached a conclusion, you were there bowling down the alley and hitting the pins without mercy. If it means my changing profession, becoming a chef or an archaeologist then I would do it, as long as you were in my life Lucy and not just as a friend.'

She drew the rim of the glass across the edge of her lip as she mused over what I had just said and in typical Lucy fashion she answered exactly as I imagined she would.

'A chef works too many hours, with little reward whereas an archaeologist digs up the past and brings back home a mummy or perhaps two. I would rather you did neither Quinn, but stay just as you are and keep sending the text.'

We made a pact there and then without needing anything to be said. At last I could stop wondering why Lucy hadn't been snapped up long before now, but maybe, just maybe she had been waiting for me to make the first move. She settled her knife and fork on the plate then patted her stomach.

'That was good Quinn and I needed that.' She blew out her cheeks taking hold of the glass. 'A lowly slice of toast for lunch doesn't quite cut through the hunger barrier!'

'You got home late?' I asked, not prying, just interested.

She smiled mischievously.

'Sometime after three.' She topped up her glass and did the same to mine. 'For the past two weeks I've been stalking the movements of a certain junior minister, nobody publicly special, but hotly tipped to be in the driving seat one day. His agenda however has been rather mundane up until this Friday lunchtime when he'd met a tall dizzy looking blonde at a Soho wine bar.' She saw the questioning look on my face and immediately defended the implication. 'I know, but some are dumb as well as being blonde and leggy Quinn!' Adding the latter knowing that I would find the long legs interesting. 'My vibes told me that it wasn't anything official, but more of an intimate arrangement, then minutes before I left the office a tip came in that they would be seeing one another over the weekend. I blew out Friday night, but last night I hit the jackpot.'

'What did you do, hide in the wardrobe?'

'No... I was on the flat roof opposite, armed with a camera.'

'Remind me not to upset you!'

Lucy raised the glass to her lips as she smiled. Her eyes, dark brown and deeply sensual looked over the rim sending a warning that dare I ever consider as much, it would be more than a camera that she would be armed with.

I continued. 'Is she known?'

Lucy shook her head. 'A fashion model, only just back from an assignment in Paris.'

'So was the night on the tiles was worth it?'

This time she beamed like a child who had found the best and biggest Easter egg.

'I caught him banged to rights, or I should say banging away without any right. I don't suppose that his wife will be overjoyed to see the images splashed across the front page.'

Lucy could be devilishly deadly as she could sexy and unquestioningly kind.

'A women scorned...' I left the phrase hanging.

'A wife and an unforgiving country. The commons might sweep acts of indiscretion under the carpet, but the lords tend to have long memories, despite taking an afternoon nap when they should be lobbying for a new bill. The public however, never go to sleep!'

Lucy shook her head as she remembered her night on the rooftop.

'What makes a man stray Quinn?' it was a rhetorical statement that required no reply. 'The marvel of another woman's cleavage, the excitement of the chase or simply that they can get away with it!' I was glad that she didn't add the long legs as I had long admired Lucy's, close up or from afar. Pouring herself more wine she went on, unconsciously clearing the thoughts from her head.

'The images that I took last night, will need professional attention, not for the perpetrator, but the victim, the wife. With your permission I could give her one of your business cards and I guarantee that it won't be contested and would be easy money, the case being settled out of court.'

Deadly, intelligent and ethically accurate. I agreed.

'I can't wait to see the smug little shit fall from grace.' Her eyes seemed to blaze with hate. 'I'm sorry Quinn. I'm destroying the evening!'

I shook my head and told her that the outburst was good for the soul. It was her cue to let it all go.

'He's nothing better than a pariah, a political leper without morals or conviction. Like a dark shadow he poisons the minds of others to achieve his own aspirations, leaving behind a trail of destruction and sometimes death, yet not once will he turn his head back and consider the consequences. He's a bastard!'

It was one of the rare times that I had heard Lucy swear. Suddenly she changed and I realised that it was over, the pressure cooker had simmered. Lucy put down her glass and took my hand in hers as she leant forward and kissed me.

'Not all men are bastards Quinn. Some are worth waiting for, however long that might be.'

'Do you want to go inside?' I asked, feeling the breeze getting keener up so high.

'No, outside is fine and I like it here.' She looked around as though checking to see that nobody was listening or around. 'Besides which what we have to discuss would be better dissected out in the open, where the confinement of walls and ceilings will not interfere.'

'You mean my experience?'

'Yes, but first I should tell you that I've also been appraising certain aspects of my life. I don't want to miss out Quinn on the chance of motherhood or real happiness.'

It was a surprise. 'You'd leave the paper?'

'If it meant raising a family and being with you, then yes. The appeal of climbing over rooftops and chasing down shits like a junior minister wane after a while. There are other things that I want in my life. A man to hold me, want me and have me know that I am safe.'

Like a reminder that we had something different to discuss the breeze whipped across the balcony once again. Lucy slipped into the cardigan that had been tied over her shoulders.

'Dreams are the mind's way of unlocking the mysteries that would otherwise complicate our lives. For whatever reason or however long we live this time around, if we didn't dream then we would not fulfil our purpose.'

'Are you saying that the places I go and the people I see, both of whom might be unfamiliar I would have encountered had it been possible for us to live until we were say a hundred and fifty?'

'More or less. However, what happened to you Friday night wasn't a dream. That was real Quinn. That involved the *equidistant*.'

'The equidistant, what's that?'

'Where the point of two unilateral parallel lines meet or in your case the coming together of two dimensions. Consider two revolving anomalies circling the earth, at some particular point in time and space they will meet. However, in paranormal circles this is known as the equidistant, where the dead meet the living. When a person dies the spirit of their soul is taken when the dimensions cross one another. The soul passes into a space where it either goes beyond and onto another life, or it remains unable to pass through the *gateway*. But sometimes a soul that has been taken has to wait until it can be released from an earthbound burden before they can pass through the gateway, whereas others remain forever in a dimension, a void full of darkness, without light or sound. Evil you see has a way of punishing the bad.'

'Not then a state of my mind?'

'No. You've not gone mad, but what you saw, you felt, smelt and heard.'

'So where did Pike originate from?'

'The equidistant, not Newgate. The prion was part of the scenario that had to be shown for you to understand why he need your help.'

'But, what am I supposed to do to help?'

'That's the part that I cannot explain. As I said yesterday, there has to be a connection for him to seek you out. If you delve into his past, you might find one.'

I told her about Jonathon's unearthing of certain facts concerning Pike's unfortunate dealings with HM Treasury.

'Then the connection will present itself to you soon.' She said.

'Will I have other experiences?'

'It all depends on the connection and whether it involves others waiting at the gateway.'

Up until the point when Lucy had helped us find the missing proof, I had been an ardent cynic, but now my apprehension was less mooted.

'I suppose that my keeping you waiting might be considered bad. Am I destined to end my existence in some far away no-mans-land?'

She suddenly grabbed my hand and guided me towards the bedroom. We left the crocks on the table, taking with us the glasses and bottle of wine that she had brought.

'That depends on just how good you can be and that you can prove to this girl that the day that we sat beside one another in nursery, our lives were fated to be spent together!'

Chapter Nine

We succumbed to sleep in one another's arms as the rest of the night passed by quickly, until the modern drone of a metallic ringtone pierced through the bliss shattering the moment, beginning the start of another working week. I felt Lucy roll away and pull back the duvet as she padded across the carpet to see who was calling.

'I'm sorry Quinn, I thought that I'd left it on silent.' She kissed my forehead then went to the bathroom. I pulled up the covers catching the aroma of her perfume on the pillow. From the bathroom she called out. 'If it rings again, perhaps you'd best answer it, only it could be long distance!'

The response was not meant to be heard. Several moments later she dived back under the covers to rejoin me, her naked body nestling against mine. I found her mouth and kissed her long and hard, sensing the growth down in my groin. Lucy positioned herself ready to accept me as we ignored the ringing of the mobile in the background.

Somewhere in the distance a factory siren beyond the opposite bank registered in our slumber as we lay together warm, spent of energy, but content. I pictured the workers trudging begrudgingly through the gates of a factory unwilling to start another monotonous shift, clocking on and donning protective overalls before joining the assembly line.

What Lucy had advised was right, I should stay with Wilkinson, Quinn and Hemp's. Nearing forty it was too late to be changing direction. When her mobile rang annoyingly for the third time she yanked back the cover and aggressively took the call. Whoever the caller, they received an outburst of venomous response interspersed with Italian. Lying there grinning I admired the way her body line went in and out with perfection. She turned and caught me looking.

'Have you got to go?' I asked.

'Not yet. I've delegated the job to a junior, it's only a jumper on the line over at Finchley Central. The experience of being first at the scene will assist develop her awareness. I can catch up with her later and help put together the story.'

I watched her leave for the kitchen and heard her switch on the kettle as I used the bathroom. By the time I re-emerged the coffee was made and two rounds of toast had been buttered and waiting.

'The first of day of the rest of our lives.' I said, thanking her as I took charge of my coffee.

'Are we good with this?' she asked.

'Better than good,' I replied noticing that she had slipped into the tee-shirt that I had been wearing the evening before. We took the coffee and toast out onto the balcony where the world below was slowly coming to life again.

'I love it here Quinn. You've the river, Giovanni's on your doorstep and the office, but a stone's throw from your front door. I could spend the rest of my life on this balcony and let all the stresses of modern living drift away.'

Looking around I appreciated what I had, but Lucy added another dimension. I didn't want her to leave.

'Can I stay over tonight,' she asked 'I could go after work, grab an overnight bag and meet you back here around seven?'

'As long as we dine out. I got lucky with my steak chanterelle!'

She smiled. 'We both got lucky Quinn.'

Not forgetting that Lucy had a gift, I enquired. 'Did Mama see us together?'

'Perhaps, although she never gave any hint. Mama keeps her thoughts close to her chest.'

We heard the ringtone of the mobile as it echoed off the interior walls. Lucy sighed as she went to answer it. When she came back she was holding the phone in her hand.

'Unfortunately, this time I have got to go Quinn. An aide attached to the office of the junior minister looks like he missed his footing and ended up under the train,' she looked at the ripples on the river, seemingly mesmerised by the murkiness of the water 'or alternatively he was pushed, either way he's dead. Roger Bremerton will have a lot to answer for when he reaches the equidistant!'

Lucy went back inside, grabbed her clothes and hit the shower. When I kissed her at the front door she looked sad.

'I really don't want to go Quinn. I just want to be with you!'

We neither said goodbye, it was taboo. As I watched her jump into a taxi I waved. Seven that evening seemed a long way off. Before hitting the shower I made the bed. Adjusting the pillows a handwritten note fell out and dropped to the floor, I picked it up and read the content.

'Forever... I love you Quinn'

The short walk to the office that morning seemed noticeably different as I increased my pace already wishing away the day. It was strange though, but I had the feeling that I was being watched although it was impossible to tell exactly who might be following as the pavements were packed with other workers going to and fro.

Like an unexplainable psychological sixth sense moment I felt that something was coming around the corner, although not knowing precisely what it resembled. When I stopped walking the pedestrians approaching and passing by looked at me oddly, but they weren't experiencing what I was feeling. The odd thing was that I couldn't tell if it was living or dead.

Chapter Ten

I must have looked perplexed as I walked through the door of the office because the receptionist asked if I was alright. She said that I looked ashen as though I had seen a ghost. I had expected to find Jonathon at his desk and already going through the case that we had middle of the week, but as yet nobody had seen him. I wasn't overly concerned as Jonathon was the matrix of our office, an embodiment of life and wisdom. I was amused when he did finally show around eleven thirty beaming from ear to ear like a child who just visited a sweet shop.

'Had a good morning?' I inquired.

'Rewardingly successful,' he begun 'I've been pounding the cobbled streets down at the East India Dock.'

I couldn't recall any of our cases being represented from that area of the city, but I wasn't to worry because Jonathon was eager to explain. He settled in the desk opposite mine laying down several paper records. Even sitting his chiselled looks, mop of blonde hair and broad shoulders did nothing to detract from his imposing stature.

'Pike and Byrne. They had dealings with a Mitcham based company, owned by a Henry Kelling. Just shy of London by ten miles the smelting works was a lucrative smelting venture and had many contracts in the city and surroundings counties. My enquiries established that like Pike and Byrne, Henry also had dealings abroad, albeit not always legitimately.' He looked up and smiled. 'It must have been a thing of that era, although underhanded dealings have hardly diversified to this day.'

'Dishonest trading and concerning precious metals!'

'To name, but a few of the many practices around.' He pushed across the records and as I scoured over them, he continued. 'We seem to have a common denominator in that the smelting works had serious dealings with Byrne, but the records never mention Pike.'

It wasn't the link that I was looking for, but Jonathon was a marvel to behold. I didn't reply not wanting to break his level of concentration.

'Unbelievably and more sentiment than necessity the current Henry Kelling Works have kept under lock and key the company records going back at least two hundred years. If you look at where I've used the highlighter, you see Byrne's name recorded against a particular transaction. Look closer and you will see the last which involved Pike's arrest.'

A sudden chill swept through my body and I knew from whence it had come. Poor Reginald Benjamin Pike had naively fallen foul of a well-rehearsed scam. I didn't ask how Jonathon had obtained the records, you only had to look at him to know that he had used his good looks and glib tongue to melt another unsuspecting heart. If only they knew that it belonged to Arabella.

'What are the weights and prices beside the entries?' I asked.

'Shave off a little here and a little there and the weight changes, but only slightly. The only main ingredient that changes significantly is the value. Originally each coin came from a good grade gold ore, but when tampered with lesser graded metals, the smelting company could almost retain the exact weight, but produce a coin at least eighteen percent less of its original value. With a ship load of coins, that amounted to a very profitable margin. Enough to resettle Byrne abroad, never to be found or held accountable for the crime of treason.'

I traced down the margin stopping at an entry dated the third of January, eighteen sixty eight. Next to it was a small symbol.

'The date of each transaction doctored?' Jonathon nodded.

'Once the treasury officials had established that a fraudulent practice was taking place, they immediately initiated changes and cancelled all existing contracts. Many lives were affected because of Byrne's underhand dealings. I can only surmise the devastation that it must have caused many families, who lost their job in a socially and economically difficult period of history.'

We had the evidence that had been missing at Pike's trial thanks to Jonathon, but the task now was presenting it to the Home Secretary in a fashion that would see Reginald Pike exonerated of all blame. It still didn't entirely show that Pike was innocent and naïve of all that was going on around him.

Around midday Lucy called. She was standing outside Downing Street awaiting an official announcement regarding the resignation of the junior minister. Even though I couldn't see it, I envisaged the look of triumph etched on her face, although I doubt that the ex-minister was anywhere to be seen. She said that copies of the photo stills had been delivered to the home address and that she had included my business card. No doubt at some time I would get a call from the wife. I told her that I had found her note and said that I was looking forward to seven. I omitted mentioning anything about the feeling that I'd had on the way into work. When I replaced the receiver Jonathon was looking directly at me, his discerning expression one of knowing as though he was saying *'there you go, it was only a matter of time.'* Shortly after the call I sent Lucy a text message mentioning one word *'forever'*.

When the telephones finally stopped ringing I decided to close down my computer and excuse myself from the office taking the five minute journey across to where I knew that my father was sitting on the bench. Away from the house and with mother absent I could ask his advice. At a few minutes to five he found me sitting comfortably in his chamber awaiting his arrival.

'Richard my boy, you're a sight to behold after the shit day that I have just endured. Be a good chap and pour me a hearty brandy please.'

We sat opposite one another, my glass much less full than his. I wanted a clear head when I saw Lucy later. I let my father ramble on few the next few minutes letting off steam about his present case.

'Do you remember that bloody fool that represents Levers, Stocks and Everson?'

'Andrew Simpson.'

'Yes, that's the one. Incompetent fool that he is. If I had the authority I would send he and his client down for a good long stretch. They're both as bad as one another!'

After a while the brandy began to unwind his jangled nerves and calm his mood. After a while he managed to laugh at the ludicrously long day.

'There are times when I envy your great grandfather Richard. At least he had the power to send a fellow to the gallows. Hanging about for a few seconds would teach Simpson a valuable lesson.'

It was an appropriate moment to interject why I had come visiting. Not to stretch out the story I briefly outlined the case of Reginald Pike and Samuel Byrne, telling my father that it was a case that I had taken on for a wealthy client who wished to remain anonymous. He never questioned my motive, but was pleased to be asked.

'It's about the right era for that old bugger to have been sitting on the bench. Take a look the next time you sit in the restaurant upstairs, the portrait of old Septimus is as imposing as the day that the artist put brush to canvas. Just looking at him would strike a chord of fear through an innocent man. With an unscrupulous jury out for the lucrative contract on offer, I doubt that this Pike fellow had much chance of an acquittal.' Horatio Quinn pondered his thoughts for a moment as he contemplated his next sentence.

'You know that Michael Cattigan is no fool Richard. Records, however good can be doctored, altered and as Home Secretary, Cattigan will ask for more proof than what you have to offer.'

'Is there any way that the court records would show who presided over Pike's case?'

'Of course. I'll get Margaret to check them out first thing tomorrow morning. She'll have packed up and gone by now. Will tomorrow do?' I told him that it would do fine.

'I've heard that old Septimus had a reputation, not just in the courthouse. Is it true?'

My father chuckled. 'You mean regarding his womanising and drinking. Regrettably, yes it's true. Your grandfather would remind me often that drink and service do not go hand in hand.' It seemed inappropriate to mention that he had hold of a large brandy, although in his defence the day was over.

'So it was possible that old Septimus could have presided over the case being under the influence?'

'More than just possible. I'd say that there was every chance he could have.' It didn't bode well for Pike. I remembered a previous discussion where father had told me about Septimus sending a good many to Newgate and the gallows. My father continued.

'The death certificate recorded that Septimus died of a pulmonary embolism, although I've always had my doubts. My father scornfully stated that the old bugger died of syphilis and consumption. I know that your late great grandmother died much younger, a blessing in disguise I would say.'

'Ghosts in the cupboard...' I remarked.

'More like ghouls than ghosts.' Father replied.

I wondered where exactly old Septimus was wandering now. Had the gateway refused him entry and was he existing in the void where it was perpetually dark and quiet. Quite unexpected father changed the subject.

'Now about this Italian girl. When are you two going to get it together?'

'I've a dinner date at seven tonight.'

He topped up his glass and sat back down letting go a long deep sigh of relief.

'Thank goodness for that, only I've heard nothing else since your visit.'

Chapter Eleven

Entering the restaurant Lucy turned a few heads especially carrying an overnight bag. She quenched the other diner's imagination by kissing me passionately before seating herself opposite.

'Sorry, I tried to get away early, but the editor asked for a re-run on the Downing Street statement.' She scooped up the menu and devoured what was on offer. 'This looks good!'

Before the meal arrived she had unwound and told me about her day, the body under the train doing nothing to destroy her appetite. She was mostly enthusiastic that the wife of the junior minister had agreed to an interview, believing that it would bolster her chances of a much bigger settlement. I couldn't disagree. When it came to my turn, I explained about Jonathon's success and my visit to see my father.

'We've all got skeletons in the closet Quinn, only some manage to stay hidden more than others. If you delved into my family connections you'd probably find a few of the underworld in the number. It's not something that I would go shouting about. At least getting together we've a chance to change all that!'

'Coming from the same streets, or on the wrong side of the law. Old Septimus didn't exactly uphold it to the letter.'

'He might have strayed, but your slate is clean.' It managed to turn the heads again, but Lucy was fired up, luckily in my defence. 'Somehow we need to unravel this connection.'

'Margaret, my father's personal attendant might do that come the morning. She's going to check the old court records and see if Pike was tried by Septimus.'

The waiter arrived with our meals and topped up our glasses. When she asked about my mother I told her the truth, rather than play it down.

'It's a feminine thing Quinn. I've had similar from my mother and Mama Maria. Mama's even measured my girth to make sure that I'm not getting too fat!'

I laughed. 'Well next time she wants a second opinion, tell to ask me.'

Lucy shook her head and lowered her eyes in feigned shame. 'You don't think that she doesn't already know!'

I hoped that Mama Maria didn't see all.

Later that night our coming together was more relaxed than the night before as we made the bond stronger. Moments before Lucy fell asleep in the crook of my shoulder we realised that we had reached a level of understanding where we felt comfortable thinking for the other. It was impossible to tell how long I listened to her breathing, but with each rise and fall of her chest I realised just how much I had been missing. Pushing away a loose strand of hair she murmured, but didn't wake, her dreams and my arms keeping her safe. At that point I decided to close my eyes and join her dream.

Like the time before I felt the presence nearby. I resisted opening my eyes, knowing that it would be there. When I did I was already gone from the bed and bound for another place. I tried to turn and call out for Lucy, but the force taking me was too powerful. All around me I detected some sort of subatomic cloud, a mist. Sensing that the ground was hard and unwelcoming I realised that I had arrived. Once again the smell was the first thing that I perceived, the air was thick, laden with death and the pungent aroma of urine and human waste. My initial reaction was to turn around and run, but my feet were rooted to the spot.

From the side a bony hand suddenly gripped my shin and held on tight, the grip surprisingly strong as I tracked the arm up to the shoulder arriving at the face, which belonged to an old woman. She was extremely emaciated and without any hair, not that it would made any difference. If she hadn't been so strong I would have surmised that death wasn't long in coming.

A figure stepped out of the shadows ahead and approached. This time it was a young woman, not as thin and she had hair, or what was left of it. Loose threads hung from her scalp in limp disarray as the torn and shredded nightdress that she wore barely covered her body. She reached down, gently spoke to the woman holding my ankle and made her let go. I heard the reverberation of hesitation in my throat as I spoke.

'Where is this place?' it was no more than a whisper.

She swallowed and cleared her throat. 'Why Newgate of course. Do you not recognise it Sir!'

I wasn't sure why I asked the next question, but in the circumstances it seemed appropriate. 'Did Septimus Quinn have anything to do with you coming here?'

She scoffed and I heard other mutterings further back in the shadows.

'Myself and many others. I told them that you'd be coming. They're keen to see the great grandson of a monster!'

I felt my legs take a step back, but as I did so, so the shuffle of feet edged forward menacingly.

The young woman held up her hand and the shuffle ceased. 'Do not fear them, I will keep you safe Richard Quinn.' I noticed that the wrist was bandaged in the torn hem of her nightdress.

'Who did that to you?'

She lowered her arm. 'I did. I thought that a rusty nail could cheat the hangman his purse, but even god cannot penetrate these walls. Down here mercy is a word rarely used.'

'Why was you sent to Newgate?'

She smiled, but the look in her eyes told a different story. 'For being in the right place at the wrong time!'

'I don't understand.'

'And neither did Septimus Quinn or moreover that he didn't believe me.'

She then explained that she had been in the employ of Lord and Lady Halsham, noble residents of Halsham Hall in the prosperous district of Highgate. One fateful night the house was entered into by a burglar out to steal the silverware and anything else that was considered valuable. Being awoken by a noise downstairs the master of the house left his bed to investigate, where he soon confronted the intruder and thus entered into a violent struggle to apprehend the thief.

When the maid hearing the scuffle came to his rescue, the burglar promptly produced a dagger and without hesitating stabbed the titled lord through the heart, ending his life instantly. As others in the house hurried from their quarters they found the maid knelt over the master. Her mistress took one look at the scene, screamed and sent for the police accusing the young maid of complicity and murder. It didn't take the jury or Septimus long to find her guilty and sentence her to death. Languishing in Newgate, she awaited the detail of the jailers that would take her to the gallows. She lifted the torn hem of her nightdress.

'This was what I wore that night. See the stains where his blood was soaked up in the cloth.'

'Who are you and what do you want from me?'

'I am Mary Jane Garman from Old Billingsgate.' She paused and sighed. 'What do I want of you Richard Quinn, why justice of course. I am innocent of the crime that I am accused of. There was another who saw what happened. Somebody that can help take me away from this place.'

'Who?'

'A footman, Oliver Grey. We were together that night and he was not far behind me when my lord was murdered. He must have seen what happened.'

'Why did he not speak up when the police were called?'

Mary shook her head. 'I do not know. I have asked myself that question many times.'

'Was Oliver Grey not at the trial?

Mary lowered her head, not wanting me to see her eyes. 'Yes...' it was no more than a whisper 'only he was sat alongside another, a scullery maid. When sentence was passed she smiled at me then they left.'

My attention was interrupted by the sudden commotion out in the corridor where two guards were dragging another prisoner to the cell opposite. The prisoner another woman was heavily drunk and slurring her words as she remonstrated with the two burly men. In one swift movement the door to the cell was opened and they tossed her inside like a rag doll. When the catch of the door lock fell into place the woman was pounced upon by other inmates. The clothes were torn from her body disappearing into the darkness as those not fortunate to grab anything from her body kicked, punched and spat at her. She groaned once before she allowed her mind to shut down and let sleep take over.

'Is it always like this?'

'I was lucky, I only had on a nightdress so I had nothing to offer. The only thing left that I have to give is my life.'

I remember seeing the look of desperation in her eyes as the vision started to fade. I held out my hand to take Mary with me, but the next thing that I was aware of was Lucy holding me down. She was gently repeating over and over that I'd had a bad dream. I looked around the bedroom expecting to see Mary Jane Garman sitting in the corner.

When we did eventually settle again we went to sleep with the bedside light on, not that I believed it would do any good.

Chapter Twelve

We took our coffee with Giovanni later that morning giving me time to reflect through my experience and have Lucy untangle the web as I tried to recall everything. At one point I thought that I detected a connection between them and not just because they both hailed from Italy, but something more tangible, perhaps physical, maybe darkly spiritual. It was strange as well because I felt safe, protected as though surrounded by angels.

When the trade died off Giovanni came and sat with us. We talked as friends and about nothing in particular, but it was good to be part of a living world. I was happy to hear them argue with one another, fiercely defending their part of Italy. Lucy had called in and told the paper that she was chasing a lead for a new story and I had texted Jonathon stating that I would be in later. In the text I had asked him to check out Mary Jane Garman, Halsham Hall and lastly Oliver Grey.

What was meant to be a few hours together turned out to be much longer, not that either of us cared. Lucy said that she felt it was best that she stayed by my side and I wasn't about to argue any different. Sometime around four Jonathon called.

'That was a tough nut to crack,' he started. 'Halsham Hall did exist until it was ravaged by fire fifteen months after the death of Lord Halsham. A number of the household including Lady Halsham perished in the fire that according to the report which had allegedly started in the wine cellar. It was also difficult to say whether Oliver Grey was among the dead.'

'And Mary Jane Garman?'

'Records show that she was tried at the Old Bailey, found guilty and sentenced by your late great grandfather and that she did hail from Old Billingsgate. Her father had been a millinery trader, but by all accounts had lost much of his wealth employing a city firm who were supposed to have defended his daughter at the trial.'

'It's always the same,' I interjected 'those left behind, continue to take the fall.' I envisaged Jonathon nodding in agreement. He carried on.

'I did wonder about Oliver Grey so took my enquiry to the shipping companies of the day. An entry at the Liverpool docks stated that a Mr Grey and a Miss Parson boarded a liner for America three weeks after the date of the fire. An Elizabeth Parson was listed on the household employ as a scullery maid. The shipping log also stated that her cabin was near to the ships nurse as the young woman was pregnant.'

Jonathon paused to catch his breath and like a dog leaving no meat on the bone, he left the best bit till last.

'Through a friend, police records at Hampstead state that known burglar, who went by the name of Charles Henry Higgins was arrested some months after the burglary at Halsham Hall. When detectives raided his digs they found several small items still in his possession linking him to the house at Highgate.

'And as if this wasn't damning evidence, at the trial where he was accused of Lord Halsham's murder, whilst standing in the dock to receive his sentence he called out the name of Oliver Grey, accusing him of aiding and abetting the crime of burglary. Higgins was hung outside Newgate two days later and to this day a warrant still exists for Grey.'

'I hope Mary was listening to that,' I said as Jonathon finished talking. Once again he had come up trumps. I ended the call stating that I would be back in the office the next day. He didn't question my reasons, but I was sure that he'd heard Lucy moving about the apartment.

Later that evening we travelled to Rickmansworth where we visited Mama Maria. Standing to one side I watched as she affectionately hugged and kissed her grand-daughter before turning her attention to me. Anna Maria Grammazzio looked me up and down as though studying everything about me. She shook my hand then invited us into the lounge, where a tray of tea and freshly baked biscuits were already waiting.

'Mama, you remember Richard, he is the lawyer who lives by the river.' The introduction made me sound like a ferryman in my spare time. 'He was the one that brought the bouquet of flowers to your eightieth birthday party last year.' The old woman nodded as she continued to study me. Her eyes appeared slightly watery and her body frail, but her senses were as sharp as the day that she had been born.

'Si... si, I remember.'

The cottage was just as I had remembered, each wall was adorned with framed photographs, some black and white, others colour. Each a family memento, but pride of place was taken by her late husband, Bernado. Wherever you sat his eyes would be watching you. In a way he reminded me of Giovanni. Wherever I sat in the coffee shop he would watch me constantly, waiting to see when my cup needed refilling or whether it was convenient to talk,

'Here…' she pointed 'you sit beside one another, you lie together, so be together!' I saw Lucy smile as we sat. Again it made me wonder just how much Mama saw.

'You knew that we were coming Mama?' Lucy asked.

Mama nodded. 'Si… si. Papa tells me things when we talk.' I took it that shew as referring to Bernado. 'He tells me that Mr Quinn wants my help.' She looked my way and passed over the biscuits, they smelt temptingly good.

'I've become involved in some bizarre experiences Mama, things that I cannot make a connection, although they may involve a past member of my family!'

She munched around the edge of her biscuit making sure that her tongue sucked off the sugar before answering.

'They only come when a balance needs to be restored. To right the wrongs of others they need our help, so that the dead can pass through the gateway. Lucetta has already explained this, but at the time she did not know about your great grandfather.'

'What happens if I cannot give them the justice that they seek?'

'That I cannot answer because I do not know who decides. What I do know is that everything as purpose. Being in the wrong place at the wrong time was part of that person's fate. You waited a long time to be with my

Lucetta. It would not have happened until the time was right. We do not influence our lives, we live them as they should be lived.'

'You mention a balance, what do you mean?'

'Evil exists where you least expect Mr Quinn, but when it strikes it causes an unbalance in the forces that control our destiny. Just as we live out our lives as fate determined, an unbalance can alter the path of an individual's existence. Giving back what they had lost, will tip the scales back in their favour. Lucetta has told you about the gateway and the space in between. Evil cannot go forward, it has to be stopped.'

'Does this apply to me as well?' I asked, looking at Lucy then Mama.

'Si... si. They not only seek your help to redress justice, but they too send you a warning to be careful. You deal professionally in a world of violence and pain, but you are not immune from either.'

I wanted to ask if I was to encounter either, but Lucy had already told me that Mama could not interfere in the future, she could only see sometimes what might happen. Mama hadn't finished.

'Death is not the end Mr Quinn, but the beginning, but it is how we leave that affects our journey.' On the mantel piece was a large wooden cross, a symbol of her catholic faith.

'So the good go to heaven and follow the path of righteousness of Jesus, whereas the bad go straight to hell.'

'It is not as simple as that, but for the present it will suffice. The dark must have light to survive as much as silence has sound. The forces of nature needs balance.'

She looked over at the photograph of her late husband.

'My Bernado toiled the land and helped raise a family. He left of his own accord, but others are not as fortunate. Without your help, they can only wait Mr Quinn. You will find the peace that you have been seeking lately with Lucetta, but so often there is a price to pay.'

We neither understood to what she was referring, but we did take comfort from knowing that she accepted our being together as our destiny. I felt that our visit was to get her seal of approval as much as help me. Reading my thoughts she smiled at me.

'Si... si Richard, you look after my Lucetta and others will look out for you. That is not the law of the universe, but the law of the living.'

I thought about Pike and Mary, who had looked out for them. When Mama put her hand on my arm and closed her eyes, she had one last thing to add.

'I know of Mary Jane Garman. She did not suffer the hangman's rope as you thought happened, but instead she cheated the gallows ending her life with use of her shredded gown, when she thought that the time was right, not the executioner. *Il destino* Richard and the things that we perhaps do control.'

On the journey back to the city I felt woefully ashamed that I had not done enough for Mary and somewhat bemused that I was possibly more confused than when I had arrived at Mama's. On the outskirts of town a light drizzle began to fall on the windscreen, reminding me of the tears that I had seen fall down Mary's cheeks moments before I was transported forward in time.

Chapter Thirteen

Like a train track running through a dark tunnel my thoughts kept emerging then disappearing as I desperately tried to calm my mind. The fact that Mama had insisted upon part of my experiences as being a warning did not help and the unknown was keeping me from shutting my eyes. Physically I was exhausted, mentally I was tuned in to every noise inside and out. Come the first rays of a new day I was ready to hit the shower and glad to be out of the bedroom, although I wouldn't have said as much to Lucy.

Just managing to open her eyelids she peered over the duvet and mumbled 'Is it that time already?' before sinking back into the warmth of the mattress.

'That and maybe a bit more. The coffee pots on... do you want some?'

Lifting her head above the covers she saw that I was shaved, showered and dressed. Her expression was one of disappointment.

'Have you had enough of me already?' she asked.

I went across and kissed her long and hard before resisting the urge to undress and get back in. For the second morning running her mobile sprang into life. Begrudgingly Lucy pressed *accept* and answered the call.

'I'll lay odds eight to one that it's Duncan Donaldson from the newsroom. He has a face like a slapped camel and a personality to match.'

I walked through to the kitchen to fetch the coffees, when I returned Lucy was sitting up in the bed with her knees pulled tight up under her chin. Big droplets of tears were cascading down her face and onto her chest. She looked up and begged me to hold her tight.

'My friend... and her sister, they've been murdered!'

I was due in court at ten, but Jonathon was up to speed on the case. I reached for my phone to make the call, but Lucy leant over and held onto my wrist.

'No Quinn, whatever happens we must carry on with our lives. Remember what Mama said about fate and destiny.'

'But... your friends. There must be something that you want to do to help?'

Lucy shook her head as she sipped her coffee.

'I tried to warn Penny when we spoke the other day. The man that she had been following around Brighton is extremely dangerous and so unpredictable.' She looked at me as I recognised the thoughts going through her mind. 'I don't need to lay any odds that he is responsible for their deaths.'

'You'll need to tell the police all you know!' I advised, pulling over the box of tissues.

'I already did. I'm surprised that acting on my information they've failed to pick him up.'

'Maybe they have, but they keeping a low profile only once a case of this magnitude hits the streets it will send a ripple of fear through the local community and have the media swarming over the area like an infestation of flies.'

She nodded sensing that I was right.

'Its things like this that test my beliefs Quinn. I'm a catholic by birth, but despite what Mama says, senseless killings don't make it right.'

What was more worrying was the calm that surrounded her. Ordinarily, a true Italian Lucy would have been ranting and raving until she had got it all out of her system, but today she was almost composed except for the tears. Suddenly, she sprang up from the mattress and put her arms about my neck and pulled me close.

'How many Quinn. How many children can we have?'

I pulled her back gently, not shocked, a little surprised perhaps startled.

'How many do you want?'

'Four, at least two of each. Boys so that they can grow into big strong men and girls so that I can go shopping with them when the sales hit town!'

'Are you proposing to have them in one go or through the natural rhythm of creation?'

She sniffed and surprisingly laughed.

'Definitively one at a time only why miss out on all the fun, but the sooner that we get started the better!'

I checked the time with my watch. If I was going to have Jonathon cover then I would have to call soon, but Lucy was already way ahead of me. She dialled his number for me and handed back the phone when he answered. Some things in life are more important than work and sorting out other people's lives. Mama was right, destiny was beyond our control and however much any outside influence tried to thwart the course with which we should be following, at some point it was inevitable that the balance was restored.

Later that morning Lucy would contact the Schuchel family and offer her condolences and we would send flowers as a fitting tribute. Life went on regardless as babies were born and others departed this world.

*****

A few minutes to one her mobile rang incessantly begging to be answered. When she came back into the kitchen her face was full of apology. She folded the paper that was in her hand and tucked it into her back pocket.

'This one I have to take Quinn. A cameraman and a driver are on their way over to collect me. I'm really sorry, can we take up where we left off later!'

There was no need to apologise as I followed her to the door and told her to take care. I watched from the balcony as a white van pulled up sharply outside Giovanni's and Lucy hopped in, she waved as the driver engaged gear and then they were gone. I realised that until events took control of our lives, we were always going to be shackled to our respective professions. Children was a good idea and I liked the prospect of Lucy being safe, not tied to the kitchen sink or laundry basket, just safe.

*****

'So what do we know?' Lucy asked.

The man sitting in the middle, the cameraman did most of the talking whilst the driver concentrated on weaving in and out of the traffic.

'We received a call from a male just prior to coming to collect you. What he had to tell sounded interesting, so checks were initiated and it was decided the call was genuine.'

'And...' Lucy asked, expecting there to be more.

'The call originated from a public call box sited near the old gasworks at Bure-Upton.'

Lucy shot her head around in surprise.

'That was where he assaulted the prostitute and left her for dead.'

George Thwaite holding his camera ready nodded.

'Madeleine Shaunessy. Poor kid just managed to cling onto life, although she'll never be able to conceive.'

Lucy held onto her abdomen and breathed in hard. She leant forward so that the driver Joseph Crane could see her face.

'Step on it Joe, I want this *bastard* burnt today. It's about time somebody ended his reign of terror and destruction!' The men looked at one another sensing the anger in her voice.

'Are you okay Lucy?' George asked, having known her the longest.

She peered out of the window looking at the faces of the pedestrians as they flashed by.

'Fired up George, but nothing that I can't handle!'

George Thwaite knew better than to question her reasons. Lucy had a reputation amongst the outside crews of being fanatically dedicated, thoroughly professional and unwaveringly direct when it can to an assignment. If she was fired up, it was fine by him.

'Did he give any other information?'

'Only that we would find our man on a river cruiser named the *River Prince* and that it could be located a mile west of the public call box on the Kennet. Do you think it would be wiser telling the local plod rather than us turning up unannounced?'

Lucy was adamant as she shook her head. 'No. the police will arrive mob handed if they believe that Chancery's on board. We'll miss the scoop of the decade if we leave it to them. Whereas we can be in the locality and ascertain that it is him. Then we can put the call in, but at least we'll be able to get exclusive rights to the arrest, newsreel and story. I've waited ten years for this chance George. I've a feeling that it won't come knocking on our door if we let it pass today for at least another ten!'

Heading out through Shepherds Bush, towards Slough via Maidenhead Joseph Crane kept the van travelling at a constant seventy to eighty only slowing when a speed camera loomed in the distance. Lucy closed her eyes and rested the back of her head against the cushioned panel as George and Joseph talked casually about the previous night's match, each avoiding the reason for their journey. They sensed the foreboding danger that would greet them once they arrived and neither liked that the police had not been informed.

Lucy tried to think about Quinn, but annoyingly the image of Jason Chancery haunted her every thought. She desperately wanted not to think of Penny or Sienna Schuchel or how they had died. Mile by mile Joseph Crane covered the distance. Reluctantly her thoughts homed in on her first meeting with Chancery at Middlesex Magistrates Court where a young, unshaven man brazenly entered the courtroom catching sight of the junior reporter sitting at the side. It was a look that she had never forgotten.

Chancery was unlike other men, he revelled in the terror that he left behind, sensing the control that he had over men and women alike. Grown men would quake in his presence never knowing when he would strike, but unlike Achilles the authorities and specialists had yet failed to find his weak spot. She remembered that chancery had refused to swear on the holy bible calling the book a parody of the living. The lady magistrate officiating had demanded that he observe the court, but it was plainly obvious that the young defendant was already out of control.

Lucy remembered his eyes the most, chillingly cold and dark, like the mirrors of hell as they undressed you, abused you and left you for dead. During the case the magistrate ordered that the female usher be replaced by a male colleague to prevent the young mother from having to endure his constant watching.

When his name was read out for the record adding his date of birth, the first of April, nineteen sixty nine, nobody felt like laughing. Chancery was nobody's fool, in fact far from it. He followed the case without interruption and enjoyed the occasion all the more when the arresting officer, a female probationer took the stand. With her pocket book held in her palm she conveyed the facts to the court, avoiding the stare of the defendant as much as was humanly possible.

'At ten twenty two on Thursday the twelfth of June, nineteen ninety seven a call was received concerning a street robbery that had taken place at the rear alleyway of Ashenhurst Garden Terrace. Upon attending, officers found a middle-aged victim being attended to by a postman. From the description given the defendant was apprehended several streets away and arrested.

'When searched at the police station a number of items of ladies underwear were found on the prisoner. It was later established that they had been taken from washing lines that morning prior to the offence for which he was arrested. During interview the question was raised as to why he had taken them, to which he replied because he could.'

Taking the place of the officer, the victim stood hesitantly in the witness box avoiding any contact with Jason Chancery knowing that his eyes were burning through her. Whenever the council acting for his defence required that she look, Maggie Jamieson had to endure the torment of seeing his tongue travel across the underside of his upper lip as it lasciviously suggested what he would like to do with her.

She told the court how laden down with shopping bags she was approached by Chancery who had demanded her purse. When he tore open her blouse and assaulted her, she had expected the worst, but for the fortunate intervention of the postman she was sure that she would be left for dead. When asked how she had come to this conclusion, Maggie Jamieson had replied, because you could see the intent in his eyes. Having given her reply she made sure that she didn't look his way again.

The consensus of Amelia Evington, leading the bench and the court was that Jason Chancery was a calculating, evil menace that did not deserve to be walking the streets. She recommended the case be tried at Crown Court before a judge and jury, where appropriate punishment could be bestowed. Licking his tongue across his mouth Chancery's only reaction was to smile.

Lucy quivered as the memory sent a chilling shiver down the length of her body. She doubted that Maggie Jamieson would ever forget the experience, she opened her eyes again when George Thwaite held her wrist.

'Are you alright, only you made us jump!'

Lucy stared ahead at the tarmac and traffic, determined to show that she was in control.

'I'm okay George. I just walked through a nightmare that's all.' She noticed the look of concern coming from Joseph Crane as he glanced her way.

'You want me to turn the van around at the next junction?' he asked.

'No Joe… we'll be fine, keep heading west.'

Five miles later Crane took the slip road down and onto the Kennet Road. The closer they got the quieter the tension took hold of the passenger compartment. Taking the vehicle through the traffic restrictions Joseph slowed then pointed to the carpark coming up on the left.

'This looks like it!' he said.

George Thwaite an amateur box in his youth flexed his arms as though preparing himself for a fight. Lucy nudged him with her shoulder.

'Always watching my back,' she remarked, getting a smile in return. Joseph brought the van to a halt and removed the key from the ignition.

For several seconds none moved, meticulously observing watching for signs of movement. Bure-Upton was like many other hamlets tucked away quietly in the Buckinghamshire countryside, dotted here and there with chocolate box cottages, a convenience store that housed a small post office, a counter that sold bread and other groceries, keeping the local community stocked whatever the season, day or year. Overhead the clouds were unsettled, sunny one minute and being obliterated the next in dark menacing blotches.

'A storm's coming!' Joseph remarked as they got ready to exit the van. From down the side of the door he took a length of metal pipe.

'What's that for?' Lucy asked.

'Protection,' he replied 'if Chancery's all that he's cracked up to be, then I might have need of this!' Lucy didn't protest, Joseph was right, only it might take more than a length of metal piping to stop him in his tracks.

Like the camera still from a spaghetti western they walked towards the river in a line, idly chatting although forever watching just in case, each feeling that they were the prey rather than the hunter as the sun decided to wisely take cover behind an ominously sinister black cloud.

With each step that Lucy took she heard the voices inside her head telling to turn around and leave, but professional pride and her dignity kept one foot moving before the other.

Chapter Fourteen

Bure-Upton had a heart beat that a cardiologist would be proud of, slow and unhurried. They passed one local out walking his dog, who seemed more interested in the inside pages of his paper than the strangers from out of town. The air was fresh, keen and coming from the north where the rivers had been bursting their banks for the past week, but as yet the bad weather had not affected the south. Further up the bank a gathering of river cruisers sat idly bobbing gently in the sway of the river.

Progressing through the years and avoiding the courts Jason Chancery's interests had grown since Uxbridge, his appetite yearning for more adventure beyond stealing ladies underwear to vicious assaults and possibly murder, although any evidence left behind was scant and unspecified. As yet he was still at large and terrorising every community where his feet took him. Sensing their apprehension Lucy volunteered to go ahead and check out the cruisers, but they insisted on seeing the assignment through. Reaching down into her pocket Lucy checked that she had her pepper spray handy.

Every so often they came across an accumulation of discarded rubbish, dog ends, soft drink cans and advertising leaflets, but when Lucy saw the familiar cigarette packet she stopped and stooped to check it out. Using her pen she turned it over, acknowledging the brand.

'This is Chancery's favourite.' She said, leaving the empty packet where she'd found it. 'It proves that he's about.'

'Anybody could smoke those.' George claimed, but Lucy shook her head as she stood back up.

'No George. Only certain tobacconists stock this brand. They're Turkish and more expensive than ordinary brands.'

At the first cruiser the boat looked unoccupied, clean, but like it hadn't been used for a while. They moved onto the next.

'Remember if Chancery should appear let me do the talking. If we get separated and he asks, we're doing our bit for the local tourist trade. Make sure that the camera is rolling George at all times. When we identify that it is Jason Chancery, Joseph can make the call to the police.' They both nodded that they understood. To help out the sun reappeared from behind the cloud making their *tourist* pretext all the more plausible.

George went first, followed by Joseph with Lucy bringing up the rear where the bank narrowed. They stepped over lines lashed around large metal stays which kept the cruisers secured to the bank, checking the boats identifying each by their name, until Joseph signalled to Lucy that the *River Prince* was the last in the line. He checked the metal pole jammed up the inside of his sleeve.

'Remember, let me do the talking if he appears,' she whispered *'he might go on the defensive if confronted by a man. You two look like you stand outside nightclubs and control the crowd rather than take pictures and drive a media van.'*

Stepping over the hawser line George zoomed his lens up and down the down recording every aspect of the cruiser. Suddenly the door to the cabin burst open and out stepped a man brandishing a long bladed knife. Lucy recognised Chancery instantly, but she was unsighted by Joseph who had stepped forward to protect her.

'What the fuck do you want?' he asked, exposing his immediate distrust of their presence. Forgetting what they had planned Joseph spoke up before Lucy could around him.

'It's okay mate, there's no need to get all fired up only George here is just filming along the riverbank for a tourist company!'

But the media driver didn't know Jason Chancery. The hesitation in his explanation was enough to convince Chancery that they presented a threat. He leapt up from the rear deck and drew the knife across George's throat before he could dismount the camera from his shoulder. Both camera and George fell forward slipping beneath the water line with a loud splash. Joseph released his hold on the steel pipe feeling it slip down the inside of his sleeve, but he hadn't reckoned on Chancery being so fast. Seeing the killer rush towards him he missed the end of the pipe and felt it drop, he turned and ran pushing Lucy to one side. Joseph Crane took three more steps before the knife embedded itself in the centre of his back tearing aside the two halves of his heart where it sliced through. He fell to the ground dead before he came to rest on the gravel.

Extracting the knife from the driver's back Jason Chancery smiled as he recognised Lucy.

'It's been a while since we've seen one another Miss Tate, but I knew that you'd come running today, like a rabbit finding a field of fresh corn, I knew that you couldn't resist it being me!'

Lucy swallowed the saliva at the back of her throat as she reached for the pepper spray, but her right hand trembled uncontrollably in her pocket. With long strides Jason Chancery was upon her before she had time to take her hand out. He grabbed her arm and pulled her to him.

'We should make up for lost time,' he announced, as he casually nudged Joseph's body into the river with the heel of his foot, where it floated momentarily before joining George below in the reeds.

Stepping down on the rear deck he pushed her roughly through the cabin door and slammed it shut, where the curtains had been pulled shut. The tip of his tongue creased the underside of his upper lip.

'You've filled out nicely since we last met. Are you going to co-operate or fight me for the chance to live through this ordeal?'

Lucy wanted to stand, but her legs felt like jelly. She tried to avoid looking into his eyes, sensing the evil that dwelt behind the hypnotic black orbs, knowing that they already had her naked.

'Like the chance that you gave to my friends in Brighton?' she spat back.

Taking the nylon twine from his rucksack, he laughed.

'Well the reporter did co-operate at the end, but only after I had ended her sister's life. It was fun though and I'm sure that they both enjoyed it, although neither would say as much!'

'You contemptable bastard, you destroy everything that you touch. Have you no ounce of decency in your veins?'

As he tied her hands behind her back Jason Chancery licked the side of her neck. Lucy tried to repel his tongue, but he was strong, very strong.

'My father knocked all morality from me when I was young. He was the reason that my mother died, the reason why you're here!'

He tore aside her jacket and blouse and yanked down her jeans pushing her onto the bed, before undressing.

'I'll ask the questions as we have ourselves some fun!'

Slicing through her underwear he tossed the items to one side as he climb on the bed beside her. Lucy wanted to scream, but the sound wouldn't emerge from her vocal chords, where fear had paralysed the muscles in her throat. As Jason Chancery raped her, he asked a question getting the answers that he demanded. When it was done, she lay on the bed feeling the tears wash down her cheeks thinking only of Richard Quinn. Derisively Chancery put her bra to the underside of his nose and sniffed hard.

'I bet the lawyer has never taken you like that?' he mocked.

Lucy looked up at him, her eyes full of contempt and anger.

'He's a real man, you on the other hand are nothing short of a monster, but eventually all monsters meet their match.'

He laughed as he toyed his knife along the underside of her breast.

'That time at Burnt-Upper-Kirby, I knew that it was you watching. You went to a lot of trouble and expense renting that hovel just to keep tabs on my movements. Had I not been so preoccupied at the time I would have come across and made our acquaintance more concrete then. It was fun though because you were watching me as I was watching you. That bathroom window did little to disguise when you took a shower.'

'What did you want me for today, other than to abuse me?'

'The *gift* that you possess, I want it, I need it.'

Lucy shook her head realising what a fool she had been, she should have listened to the voices and seen through the warning that Mama Maria had given Quinn the evening before. Destiny took a path along which we all walked, but fate could intervene without showing any mercy.

'The gift cannot just be handed over Chancery. It is given at birth, a bequest handed down by god and to be used for the good of mankind. If this is what you seek then you have wasted your time and energy!'

Jason Chancery suddenly became angry, he cut a line across the top of her shoulder, but Lucy had suffered the humiliation of being violated, she had become resilient, stronger both in body and mind. The tears of pain and degradation had gone.

'Why do you need it?'

'I need to communicate with my mother. I need to know that she still loves me!'

This time Lucy laughed. It sounded ridiculous and unwarranted in the present circumstances, but she knew that the end was near. In a final act of defiance she turned the balance of power in her favour. As Jason Chancery slashed and cut, she felt her life ebbing away.

When the blanket of death finally fell a hand, a loving strong hand reached out for hers as Papa Bernado took hold and pulled her soul through to the other side where he could wrap his arms around his grand-daughter and have her know that she was safe. In the void where Lucy could see the gateway, he would wait with her until such a time that she was avenged.

Just shy of forty miles away Mama Maria sat beside the fire place cradling the photographs of her late husband and the girl child with the long black ringlets. She felt the weight of death pulling down on her heart as the tears fell upon the glass keeping the images safe. Inside her mind Bernado had told Mama that Lucetta was with him, she was glad. One day she vowed to have her revenge, but for the others still living, those left behind the pain was just about to begin.

Chapter Fifteen

Jonathon used the services of a friend to tediously search through old census records and parish ledgers looking for anything that could positively identify the whereabouts of Oliver Grey. When the call came late that afternoon drawing a blank the search was passed onto an agency in America. I was glad that Jonathon had taken the challenge upon himself as I was finding it difficult to concentrate on anything specific. Something and I couldn't quite put my finger on what was asking for my attention elsewhere. I had sent a couple of text messages to Lucy and left a voicemail, but not unsurprisingly received no reply.

A short time after the first call came another to say that a niece several times removed had been found in relation to Mary Jane Garman. Tentatively Jonathon made the call as I listened in. Anne Sturgess lived in Lincolnshire was a mother to twin girls and although surprised to receive a call from our office, was delighted to hear the intention why. More surprising was that she herself had been for years wading through records and documents trying to find a way in which she could have her great aunt officially pardoned.

We both listened as Anne Sturgess read the contents of a letter that had been written to Mary's father from a detective sergeant at Hampstead, where an apology did not excuse the wrongful arrest and execution, but by which the detective begged forgiveness for the injustice served upon the family. In the letter the policeman named Charles Henry Higgins as the true offender and made reference that justice would be served on earth and in hell. Of course the letter would have to be authenticated, but it was the proof that we needed to clear her name. Somewhere inside my head I heard a voice say *thank you*. Jonathon made the necessary arrangements to visit Lincolnshire the next day. When he replaced the receiver, he appeared jubilant yet perplexed.

'You've something on your mind, would it help talking it through?' he asked, concerned that I didn't appear to be my normal self.

'We went to see Mama Maria last night, which was both good and bad. Good in that she cleared up some grey areas, but bad that I'm still confused. At one point she referred to me as the *gate-keeper*. When I asked Lucy what her grandmother had meant, she told me that I had been empowered with the souls of those waiting to go beyond. It's a big ask Jonathon and I cannot devote my entire life to each and every one.'

'Maybe Pike and Mary Garman were some kind of test to see how you coped?'

It made sense. A test run I could manage, but I didn't want many others. Lucy and I had plans and I wanted to devote my life to her.

'You've been staring at that phone most of the afternoon, are you expecting a call?'

To prove his point I picked up my mobile and saw a blank screen.

'I know that Lucy is on an assignment, but I've a gut feeling about her being there!'

'Where?' Jonathon asked.

'That's just it, I don't know.' I felt a cold shiver run down my spine. 'But from about two this afternoon I've had a strange foreboding that she's in danger. She's not answered my text or voicemail, not that there's anything strange about that, but about an hour ago I heard a voice cry out inside my head and I was sure that it was hers.'

'Have you tried the paper?'

I nodded. 'You know what the press are like, they are more secretive than the green and white monument at eighty five Albert Embankment.'

Jonathon chortled as he picked up his mobile and punched in a quick text message.

'Arabella?' I asked.

'No... Lucy. I asked her to put you out of your misery and call.'

'How did you get her number?'

'She gave it to me some time back when you were in court one afternoon, I case she couldn't reach you. I would have said, but I was sworn to secrecy. You know how manipulative Italian's can be!'

I had to agree with Jonathon, Lucy was frightening when she got going, definitely sexy and adorably fiery, but not knowing what she could dish out was what concerned me the most. His knowing her number eased my mood.

'Thanks. I'm sure that she'll make contact when the moment presents itself.'

I phoned her apartment and my home to see if she was there, but when the sound of my voice cut in, I put down the receiver. Overhead a large black cloud was looming from the west.

*****

As more and more police vehicles arrived the small carpark at Bure-Upton began to fill and resemble an emergency services extravaganza rather than the start of a murder investigation. To the side a team of dog handlers waited impatiently for instruction ready to begin the hunt having found a patch of blood on the riverbank where it narrowed, but with so many specialist units still arriving they had to wait their turn. What none of them realised was that the last cruiser the *River Prince* had already left its moorings and gone down river long before the two bodies in the water had decided to float to the surface.

Parked alongside the white van a school coach sat with the engine idling waiting for permission to take the party of children back to the junior school, where a team of detectives were already waiting to interview them. Later that afternoon the head teacher would put a call through to the education offices and arrange for several bereavement councillors to attend the homes of the youngsters that had located the dead men. In reality, although excited about their find the children, a mix of boys and girls were unaffected. They saw horror and violence as part of their upbringing playing on their older brother and sisters Xbox.

Waiting on the bank a police diver came to the surface holding a large black object. The detective nearest reached down and took charge of the video camera that had once been the extension of George Thwaites right arm.

I doubt that we'll get any images from this now,' said the detective in charge 'but send it to the lab anyway!'

The diver went back down and searched around, but could find no murder weapon amongst the reeds or the water filled cans that decked the river bed.

Chapter Sixteen

The more that I paced around the apartment the more my gut got tighter. The last call that I had placed to Lucy's mobile, it had come back dead. No reporter ever turned off their phone. Just after a quarter to seven I tried the paper again and talked to another female reporter who could only say that Lucy was still out on assignment. I thanked her, but cancelled the call knowing that something was definitely wrong. She had been on a high earlier that morning making plans, talking about having children and altering the course of her destiny. It didn't include journalism, maybe staying at home, becoming a writer and being there should the school call. When I tried around eight I was less genial.

'Okay... okay, I'll check with whoever's around!' I heard the receiver thump the desk top as the man went away to appease my concerns. I hung on the line desperate for some news. When he returned he was less aggressive. I wondered why the sudden change.

'Lucy's not come back to the office yet. She's with two other's a cameraman and driver, so I can vouch that she's safe as I know both George and Joseph. Neither would let any harm come to Lucy. Trust me, your concerns are unfounded. I'm off soon, but the sub-editor is downstairs in the print room. Before I go I'll get word to him that you've called several times. Duncan's not normally as strung out as Bill Schuchermann, the editor. If there's any update on Lucy, I'll have him call.' I was about to say thanks, but the line went dead and I was left with the receiver stuck on my ear.

Walking past the steak that had been washed, flattened down and drowned in alcohol I went out onto the balcony, where I could see her as she walked down the road, only I had a feeling that she wouldn't. A quarter past the hour I grabbed my car keys and drove over to her apartment in Knightsbridge.

*****

Oscar Bunyan stretched hard feeling the sinews in his arms drive away the stresses of the day, before inserting the key in the club house door. It was a day that he wanted to forget, a day that in which he would be glad to be home, as long as his wife didn't start nagging the minute he got through the door. It was the same old record going around and around ont eh turntable, always insults and insinuations regarding the barmaid, Sybil Ellenmore. It wasn't Oscar's doing that she had a voluptuous bosom and long peroxide blonde hair. Sybil was a nice lady, run an efficient bar and helped boost necessary funds for the yacht club. It was naïve of his wife to consider anything else. All Oscar yearned for was a hot meal and watch a good movie.

As club secretary, he had an important, but demanding role which occasionally involved some late working, especially when the minutes of the annual meeting needed recording. Earlier that afternoon he had taken delivery of a new yacht which had been transported by road from Southampton. It would have been ordinarily an easy task, signing off the delivery and making sure that the boat was in place for the owner had the transporter not been in a collision with a foreign articulated lorry. Oscar hated the slightest disruption to his military precision run agenda.

Easing himself into the soft upholstery of his car, he switched on the lights and fired up the engine. The instant that the beam of light rested upon the water ahead Oscar became aware of something in the water, he turned the switch to full beam adding more light. Initially he thought that the object was a drowned animal belly-up. Rolling the car forward to the water's edge, he realised that it wasn't an animal. In the navy he had seen both animals and deep oceanic creatures floating motionless at sea or lying at the side of the road and in the deep freeze of a ship he had come across the corpses of dead sailors who had died at sea. Fumbling around for his mobile he dialled for the police.

Standing at the edge of the pontoon he managed to avoid the forever moving and stretched lines keeping the boats from drifting away as he tried unsuccessfully to get a hold of the body in the water by casting a weighted line hoping that it would snag an arm or a leg, but the ever present arthritis in his shoulder wouldn't allow him to cast out far enough. When the incoming tide turned the body around Oscar got his first full sighting of what had once been a young woman. He felt the repulsion bubble and rise in the pit of his stomach as leant forward unable to prevent himself as the outward gush of his lunch hit the surface of the water. The first police vehicle to arrive saw the man vomit as he steadied himself and sat down on the back of the nearest boat.

'I take it that the caller went for a closer look!' remarked the driver as he pulled up next to the pontoon. The passenger didn't reply. This was his first body and he was already somewhat apprehensive. Not far behind an unmarked car entered the marina carpark.

Due south and not more than four miles away from the marina at Harpsend Common Trevor Baines dropped the remains of his cigarette onto the towpath then crushed the dog end with the heel of his shoe. His mobile was pinned to his ear ignoring any background noise his end.

'So what have you got Jack?' he asked.

Jack Kelstow a seasoned veteran with only a year left before retirement watched the dead woman bob about amongst the ripples. He sighed knowing that he wouldn't be back home in time to catch the re-run of the match.

'What looks to be a young woman guv'nor, but I will be able to tell you more when our latest recruit goes in and fetches her out.'

The detective chief inspector waited patiently as the uniformed recruit waded through the shallows before grabbing a hand and pulling the dead woman to the shoreline. What Jack Kelstow saw turned his stomach.

'I think that you had best come and have a look yourself. This floater didn't die of natural causes.'

The two men had known one another for a very long time, joined the force the same day, trained together, but Trevor Baines had more ambition. Rising through the ranks he now headed a small detective task force operating out of Reading. Ambition however could not outweigh experience and if Jack said he should go look, then it didn't warrant questioning.

'Alright Jack, give me ten or fifteen minutes. I'll go find Bob Pearson then we will make our way over. We are almost done here anyway.'

Jack Kelstow patted the recruit's wet shoulder, praising him on doing a good job.

'Jobs like this are never easy David, but unfortunately this will be one of many that you'll attend during your service. Throughout the summer months the idiots coming boating thinking that they know everything there is to know about the river. Add some alcohol, hot lazy days and you instantly have a cocktail for disaster. This river is without mercy and the undercurrents are notorious.'

David Jackson tousled the water from his hair then put back on his shirt as Oscar Bunyan helped the other, older officer to place the dead woman onto a plastic sheet.

'What kind of sick bastard does this?' Oscar Bunyan asked, as his eyes travelled up from her feet to the top of her head.

'The kind that shouldn't have been born.' Replied Harry Simmons, a year behind Jack Kelstow in service. 'Do you want me to cover her completely Jack?' he asked.

'No, leave her be Harry. Trevor Baines is on his way. As long as she's protected from whatever is on the shoreline, forensics can do the rest.'

'I need a drink,' remarked Oscar as he looked away not wanting to look any longer 'can I interest anybody else?' Jack Kelstow shook his head, but suggested that Harry accompanied David Jackson and Oscar to the clubhouse.

Standing where Sybil Ellenmore had stood only hours earlier Oscar poured three whiskies, offered Harry and David theirs then topped up his glass almost instantly. He saw Harry watching.

'Don't worry officer, I might have another couple after this, but I'll call for a cab to get me home. I don't think that I've the stomach to drive.'

In the carpark outside another car had arrived. The occupants got out and walked over to the water's edge.

'Things don't look like they're getting any better, do they Jack?'

Jack Kelstow nodded at Bob Pearson and raised his eyebrows at Trevor Baines.

'I thought that in all my years I had seen it all, but this adds a new dimension to the slice and dice brigade. Whoever did this to this poor woman, must not only be short a few bob mentally, but must have a pact with the devil himself.'

Trevor Baines looked his the man that had accompanied him to the marina.

'What do you think Bob?'

Bob Pearson knelt down to examine the flesh wounds closer.

'I've seen similar injuries before on a victim, only I cannot remember exactly where!'

'Have you called forensics Jack?' Baines asked.

'They should be here any minute.'

'And the club secretary, what's his name…Oscar Bunyan. Is he giving a statement?'

'He's in the clubhouse trying to forget what he's seen.'

'As long as he gets it all down on paper first, after that he can drink as much as he likes. And young Jackson, is he okay?'

Trevor Baines gave the impression that he had a hard exterior, but those that knew him best also recognised the soft interior that still had compassion for others. He had never forgotten his earlier years on the beat and what he had been asked to endure to earn his spurs.

'He's alright…' replied Jack Kelstow. 'He'll notch this one up, never forget it mind, but soon he'll be telling all that will listen about the night that he fished out the woman from the marina. We've all done it at some stage of our career.'

'She's the right age group for the report on the missing reporter.' Bob Pearson added before he came away from the body. 'She was a looker as well, still is… only dead!'

'Until anybody else reports her missing, you'd best get back in touch with that sub-editor Bob and have him formally identity all three bodies. This is turning out to quite a day.'

They watched as the forensics team set about erecting a tent and laying out the examination equipment. Trevor Baines asked only one question of the lead examiner.

'Can you estimate how long the deceased has been in the water?

The white suited officer checked various areas of the body before replying.

'Not long, a couple of hour's maybe, but I'd say no more than that.'

Trevor Baines turned to both detectives.

'Then our killer could still be in the area, although given that he's got a two hours head start he could be anywhere, but my gut tells me that he's still somewhere close by.'

Calling his wife to explain the reason why he was so late in getting away from the marina, as was expected Shelia Bunyan gave Oscar a hard time, yelling down the receiver at him that Sybil Ellenmore was a no good tramp, a philandering whore and the only attraction that men ever saw in her was the way she wriggled her arse. Propping up the bar the two uniformed officers heard her describe the barmaid as all tits and teeth.

'I bet that makes you feel glad that you're still single.' Whispered Harry, as he playfully nudged David Jackson's arm.

*****

Tucked out of sight and concealed amongst the undergrowth on the far side of the marina entrance Jason Chancery put down the binoculars and rubbed the bridge of his nose where he had been observing the detectives mull over the body stretched out on the plastic sheet. He had become disinterested when the tent had been erected and placed over Lucetta Tate.

With a nudge of his arm he watched as the black bag weighted down with a heavy boulder dropped below the surface of the water and quickly disappeared into the dark void below the river cruiser. The splash sent out a series of ripples that fascinated him. As a boy he had liked throwing things into water to see how many ripples he could create. Standing on the water's edge the three men heard the splash.

'What was that?' said Bob Pearson as they scanned the horizon, but saw nothing to help.

'Probably only a large fish, they come out at night to feed and catch the fly's hovering above the surface.' The lead examiner pulled aside the tent flap and went inside. It seemed that he could be right as the silence returned.

Running the lace of her knickers along the underside of his nose Jason Chancery smiled to himself, the police were always one step behind and he was always one step ahead. It was a pity that Lucetta Tate had, had to die so abruptly, if only she had been more accommodating he wouldn't have gotten so angry. Sniffing long and hard he could feel himself getting aroused, wishing that she was still tied up and waiting for him to join her on the bed.

Sucking hard on the end of the cigarette he felt the calming effect of the nicotine as it filled the chambers of his lungs and brain, and like the river it washed through his mind sending him to another place. Adding cocaine to the tobacco had been a good idea. *Aphrodite's gold* was what the teenager had called it, from whom he had made the purchase. As he closed his eyes he recalled the afternoon that he had spent entertaining

Lucetta Tate. He had waited so long for her, but the wait had been worth it. He nodded to himself as he drew on the cigarette and agreed that it had been a real shame that she'd had to die.

Chapter Seventeen

Taking the stairs two at a time I pressed the doorbell several times before inserting the key, justifying to myself that this wasn't just me being over protective, but my coming to find Lucy had become necessary. I called out, but the silence was deafening. The only sound that I could detect was the small motor working the fridge freezer. I checked each room and although there were no doors or windows open the place appeared cold, much cooler than it should have been. Ordinarily the apartment, imbued with light and energy seemed to have had the life been sucked out of it.

Going around a second time I noticed that nothing was out of place, neither the kitchen nor the bathroom had been used and perhaps the only thing missing was the space in the wardrobe shelf where Lucy had removed the overnight bag and that was still at my apartment. The different thoughts racing around my head kept asking the same question, but without answers the cycle would not stop. It might have been better had I closed the door made sure that it was secure then returned home, but suddenly I was overcome with anxious exhaustion. I sat on the settee and closed my eyes. The next time I opened them I was in the midst of a darkened hospital ward with a line of occupied beds either side. Whoever had come to collect me was standing at my side and pointing down at the women nearest to where I had landed.

'Do not concern yourself with her because she will not wake.'

'Where are we?' I asked.

'Palmerston General Hospital.'

For the first time I noticed that she alike all the other patients was wearing a hospital gown, but it was her face that concerned me most. Her features were set hard, not cracked, but as though she hadn't laughed in years. At the other end of the ward a lone nurse was busy filling in medical records as she beavered away at the desk, she didn't look up nor seemed interested in that I had arrived, I wondered if she actually knew I was there.

'She will not disturb us, of that I am sure!'

'Who are you?'

'Linda Cunningham or at least I was, when I was last in the ward.'

'Is this going to take long?' I asked, feeling slightly irritated that I had been taken once again when I wanted, needed to be elsewhere. The woman smiled.

'Time is irrelevant, has little meaning here. What controls your life Mr Quinn is lost when we pass over. I know too why you went to the flat in Knightsbridge, but don't worry because you will see Lucy again soon.'

I wanted to ask how she knew that I had made the journey across town, how she knew where I would be when she came calling and how did she know Lucy. I didn't ask because I feared the reply.

'Alright... but, why the hospital ward?'

'Because this is the last place that I breathed air before my soul departed my body. Because I need your help.'

I knew it. This couldn't keep happening only I didn't want my life dominated searching into the past lives of others. I wanted to lead a normal, happy existence with Lucy, raising children, going on holiday and building a home for my family. It was inevitable also that Jonathon would one day venture further afield, start his own practice or emigrate, he had ambition and goals to achieve and I wanted the same. I had forgot that *they* could read your thoughts.

'Your scorn is justified, but if you hear my story out, perhaps then you will understand why I brought you here.' I nodded, staying silent so that she could explain.

'*Ten years ago I made a fatal mistake, taking up with an evil, wicked man who went by the name of Jason Chancery. At first he seemed perfect, my ideal choice of partner, but soon after moving in with me he changed. Physically he had a problem, but I was patient, helpful and got him through some difficult times, but it seemed the more I tried to help the more he channelled his aggression against me.*

'*Prior to meeting Jason I had been experiencing a low period of my life, crawling out of the gutter having gone through a messy divorce, struggling financially and I was at my lowest ebb. Jason recognised the signs, he took advantage of the situation and quickly manipulated the situation to fulfil his own sick fantasies.*

'*Like a disparaging black cloud he had descended upon my house bringing with him unpredictable moods and demoralising demands. Within a month I had been transformed into a recluse and his slave. I prayed for a way out, but my prayers went unanswered.*

140

'Before my husband I'd had men, but other than my husband, Jason Chancery was the worst of them all. What he would do to do me physically went beyond depravity. I felt like I was an animal there to satisfy his weird fixation on lust. Sex wasn't normal, a pleasure, it was something that had to be endured. I never felt clean Mr Quinn. Have you any idea what that feels like for a woman?'

She quickly shook her head.

'I doubt any man, however good, really knows. Men don't walk the same path that women do. We endure more, accept more whether we like it or not. Our body should be a shrine, not something to be abused. Self-preservation becomes our only hope of survival. It's like fighting an enemy that we cannot see or defeat. Men like Jason Chancery somehow know this. He would tie me to the bed ends, abuse me physically and mentally then end the session by cutting me!'

In the half-light Linda Cunningham suddenly let the hospital gown fall from her shoulders all the way down to the floor. Instantly the dark scars that lined her body, her breasts, abdomen, thighs, arms and back were shockingly evident. If I could be grateful for anything, it was that her face had been untouched. Moments later she reached down and covered herself once again. Somewhere towards the end of the ward where it was darkest I thought I saw something move. I tried to peer into the gloom, but saw nothing.

'As he cut through my flesh, Jason would tell me that he was protecting me. He said that it would bond us together. Believe me Mr Quinn, it was last thing that I wanted with the monster.'

141

'Why did you not just walk out when he wasn't around and go to the police. They would have protected you. They would have put him away for a very long time?' She came closer.

'Have you ever seen a caged animal, they prowl back and forth seeking the moment that the cage door is left unlocked. That's how I felt, only the keeper always made sure that the cage was locked down. If Jason went out, he would place a gag across my mouth and tie me to the bed. When he returned that was when I was attacked. I remember his breathe smelling foul as though he had been smoking heavily. I could not escape.'

'But why the hospital... why here?' I asked.

'One morning whilst Jason was out the police came and forced their way into the house, when they found me, I was untied, the gag removed and taken to hospital. I was so badly beaten that I couldn't even tell them where he was. An ambulance with a police escort brought me to Palmerston General, where a police officer guarded the side ward day and night. A warrant was issued for his arrest and media bulletins warned the public not to approach him.

'When I did regain the use of my vocal chords I discovered that the police had come that morning to arrest him as part of an ongoing investigation into the rape and murder of a student from the nearby university. Jason had been identified by a milkman out on his rounds. He picked out Jason from the photofit files that the police had on computer. By chance the same milkman had been out delivering again when Jason left the house. The rest you can work out. The milkman became my angel for the next few days as the doctors and nurses healed my wounds and began giving me back my dignity.

'A reporter from London got wind of the police raid and she came to see me at the hospital, but was refused entry by the police officer. I never did get chance to talk with her, but I saw her looking at me through the viewing window. Much later I discovered that she had been tracking Jason all over the country compiling a dossier on him. I remembered him talking about her when he was raping me, although at the time her name was as insignificant as any other woman's.'

I felt a dagger plunge through my heart at the mention of her name and feared the worst. Again I thought that I saw something move at the end of the ward, but the light was playing tricks with my eyes.

'The student from the university. Did he cut her too?'

She nodded then lowered her head as though feeling responsible for what happened.

'When he eventually came back in the early hours of the next morning I just knew that he had committed some atrocity. He would never tell of course, but when I saw on the news that a student had been raped and murdered, I instinctively knew that Jason was responsible. I begged him to stop, but the more I pleaded the more he beat me. If the milkman had not tipped off the police I think I would have died the morning they kicked down the door. All the time that he hit me he kept repeating over and over again 'leave no loose ends, leave no loose ends!'

'On the third night after a small operation to repair some internal damage, Jason calmly walked into the hospital, found a nursing orderly working alone in a store cupboard, he left the orderly for dead taking his uniform. With the policeman outside the room he entered my room where I was sleeping and slit my throat, leaving the hospital before I was found. This is where I died.

'But why kill you. You didn't tell the police anything that they didn't already know?'

'Because I cannot pass through the gateway without your help. Jason Chancery is connected to you now, although you don't know it yet, the same way that Ashley Jones, the student is too. With your help justice will be done.'

This time the shadow did emerge, did reveal itself, not that I wanted it to. Before Lucy walked towards me I already knew that it would be her. I felt my heart crushing inside my chest as the words 'Nooooooo' left my lips.

The sound of the lift arriving in the lobby beyond the front door interrupted the scream and when I opened my eyes I found that I was still sitting on Lucy's settee. I wanted to rush from room to room to check again and for the first time I wanted the experience to be nothing, but a dream, but the rapid beat pulsing through my wrist told me that what you wish for, doesn't always come true. The experience had been too vivid not have been real.

Chapter Eighteen

The two detectives passed through the wooden door without any windows and proceeded down the long corridor, their footsteps echoing on the tiled floor. Trevor Baines held open the door at the far end ignoring the small dish containing coffee granules.

'This has got to be the only place where the smell of formaldehyde hits you before you reach the cutting room!'

Dr Anthony Bremmer, pathologist and keen golfer was already attired in green scrubs and stood ready beside the first cadaver.

'Finally gentlemen,' he declared, 'perhaps I can make a start.'

Lying adjacent to one another, naked and their heads supported by a small wooden block the bodies of Lucetta Tate, George Thwaite and Joseph Crane waited to be examined.

'I have already made some preliminary checks, but nothing which will detract from the main reason why we are here today. I have to say chief inspector that you don't believe in doing things by half, three dead is a bit excessive and I have a charity tournament arranged which is due to start at two.'

'Then we best move along and not delay you!' remarked Baines who professionally respected Bremmer's work, but wouldn't choose to have him as a friend.

Standing back so that the pathologist and his assistant could move about the stainless steel tables with ease Baines and Pearson watched and listened. Going to Lucetta Tate first Bremmer switched on the overhead microphone.

'Victim one – is a female, white Caucasian of European extraction in her mid-thirties. Height one sixty seven point five centimetres and weighing fifty nine kilograms. Initial examination rules out any previous medical trauma, procedures or conditions and there are no signs of drug abuse.'

He pulled back the eyelids then closed then again. 'No asphyxia present, but the torso and limbs have suffered multiple laceration trauma.' Using a metal rule he gauged the depth of several cuts. 'It would appear that the cuts have been meticulously applied, appear unhurried and are detailed in pattern. It is not certain whether the victim was alive or deceased at the time that they were administered and of course with the intervention of her being in the water for at least two to three hours, certain other factors have to be taken into consideration. In my humble opinion however, I would say that she was still alive suggesting that the victim was tortured before she died.'

Bob Pearson looked at Trevor Baines. 'This has similarities to the case of the two young women from the Brighton area!'

Bremmer nodded 'I spoke to a colleague before you arrived and yes, there are as you say similarities.' He scraped clean the fingernails collecting samples of fibre and skin tissue, hoping that some might be the perpetrators.

'At some stage of the attack the victim was struck with a blunt instrument,' he took measurements and photographs 'and I would say that she was rendered unconscious, with the blunt end of the knife handle. No doubt fighting back!'

'Was her neck broken?' Baines asked.

Bremmer examined the area of the neck with deft fingertips feeling around where the handle had struck. 'There is a partial displacement of the cervical osteophytes in the upper spine and the small veins have been ruptured as a result of a severe blow to that area, but it would only be a contributory factor. The heart, one's body and the soul can only take so much Mr Baines. This level of torture is far outside of any comprehensible acceptance.

'During times of war, conflict and terrorism, the questioning of a prisoner might prevail upon using physical violence to extract say vital information, going outside the boundaries of the Geneva convention, but I doubt anything as drastic as this would ever have been inflicted upon any unfortunate soul. This poor creature however suffered terribly and only Satan could do such a thing.' For the last part Bremmer had turned off the microphone.

'Would he have need medical training to inflict such injuries?' Bremmer looked up at Bob Pearson and shook his head.

'No sergeant. But I would say that this wasn't his first time!'

'Ritualistic?' asked Baines.

Again Bremmer shook his head. 'The black arts can be idiosyncratic, but this is more personal, this attack had revenge stamped all over it.'

The pathologist then performed an internal investigation to which he confirmed that Lucy had been sexually assaulted. Samples were taken and would be sent to the lab for analysis and when run through the system they would identify Jason Chancery as the offender, but by then he would have attacked again. What Bremmer wouldn't know was that one of the chromosomes already in the womb would belong to Richard Quinn and that it had already reacted with that belonging to Lucetta Tate.

'Somewhere in the system you'll find that this offender has left behind similar havoc chief inspector.'

'Are the cuts a calling card, the killer's signature?'

Bremmer didn't want to get drawn into areas where he confessed to not being an expert. He did however, have an opinion.

'Off the record, I would say that the perpetrator is a calculated madman. The woman's injuries state as much. Whoever inflicted this level of pain and you cannot discount another woman from being present at the time of the attack, the rape no, but the cutting yes, whoever tortured the victim has an agenda by which they operate. Madness is a complex issue, a defect of the human brain and some hear voices which they offer as a poor excuse for the atrocities that they perform, but very few kill for the sheer fun of it. The dark arts will need investigating, but a calling card chief inspector, maybe. Or perhaps a warning!'

Bremmer quickly moved onto George Thwaite ascertaining that he had died instantly from a knife wound which had severed his throat and finally recording that Joseph Crane had met a similar death suffering a punctured aorta. He took water samples from each of their lungs, but it was only to satisfy himself and the police that a full examination had taken place. Each man had died as a result of a violent meeting with Jason Chancery. The only other outside fact was that Joseph Crane had been suffering from pancreatic cancer. It had not reached the most aggressive stages of the disease, but it would have in another few months. All the same he did not need to have his life ended prematurely.

When at last he switched off the microphone, Anthony Bremmer sighed and stretched out his upper limbs as far as they would go. He removed his gloves and threw them in the surgical waste bag pegged alongside the three tables.

'I'll have the reports typed up and sent across to you by late this afternoon.' With that he bade them farewell and left the examination room to change in readiness for the charitable golfing tournament.

In the grounds outside Baines and Pearson shared a few moments to reflect the morning. As the smoke from their cigarettes disappeared above their heads Trevor Baines felt that he needed to say something.

'We need to catch this bastard and soon Bob. Bremmer was probably right that he's done this before and will do it again.'

Bob Pearson stubbed out his cigarette then snapped the ends of his fingers together as a thought, a memory flashed through his head.

'We need to get back to the office, only I have just remembered where I had seen these kind of injuries before. It's a long way back in the past, but the photographs and statements should still be in the system.'

Within ten minutes they were back at the station and eagerly trawling through the data base searching through the criminal variants. Soon a match would be found, along with a name.

*****

Not that far away the *River Prince* bobbed up and down on the water, but now minus its name where it had been painted over. Finding a suitable place to tie off Jason Chancery gathered together his rucksack before dousing the interior with petrol. When the explosion ignited the cabin he ducked then walked away across the field to the village in the distance. More explosions destroyed all evidence that he or Lucetta Tate had ever been aboard the cruiser. He smiled to himself, satisfied with how successful everything had been dispatched.

Not too far away the residents of Burtonmoor heard the blasts, but none could determine from which direction they had come, until the black plume of smoke rose high in the sky. Had they known too what was coming their way, they would have run and shut the doors and battened down the hatches.

Chapter Nineteen

Coursing through what had been left behind by the downpour I could hear the traffic travelling up and down the Knightsbridge Road washing down the pavements amidst the occasional shout from a unfortunate pedestrian who was too slow to avoid a sudden shower. Standing on the balcony outside I needed to see and hear people going about their business, some leaving restaurants, others doing some late night shopping. The air all around felt charged, alive and ready to do battle with the night.

When eventually I went back inside having unscrambled my thoughts I checked the ansa-machine and listened to the fourteen messages saved. Ten belonged to me and I deleted them, hating the sound of my own voice. One was from a florist to say that Lucy's order had been dispatched south, another from a man called George who would try her mobile. Mama Maria left one, but it was in Italian so I didn't understand a word of it and finally the last from the news desk, asking Lucy to call as soon as she got back home. I had to smirk to myself when the caller, a vexed male stated that a man purporting to be Richard Quinn had been pestering the newspaper since early evening asking about her whereabouts. When the message ended I felt suddenly flat, spent of energy and without direction. Every aspect of Lucy's existence had been played out. Like the messages, memories could be played back, not forgotten, but not ever physically re-enacted.

The experience with Linda Cunningham had answered some nagging questions that had been plaguing my mind, but also opened up others. I realised that to put a stop to this episode of evil I would have to stop Jason Chancery myself. At the moment I didn't know where to start, but I was sure that when the anger intensified then I would know.

Leaving the last four messages recorded, I switched off the message facility as it made no sense to leave it available. In her bedroom I found a framed photograph of when we had been teenagers, young and trendy, our mode of dress now outdated, but irrespective of opinions we looked cool and ready to take on the world. I removed the photograph and slipped it into my coat pocket. As I went through her personal belongings, I found myself searching for clues, knowing that Lucy would not have kept everything inside her head. Females had many habits that annoyed men, but one was hoarding. They kept old memories, trinkets, photos and school memorabilia in shoe boxes or under the bed. Like a burglar I rummaged frantically.

Moving her jumpers to one side I found it, a box patterned in news clippings and slightly worn down one side where the lid had been removed then replaced many times. When I pulled open the lid the first thing to hit me was musty smell of age. Inside was a stockpile of clippings, photographs, reports and written notes, dates, times and places. One by one I went through the contents spreading them out across the kitchen worktop. One photograph in particular stood out more than others. A man in the foreground had been circled with a thick red marker, but as important was the second circle surrounding a woman standing in the shop doorway. She wasn't as clearly visible, although she would be recognisable if matched against another image. The photo had been taken in Leeds City Central.

Delving deeper I removed a buff envelope and made space on the worktop. Inside was a single still image from a security camera dated June, nineteen ninety seven, an official typed report and a small article from the newspaper, written by the reporter, Lucetta Tate. On the reverse side of the still was the name *Jason Phillip Chancery – 1st April 1969.* Chancery was smiling up at the camera and had raised a two finger gesture. I read through the contents digesting every detail. One article in particular seemed out of place, concerning a young man named Alexander Machin a former pupil of Brancaster Grove Secondary Modern who had been found fatally stabbed in an alleyway not far from the school gates. Machin had last been seen frequenting a gay club in Leeds City centre, but none when questioned remember him leaving the club or whether he had been with anybody.

The official report however did interest me. It was a psychiatric evaluation that had been compiled for the North Nayworth Court and concerned Jason Phillip Chancery who was accused of sexually harassing and abusing a teenage female in the area. I read through the details of the arrest, then settled myself to read the rest.

Demographic of Patient:

Born at home address on Tuesday 1st April 1969. 35 Shelton Road, Harbonworth, Leeds. Parents – Mary Anne Chancery (nee Wilkes) and Phillip Arthur Chancery.

Jason's birth was a difficult breech and the midwife had to prevent the umbilical cord from strangling the new-born infant. Precious seconds of oxygen starved the infant's brain and lungs until at last he cried and was placed on his mother's chest.

Jason Phillip Chancery is a white Caucasian male, 21 years of age.

He is of medium build, although strong and appears athletic.

Initial clinical impressions suggest long-standing psychotic tendencies.

Background Information:

A working class family who struggle on a low income with the father often out of work and supplemented by government benefits. Jason struggled at school between the ages of 5 – 16 years, although the last terms at Brancaster Grove seem to have changed his outlook on life. He left behind an education with no qualifications. Jason was fostered out several times, but never successfully.

Jason was hesitant to offer any personal information about his school days or since walking away from Brancaster Grove other than to add, that his father arrived home early one evening having been in the pub from the time it had opened and promptly accused his wife of being involved with a much younger man from the next street.

A violent argument ensued resulting in Mary Anne Chancery being hospitalised for her injuries. The accusation, which father had overheard in the pub was never substantiated, not that it mattered to Phillip Chancery. He had to be seen to save face. After hospitalising his wife, he went around to the next street to do the same to the alleged lover.

Jason was left confused. Had his mother been guilty of such indiscretion? Had she taken a younger lover, not that he could have blamed her? But, most of all did it mean that she did not love him as well. Not loving his father was easy, but Jason needed his mother, needed her love.

When Mary Chancery died of her injuries, Jason's world fell apart. His views changed also, he saw women as objects of desire, but nothing more than harlots who gave and took love whenever it suited their personal requirements.

Forcing his son to go with him Phillip Chancery went on the run accompanied by his teenage son. They were picked up just shy of the Cumbria boarder and both arrested until the facts could be determined that Jason wasn't involved in his mother's demise. Phillip Chancery is due to be released from prison in March 2022.

Jason suffers periods of changeable mood swings with complex neurotic episodes which he is adamant take control of his life. He has no recollection of ever being affected by any childhood illnesses and states that he is rarely unwell. Jason states that he feels inadequate when he is with a woman, but will quickly become angry if derided.

Results of Evaluation:

Jason appears to be a focused, intelligent individual who responds quickly to questioning. His answers can be subjective depending upon whether it involves personal information or concerns others. It is difficult to determine just how much of his childhood has left him scarred. I feel that there are underlying currents to Jason's character traits that no amount of counselling would ever open or that the authorities would understand. Despite his school reports, Jason has a quick thinking brain, is alert and aware of his surroundings, although cognizant of authority. He has a dislike of social workers and especially foster homes. He is wary of all police officers.

Summary:

Jason displays psychotic tendencies and is sometimes delusional, a state of mind that he quotes will get him through a day. He hears voices that belong to his deceased mother with whom he says he communicates, although he is still waiting for the day when they will be reunited. I could not get him to explain how, where or when.

Throughout the evaluation Jason smiled a lot, appeared friendly and unthreatening although I have to challenge whether this calm approach was part of a game that he liked to play.

He clearly does not like other's meddling in his affairs or interfering with any aspect of his life and will deal with anybody accordingly. Again Jason would not state how this would be executed.

His general opinion of woman is that they are there. They look nice, but he does not trust them. He goes on record saying that his role in society is to save them from the evil of other men. I took this to mean that Jason is still affected by his mother's alleged indiscretion.

The big question that needs to be considered is, is this all a game? Does Jason know what he is doing or does he use his past as an excuse and lastly how much is fact and how much fiction?

When I touched on physical love Jason became extremely defensive, dealing with such emotions through fantasy, erotica and graphic stimuli. This could account for the present charge for which he is accused.

Jason Phillip Chancery is a young man with a controlled aggression that will explode without warning and respective authorities should recognise this and take any necessary precautions should he wander into their jurisdiction.

When asked, Jason refused to comment on any question regarding death. From my own personal observations I detected that such a subject is met with a cold indifference, meaning he neither cares nor worries about the matter by which it is sent or administered.

Signed: Dr Julianna Hesseltolph – Psy.D.

I studied the circled photograph of Jason Phillip Chancery and saw the mockery in his smile. His eyes were exceptionally dark as though no light had ever penetrated his mind and showed him that outside of the shell, beauty and harmony did exist. Whatever his reasons for going down the psychopathic path of destruction, he could not use the past as an excuse. Everybody could change destiny if they wanted. I replaced the contents in the buff envelope and gathered up the rest wanting to take it all with me. I needed to decipher closely what Julianna Hesseltolph had said in her report. There were some strong points contained within, strong perhaps personal opinions and not just professional based.

When I pulled shut the front door I turned and walked away without looking back. Overhead the night couldn't decide how to play out the storm, but one was certainly coming. Although we had never discussed our respective jobs in depth I wish Lucy had told me about her secret quest to find out as much as she could about Jason Chancery, had she done so it might have saved her life.

A short distance from where I had my apartment I had to pull over the car and park up grateful for the rain on the windscreen that shielded my face from the pedestrians passing by outside. My emotions were private, but needed to be released and it was not something that I could contain any longer nor was the world invited to share. With the photograph placed on the dashboard where I could see it I continued to weep shaking my head. We looked so happy standing beside one another, so together and we had everything to live for. Jason Chancery had a lot to answer for, but for me personally he had destroyed my future. For that I was determined to bring him down and illegally if needed.

Chapter Twenty

It was a strange argument going around inside my head and thoughts. I knew that I should pass the contents of the box over to the police to help with their investigation, but I wanted every snippet, photograph and record copied first so that I was able to plan my revenge. The other argument going on came from the heart where I knew that it was wrong to feel such emotion, but anger came out in different ways, love could forge hate as quick as amity and despite all my legal training and the morals by which I lived my daily life, there were things that could only be resolved by stamping out, eradicating the problem. I had long thought that the removal of the death penalty from our shores to be a mistake. With the coffee pot cold at my side I made my own notes, forming a picture in my mind of how and when I could trap Chancery.

When Giovanni inserted the key in the door and pulled up the shutter I was just about finished. If anybody had come wanting me elsewhere I would have told them to fuck off. When I put down the pen I had a plan, not one that others would appreciate, because it was flawed, but all the same it was a plan. Regardless of the rain which had turned to a light drizzle I sat outside where I could watch the movement of the river as it flowed on by. The murky swirls of grey and brown seemed appropriate for my mood. I was still lost in my thoughts when Giovanni put down a plate of food and hot coffee.

'You eat and you drink Riccardo... only you need both to do you good.' It was difficult to refuse a man who towered above me. 'I see the look in your eyes and it does not disguise the pain you feel inside. My Anna, she always say you should eat to fill your belly because when the body has food, there is nowhere left to be sad. Eat and drink, fill up your body and remember that one day soon you will smile once again!'

Giovanni was like a free tonic, I did as he requested, but the abhorrence of Chancery had already filled the empty voids.

'Maybe my friend... maybe.' I put my hand in my pocket to pay for breakfast, but Giovanni was as perceptive as he was big. He caught hold of my wrist and prevented my hand from exiting.

'Not today Riccardo, today you are more than just my friend, today like brothers we share each other's tears and we say a prayer for your beautiful lady.' He looked up to the clouds above and crossed himself. 'Today she walks with the angels where evil cannot get to her ever again!'

I felt the pain course through my heart as I nodded unable to respond. Giovanni walked away his head hung low as though he too felt my pain. How he knew about Lucy I didn't get chance to ask, but Giovanni had never stopped surprising me, not since the first day that he had taken over the deli-cum-coffee shop. Every so often I watched him serve other patrons, his genial smile inviting them in through the door and wishing them well when they left. Giovanni was right, today we weren't just friends. As if magic really existed the clouds suddenly parted and allowed the sun to come flooding through. It landed on the river and the terrace in an abundance of blinding white light. An angel's smile, I couldn't be sure, but when I looked at the big Italian he raised his palms as if to signify that it couldn't be anything less. Jonathon sat himself down opposite an

160

almost instantly Giovanni arrived armed with croissants and coffee, topping up mine.

'How did he know?' asked Jonathon when were alone.

'Call it divine intervention!' We left it at that and Jonathon was grateful for the fresh pastries and richly dark coffee. I pushed across the photograph that had been circled.

'Contemptuous, evil looking bastard, isn't he!'

It was so out of place as Jonathon rarely used bad language, but it seemed to just pop out of his mouth.

I'm going after him,' I declared, making sure that I wasn't overheard.

Jonathon checked, looking around.

'Is that wise Richard. Chancery has a look about him that positively say's *'don't fuck with me'*. He's not only contemptible, but from what this psychological evaluation states, he is regarded as undisputedly dangerous!'

I then told Jonathon the reason that I had asked him to join me for breakfast. He was a good colleague, never questioned why or what hour I called and we were fast becoming friends rather than just working associates. It was times like this that you found out just who were your real friends and one of them sat opposite me, the other was less than twenty feet away. He snapped his fingers together.

'Holy shit...the two men that were reported upon last night on the mainstream news. They were with Lucy!'

'They walked into a trap, I'm pretty sure of it.'

'That was some trap.' Jonathon realised what he had said the moment it left his lips, he apologised, but there was no need.

'That's why it has become imperative that I do the same.' I replied. 'I have to avenge Lucy's death and theirs, to show that they didn't die in vain.'

'How can I help?' he asked.

I shook my head. It wasn't that I didn't want Jonathon or anybody else's help, but working alone was probably going to be a lot safer for all concerned.

'You can help me best by covering my caseload for a couple of days. Whatever I plan I will keep you posted, just in case, although this time next weekend I expect to have the matter dealt with.' The murky grey and brown had been replaced by soft white and calm blue. My thoughts were as calculating as Chancery's. To outwit a monster, you had to become a monster. I put everything back in the box and handed it to Jonathon. 'You can start helping by copying this lot, putting one copy in our safe and giving me back the originals.'

'And the police?'

I conceded to instinct. 'Copy it first then we'll arrange to hand it over, I promise.'

Jonathon wasn't happy being side-lined, but I soon made him see sense, stating that he had to think of Arabella and her welfare. Jason

Chancery slaughtered without any pangs of guilt, remorse or mercy. I had to live with Lucy's death, I didn't want him to suffer like I was suffering.

'And what about Mama Maria, do you think he knows about her?'

I had thought about Mama, but my mind had been held captive since seeing Lucy emerge from the shadows on the ward. It was possible that Chancery could go to Rickmansworth, although I had a gut feeling that he would be coming for me first.

'I'll contact after we copy this lot and I get in touch with the police. Mama has Lucy's cousins to look after her. If you ever get chance to see them, you'll know what I mean. Giovanni looks like a dwarf compared to her four cousins.'

Jonathon mentioned the news item regarding the journalist from Brighton and her beauty queen sister, who had been found dead in the house fire. He had made the connection with Lucy and asked if they knew one another.

'It was probably how he got to Lucy.'

Jonathon lowered his head remorsefully as he thought about Arabella. When he raised it again moments later he complained that his neck felt heavy.

'You wonder at how much he does knows.'

Chapter Twenty One

The sound of general banter hushed the moment Trevor Baines and Bob Pearson walked in the room. Baines had a no-nonsense reputation which had always proved him right and the criminals he sought wrong. As the gathering found a seat he uncovered the board which had erected moments before his arrival. Baines tapped the face on the board with the ends of his fingers making the trestle shake.

'This evil bastard is none other than Jason Phillip Chancery, born April first, nineteen sixty nine. He doesn't possess a heart, function like Dracula sucking the life and soul of his victim's adding torture before they die. Don't be under any disillusionment ladies and gentlemen this monster will carve you up as much as look at a uniform.

'Besides myself, DS Pearson and a couple of you in the room, we've already had the unfortunate experience of having to pick up the pieces of his handiwork. Chancery is a killer, a serial killer. He works alone as far as we can ascertain, has no outright objective other than to destroy, main and kill. He leaves behind no trace that he was ever present at the crime scene, but every criminal will make a mistake, I guarantee it.

'In front of you, you have a picture and a brief résumé with the main salient points that you need to digest to keep you alive. I do not joke when I say that he will kill you if cornered. Chancery has managed to evade arrest for the past ten years, so he's either a very lucky bastard or extremely adept at becoming a ghost. We're gathering intelligence at present from forces all- around the country where Chancery has been active during that period and believe me when I say that he hasn't taken much time out for sight-seeing. Any questions?'

A hand at the back of the room was the first that caught Baines attention. He craned his head towards its owner. A young woman who looked like she had just left after the last year at school blushed when a number of heads turned to look her way.

'Jason Chancery… is he likely to still be in the area?'

The question was mocked by some grunts of mockery, although most were as tight as the tension in the room. Baines looked at Bob Pearson who was first to respond.

'Okay, settle down again.' He advised. 'Firstly Amy's question is a sensible approach. There's every chance that Chancery is still lurking about. Previous forces have tried to track his movements, but without success. From the little that we know, Chancery will either run or gloat. You work it out. Secondly, I'm glad that Amy asked. The chief inspector has outlined what Chancery will do to you if you corner him. We've not long come back from the mortuary where the three bodies underwent Dr Bremmer's close examination. If you doubt our word, pop along and have a look for yourself, but heed my words that it'll make you leave the lights on when you go to bed tonight.' He looked directly at Amy Bradshaw. 'There's no telling, but this killer doesn't differentiate between genders, he will do whatever is necessary to escape.'

Trevor Baines wanted the last word before the crews left the briefing.

'Jason Chancery started small taking female underwear from the clothing lines of back gardens, but like most predators of his ilk, they quickly become brazen, gain confidence and climb the ladder of immorality. Chancery assaults, rapes and leaves his victims for dead. Your shift sergeant will double up all crews and that's how it will stay until he is caught. If you don't agree and have any opinions regarding women's lib and all the like, take it upstairs where they've more time to listen because I've bigger and better things to deal with. I work for a living. This briefing is meant to keep you safe and to have you realise what kind of monster there is in our midst. If you come across Chancery call it in. Let firearms and the dog units deal accordingly.'

When the last of the crews left the room the comments and banter could be heard echoing back down the corridor. From the briefing room window Trevor Baines and Bob Pearson watched them as they checked the equipment in the boots of the marked cars they would use out on patrol. Baines offered his sergeant the cigarette packet.

'Look at them Bob, they've just stood here and heard what we've both had to say and yet they still find time to laugh and piss about. Was we ever that relaxed when we went out on patrol?'

Bob Pearson put the cigarette to one side of his mouth as he continued looking down.

'We we're that and probably worse Trevor. I remember hitting the bars till four in the morning, grabbing an hour before we started again at six. The criminals haven't really changed that much, the level of violence has always been the same, it's just that nowadays the scruples of the game has changed. Now they don't care who gets hurt. We'll always have monsters roaming the streets.'

'Gladiator's without armour, facing the lions. Let's hope that they did listen. I've seen enough of the mortuary and Bremmer for one day and I wouldn't want to interrupt his golf!'

Chapter Twenty Two

Occupying the corner table Jason Chancery watched the waitress weave her body between the tables as she brought him his order. The day before had sapped his energy levels and they needed topping up. He was about to fork in the first mouthful when the bell over the door rang out. Three men in builders garb took seats nearest the door. The youngest of the trio opting to sit by himself where he could see both the view beyond the window and the waitress working behind the counter. When she came to take their order the young man edged closer so that he could put his hand on her buttock. She slapped it away much to her annoyance.

'Pack it in Greg... I've warned you before about this. If you do it again, you'll be banned!'

The builder laughed haughtily.

'You know you want it Monica, you're just playing hard to get!'

To keep the peace the older of the men said something under his breathe which had the younger man go silent. When their order was taken the blonde went back behind the counter and ignored the table beside the door. Jason Chancery let the grip around the knife handle go slack and felt it drop back into the rucksack. He despised men like the builder, brash, arrogant fucks that thought they could take any women they wanted, destroying families, trust and love in the process. It had cost his mother her life and somewhat destroyed his.

The unintelligent banter continued until they had consumed their breakfast and left. Jason watched the trio mount the lorry parked opposite flexing the sinews in his arms. He had a feeling that this would not be the only meeting where he and the building came face to face. From behind the counter he saw the waitress looking too. She apologised to the few customers left behind, explaining that Gregory Steadman had never been any different. He had pestered her ever since they had been in senior school and the same class. Jason knew exactly what she meant. She caught him looking her way.

'How his wife puts up with him I will never know. You'd not think that they've only been married a month.'

She cleared the table and took the dirty dishes through to the kitchen out back. Jason caught sight of the sign written name emblazoned down the side of the lorry as it proceeded along the street. Names were always handy if you ever needed to make contact with someone. When the waitress reappeared he paid for his breakfast, picked up a paper that had been left behind by another customer and smiled at the blonde behind the counter before pulling the door shut.

Frustratingly he crumpled the pages of the newspaper and threw it in the dustbin at the end of the drive where he was waiting for the next bus. The article on the woman found at the marina was less than insignificant, in fact the reporter had missed all the relevant detail. It annoyed him and there was no mention on the two men found further back the Kennet. It was as though everything was being kept low key to save the public from panicking. What ailed him just as much was when the reporter had referred to the marina body as the monster from the blue lagoon. Ridicule or clever deception, it was difficult to know which. It was strange as well because there had not been any mention of the missing boat owner for over a week.

He checked the bus timetable noting that one was due in five minutes. Resting back against the brick wall the weather was warm, dry and seemed to cleanse his soul. A pensioner was ambling his way, he gauged that she would be at the bus stop before the bus arrived. With a bit of luck he could dip her bag and remove her purse which would pay for the breakfast and maybe give him some spare cash.

Like insurance once word got around that she had been *turned over* the public would club together and come the end of the day she would probably be richer than she had been all year. Wiping the egg from his whiskers he waited and watched, but when the post van stopped and offered her a lift, Jason chuckled to himself as he shook his head in disbelief. The old woman had missed out on the fun of becoming a celebrity for a day and becoming that much richer. At the other end of the high street he saw the bus pull away from the stop and head his way.

It had been a couple of years since he had last visited Oxford, but as he threw his rucksack onto the back seat sitting next to the emergency exit Jason rolled his head around on his shoulders, sometimes it was good to go back, good to explore new adventures and pick up on one's left behind. As the bus pulled away he saw the blonde waitress wave, he waved back. He hadn't really taken that much notice of her before, but from afar she looked quite desirable. It still didn't excuse the builder, he was still an arrogant arsehole that needed teaching a lesson.

In the seat two ahead a young girl of three, maybe four with long brown ringlets and wide enquiring eyes looked back, she grinned cheekily and scrunched up her nose, Jason did the same. He had always liked very young children. They were the innocent that could do what they liked and get away with it. As a young boy he had wished for a brother or sister, but in later years was glad that one had not materialised. He had suffered enough trying to protect his mother, not wishing to heap more misery upon himself with a sibling in tow. The girl's mother pulled her young daughter down onto the seat and made her sit forward.

Half a mile up the road where the village crossed the boundary into the fields beyond he saw parked on the drive leading up to the farm the lorry belong to the builders. The young builder had removed his tee-shirt and was on the tailboard sorting through the tools, he turned and waved at the bus, but nobody paid him any real attention except Jason. With a long drawn out motion he drew the tip of his thumb across the underside of his neck. The builder looked puzzled, but by the time he reacted the bus had gone on by. At the back of the bus Jason smiled to himself. One day he would pass through Burtonmoor again, maybe then he would seek out the builder, pay his wife a visit too and have another breakfast at the café in the company of Monica Moon.

Coming in the opposite direction a police car sped towards the bus, its blue strobe light flickering like a moth caught in a purple haze as it flashed on by. Jason watched it travel towards Burtonmoor and wondered what had attracted their attention. It was improbable that anybody had recognised him. At the church in Crowmarsh the bus collected a gaggle of pensioners, who filled the bus, although none elected to sit on the back seat beside the young unshaven man. There was something about his seat that seemed unwelcome. The bus didn't stop again until it reached Oxford.

Heading down the road towards the Cornmarket he continued to look out of the window where he saw an advertisement hoarding promoting a new film. Plastered across the front was a dark and mysterious picture of a young near naked woman, her dignity protected by a bath towel. Peering out through the window slats of the blind she failed to notice the stranger standing in the background holding aloft a knife. Whoever the artist was, he or she had captured the expression in the woman's eyes just right. They were full of concern, full of doubt and fear. Jason liked the artwork, admired it and especially liked the moment of control that would follow when she realised that the man was coming towards her. Fear was unpredictable, exciting and gave him such an adrenalin rush. He noted the name of the cinema checking the time with his watch. He had a couple of hours to kill before the matinee performance, it was plenty of time to gather together some ready cash.

Stepping down from the bus he scrunched up his nose at the little girl then turned away hearing her chirpy giggles of joy as she danced in the opposite direction towards the shops holding her mother's hand. Her life was so carefree, so unsullied and so pure, he silently wished that it stayed that way for her, forever.

Blending casually with the crowds in the market he pocketed a number of women's purses where the opportunities had presented themselves so easily, taking the cash and throwing away the rest. Cards he considered only presented unnecessary problems and every cash dispenser was covered by a security camera.

Oxford was so full of unsuspecting females, many being students, some foreign and some native. Not forgetting the young mothers and trendy professionals in designer suits all caught up in the hype of the city. As he moved amongst them freely sniffing the air he caught the occasional whiff of their perfume, the scent of their hair or perhaps their body. Sensing that an adventure was imminent, he made his way to the forum where it was just a matter of selecting a target and following them home.

Chapter Twenty Three

My call was answered by a detective sergeant who introduced himself as Bob Pearson. Predictably he was cautious expecting me to be another crank out to waste police time, but when I told him of my relationship with Lucy and explained about the box of tricks that she had collected down the years the room behind went immediately quiet, I heard a door open and close, a few moments later another voice had intercepted the call and introduced himself.

Trevor Baines was polite and eager to meet, we suggested midway and on neutral ground somewhere around Windsor. Before the call ended I was advised that a total press blackout had been authorised at the highest level to keep Chancery guessing and give the police more time to establish the facts. Armed with the box which Jonathon had copied I travelled west down the A4 alone, wondering what I was walking into at Windsor.

Trevor Baines and Bob Pearson were older than I had expected, but then the officers on the front line seemed younger than me so it was inadvisable to make comparisons. We greeted one another in the foyer of the Rochester Country House where I had arranged a private room so that we could talk freely. As I spread out the contents of the box it was immediately apparent that Lucy had been treading on dangerous ground. Reporters are committed to delving deep, rooting out the stories that will best keep us interested, watching and reading, but occasionally one of them goes deeper than most others and that's when they themselves become headline news. Armed with coffee and biscuits we sifted through what she had collected.

'Miss Tate would have made a damn fine detective.' It was a compliment and helped ease the moment.

'She was a damn fine reporter, but was thinking of giving it up!' I replied.

'We'll catch, when he slips up!'

I wasn't so sure, not that I doubted their ability, but Jason Chancery had eluded the police for over a decade. It was a long time to be outwitting the authorities.

'I've seen Lucy since her encounter with Chancery.' I knew that it would immediately get their attention.

'How is that possible?' Pearson asked.

I told them about my experiences, how I was taken, where I was taken and with whom I had met. I considered it best policy to be honest and up front, the police liked that and it gained their trust. When I had finished I expected a barrage of questions and some sort of cynicism only it never came.

'That's a hell of a story Mr Quinn. Maybe and if I had been much younger I would have been sceptical, but I'm not. My sister is into this kind of thing, holds spiritual meetings with friends and regularly gives healing sessions to people who have lost loved ones. It's a different slant to the one that she promotes, but interesting.'

I was relieved to get Trevor Baines support and neither were like what I had expected. My perception of the police had changed somewhat in the last half an hour.

'I'd prefer if you call me Richard or Quinn, whatever you think appropriate, but less formal is easier.'

'We're sorry for your loss and we too have seen Lucetta. She was a brave women and didn't deserve to die. Did you know about the two women from the Brighton area?'

I nodded. 'They were friends, Lucy had arranged to go and see them the following weekend. We were both going down. I can only surmise that the information that Chancery extracted from Penny Schuchel helped trap Lucy.'

'It's possible only there wasn't too much of the house left by the time the brigade put out the fire.'

I considered telling them about Mama Maria, but she wouldn't have thanked me for saying anything and I wasn't that involved with the family that I knew exactly what the cousins did for a living. On the few occasions that I had seen them, they looked as shady as the colour of their skin.

'The two men who accompanied Lucy on the assignment, one I believe was a cameraman, did he get any footage before he was killed?'

Bob Pearson shook his head. 'Unfortunately the camera was in the water too long. Our technicians have tried everything to put it right, but reluctantly they failed.'

It was a pity, not that we needed a recent photograph of Chancery.

'Has there been any other similar crimes in your area?'

'Involving Chancery?'

I nodded indicating that, that was who I meant.

'None yet, but we believe that he is still in the area. Chancery is a cunning fox. He leaves no loose ends and covers his tracks by whatever means easily melting into everyday life as though nothing at all daunted him. He is either very lucky or extremely adept.'

I picked up the photograph that had been circled in red.

'Do you recognise the woman in the background?'

They both shook their heads.

'It would have been good to have asked why she had been highlighted. She certainly doesn't give the impression that she is a victim, more likely a friend!'

That was my sentiments, but finding out was my next move only I wasn't about to tell Baines or Pearson.

'I think Chancery's getting help from somebody and I don't mean spiritual, but living. Perhaps this woman?'

Baines studied the photograph and agreed, it was likely.

'She would be taking a chance, considering his past record.'

'Not unless she could control him!' they smiled and looked my way.

'If you ever give up law and want to come across to the other side, give me a call. We could do with your logic around the station.'

'Thanks for the offer, but I'll stick with what I know for the meantime. What's next?' I asked.

Bob Pearson carefully gathered together the contents of the box, chronologically placing each item back inside. I was impressed that he could remember the layers.

'We work around the clock, turn over every stone and go back over old cases looking for anything that might give a lead, anything that might for once put us ahead of Jason Chancery.

Trevor Baines looked at me thoughtfully, I could almost read what was going through his mind.

'In your place Richard I would be sorely tempted to go after Chancery myself, but be under no disillusion, he is one of the most dangerous men that I have ever encountered. Without a gun to hand I would think twice about cornering him.

Chapter Twenty Four

On the return journey to Reading Bob Pearson cruised past the vehicles travelling in the slow lane wanting to get back, he turned on the windscreen wipers and cleared the screen before switching them back off.

'Bloody weather can't make it mind up!' he exclaimed.

'What did you make of the Richard Quinn?' Trevor Baines asked.

'Nice bloke really, level headed, obviously affected by the death of his girlfriend and what he's experiencing from the other side. My only reservation is that I think he had something up his sleeve.'

Trevor Baines watched the countryside flash on by.

'Yes, that was my thoughts too. He gave us enough to keep us happy including the stuff that Lucetta Tate had amassed. I've an idea though that he has an agenda already set. He's a lawyer remember and thinking outside of the box is nothing new.'

'Do you think he knows who the woman was in the photograph?'

Trevor Baines nodded.

'Possibly...' he looked away from the window 'who do you think it is?'

'The clinical psychologist!'

Baines rubbed the underside of his nose. 'I was thinking along those lines. But what does she gain by watching out for Jason Chancery?'

'As Richard Quinn intimated, control.'

'I'd want him on a very short leash wouldn't you? If she is assisting Chancery, she could be playing a very dangerous game. Men like him have little control, they lash out then consider the consequences post attack. I think we should add Miss Hesseltolph to our list of enquiries Bob. First though I want to go through this lot and see if we can find us a lead. They always say that the answer stares you in the face.'

When they pulled into the rear yard of the station the first of the patrols that had been out on the streets were coming back for their refreshment break.

'Anything out of the ordinary happening?' asked Trevor Baines.

'Nothing much. An alleged assault on an old woman by a local postman. Picked her up in the high street at Burtonmoor. It didn't add up to much, but he's down in the cells, cooling down and looking at a caution.'

Trevor Baines held back the door for the patrol to pass through.

'Even the postman can't just deliver the bloody post nowadays. Do we have funny air down here or is it the season for attacking women, young or old?'

'Put it down to something in the water. I'll head down to custody and check out our boy from the royal mail. I'll catch up with you after.'

As he closed the door to his office Trevor Baines spread the contents from the box on his desk. Wherever he looked the face of Jason Chancery looked up at him from various photographs. Serial killers had become main stream news, attracted audiences far and wide, including the many undesirables that saw another killing as a mere trophy. Atrocities against fellow men and women meant so little in modern society. You could switch on the television and see similar in films, early evening viewing or playing electronic games. Society ignored what didn't touch base with their lives. Care and consideration for neighbours and others had quickly flown out of the window. By the time that he had read through the psychiatric evaluation and made several notes Bob Pearson had returned from the custody area.

'Did postie have anything to say?'

'Not much. He picked her with the intention of taking her home. Halfway there she suddenly has a dizzy fit and screams blue murder that he touched her inappropriately. Either way it's difficult to discount, so MacDonald is giving him a caution and sending around a female officer to advise the old girl not to get into any other postal vans in future.'

'I bet she won't be sending any Christmas cards this year!'

Bob Pearson pulled up a chair as Trevor Baines handed him the report.

'It's worth another look. I copied the original that Richard Quinn gave us and highlighted the areas that need investigating. Phillip Chancery would be a good place to start. Let's get a visit arranged to visit the prison only he's due out on parole in a couple of years, so any concession for information might help his case before the board.'

*****

Using the hands free I called Carole in the office, gave her Mama Marias address and asked that she send her a bunch of white lilies adding a message. I asked the whereabouts of Jonathon and was told that he was still in court defending Suzi Wang Choy. I did think about going directly to the courthouse as Suzi's case interested me, but Jonathon was more than capable of laying down a good defence on her behalf, at the junction with the New Kent Road I turned towards home.

Taking a glass of wine out onto the balcony I sipped the contents before tapping in the number that I had obtained from the internet. The call was answered almost immediately by a receptionist then transferred when I said that it was personal. Julianna Hesseltolph was professional although sceptical.

'I don't think that we have ever met Mr Quinn, so how can I help you?'

Listening to her on the phone I put a body to the face that had been in the photograph. A woman tall and slim, late thirties, fashionably conscious of modern design and colour, her hair cut and styled every week, only pulled back for the office to add that air of authority whenever required. Her thick rimmed glasses nestled upon her head as she rested one knee upon the other allowing the pumped up comfort of her recliner desk chair to mould about her shoulders.

'I have suffered a recent loss and was wondering if you had any available times in your diary where I could receive some sort of grievance counselling?'

I heard her flick through the pages of a book, possibly a diary, although for all I knew it could have been a hardback loaned out by the local library.

'No... that's unfortunately not possible. I appear to be fully committed for the next month. I could recommend another colleague, although I am somewhat curious as to why you would not choose one much closer to home?'

It was good point, but what interested me more was that she knew from where I was calling, my home line did not disclose any dialling detail.

'You come highly recommended from a colleague Miss Hesseltolph. I thought that in the circumstances I would approach you first. It's a pity that you are not available because I think you could have helped me a great deal.'

Whether she saw through my pretence or was being overly cautious it was hard to tell, but quite abruptly she ended the call.

'I'm sorry Mr Quinn. Thank you for calling, but I really should get on as another client is due any moment. Good luck with what the future holds for you!'

The receiver was replaced and the line went dead. I got the distinct feeling that there was some kind of message hidden in her wishing me well for the future. Julianna Hesseltolph was definitely hiding something and I was curious to know what.

Standing in the kitchen waiting for my pizza to cook in the oven I took an unexpected call from Bob Pearson. Unexpected because he and Trevor

Baines had promised to update me with whatever developments they established during their investigation, but I honestly believed that they had made the promise merely as a ploy to appease me. I was proved wrong.

'I called the governor of the prison where Chancery's father is being held this afternoon and it transpired that my call was an hour too late. Chancery senior had been involved in a scuffle with another inmate in the machine workshop whereby Phillip Chancery was fatally stabbed with a modelling chisel. It punctured his right lung and ended his life before the guards could transfer him to the prison infirmary. In a way summary justice has been served, although we had wanted to talk with him to see if he could have told us anything that might have led to his son's arrest.'

We talked for a few minutes longer going over old ground that we had discussed earlier. I felt that I could trust Baines and Pearson, although I did not mention the call to Julianna Hesseltolph. Making the call had only been part of my plan.

Around ten thirty I took a long hot shower and had an early night, taking with me a bottle of whiskey and a glass. Some would say that it was the beginning of the end, but I looked upon it that I needed a damn good drink. The vacant side beside where I lay was cold and full of memories. Filling the glass I sipped the whiskey, raised a glass to Lucy and told her that I would avenge her death.

When I awoke sometime around two twenty three with an unexplained jerk, the stars were out in evidence filling the night sky which was a deep dark blue. Nothing outside stirred except the sound of the traffic in the distance and at the side of the bed the glass was still half full. I didn't remember falling asleep, but I did recall everything about where I had been, although not being invited there.

Chapter Twenty Five

When the young woman with the elfin shaped face peered through the glass pane of the white washed pavilion I was drawn to her as she waved me forward. Crossing over the boundary line of the pitch and ascending the short flight of steps I walked through the open door where I was immediately swallowed up in the reflection of the moon. Other than a solitary wooden bench the room was bare and resembled a dance hall. Near the centre of the wooden floor was a large dark stain, an abstract like blemish as though somebody had crept up on a giant spider and hit it with a cricket bat.

In the moonlight the woman looked like a ghost, her features drawn and deathly white. Her hair was long and parted in the middle, her eyes sunken above prominent cheek bones. She smiled and invited me to sit beside her on the bench. I noticed that both hands and above the wrists were marked with henna. From her neck was strung a metal emblem in the shape of a dove.

'I've been waiting to be with you Mr. Quinn, my name is Ashley Jones.

'I have been expecting you Mr Quinn, my name is Ashley Jones and Linda told me that you would be coming.'

'Linda Cunningham?' I asked remembering the conversation that we'd had in the ward.

Ashley Jones put her hand on top of mine.

'I am sorry for your loss, losing one that you love so much must be very painful. I've seen Lucy and she is safe now, but we all need your help!'

She fiddled with the bangles spun around her wrists, turning them nervously as though waiting for something to happen. I felt my attention drawn to the stain in the centre of the room.

'This was where Jason Chancery attacked you?' I asked.

'Where I lost my life Mr Quinn.'

Like a small child she bit her clenched knuckle ignoring the pain, but drawing comfort from the bite, as her mind held onto the reality.

'I was coming to the end of my second year at university where I was studying humanities and social sciences that I encountered death. Being away from home allowed me the freedom to do what I wanted, I was so content with life and looked toward the future with vigour and passion. I had so many plans made. None included Jason Chancery.'

Ashley Jones suddenly got up and bathed herself in the moonlight releasing the straps from her shoulders so that her summer dress fell down to the wooden floor. She stood before me completely naked and scarred. The long dark rents went up and down her arms, her back, legs and across her abdomen in weird patterns, they were almost identical to the ones that Linda Cunningham had shown me. Other than how the monster had marked her body Ashley Jones was beautiful and would have turned many a young man's head her way. She bent down and scooped up the dress covering her body once again.

'I didn't want to die that night nor end up with these scars, but fate dealt me a wicked hand Mr Quinn.'

She came and sat beside me once again, coming much closer than before. I wanted to put my arm about her shoulder and showed her that I would do all I could to help, but for some reason I left my hand resting on my knee. She whispered in my ear as though not wanting anybody to hear.

'He has gone beyond the bounds of depravity and evil. He has to be stopped, by whatever means.'

I tried hard to put Lucy furthest from my thoughts, not wanting to dwell on how she must have suffered as well at the hands of Jason Chancery. Suddenly from seemingly nowhere an ethereal mist started to appear before my eyes the kind you would find at a magic show. I felt Ashley grip my hand as the mist produced an image. Slowly the phantasmagoria took shape.

It began with people laughing and chatting, having fun together inside the bar of a public house where Ashley was present with friends from the university, young men and women of her own age. They were celebrating the afternoon's victory over the local rotary club. Ashley looked absolutely resplendent in her summer dress, cut away at the shoulder line and delicately dropping down to just below her calves. It was the same dress that she wore when she had dropped it to the floor so that I could see her scars.

Ashley was smiling and had about her a carefree spirit as she participated in the festivities, her arm looped affectionately through that of her boyfriend, who still had on his cricket whites. When the landlord rang for last orders the group drank up before spilling out merrily onto the pavement, each of the party saying their goodbyes and heading home in different directions.

Adam Mottelson eager to have Ashley all to himself was keen to show her something special that night. He took her hand and guided her back to the cricket pavilion where he knew of a way to get inside without causing much damage. As she sat on the steps of the pavilion he re-enacted his final delivery that had won the match making her giggle as the wine spun around inside her head. She applauded when he took his bow. Dancing on the pavilion veranda they kissed and touched one another, exploring, wanting and sighing. When Adam sprung open the lock to the door he pulled Ashley through and undressed her, bathing her in the moonlight. Now I knew why she had chosen to bring me to the pavilion this night. Neither saw the figure watching from the trees nearby.

Such was the intensity of their desires that soon Adam was naked as the day that he had been born, only different, now he was a man and wanted Ashley bad. Kissing her lips, her breasts and travelling down towards the floor he pulled her down with him no longer able to contain himself. As the fires of passion ignited their lust for one another Jason Chancery watched standing in the open doorway. He pulled out the knife from his rucksack casually walked over to where they lay and hit Adam across the back of the scalp. The young cricketer slumped down onto Ashley as Chancery roughly pushed him to one side.

Ashley felt the scream rise inside her throat, but it materialised as nothing more than a squeak as Jason Chancery removed his clothes. He raped her as she struggled to get free keeping the knife close by for later. Watching it happen second by second I felt different waves of emotion pass through my body. I wanted to get up and kick Chancery away, to hurt him badly and stamp on him until he screamed out for mercy. I wanted to hold Ashley tight and tell her that she was safe, but when I tried to move I found that I was rooted to the spot.

When he had satisfied his want of her Chancery introduced the knife. I desperately tried to look away, but like my legs wouldn't move, neither would my head. Cutting into her flesh he turned her until she was marked back and front. I thought that I would throw up, but watching had only produced a bad taste in my mouth. The only thing that would move were my fingers. I opened and balled them into fists time and time again.

Calming sweeping the blade across her throat he took her life and left her bleeding in the centre of the pavilion floor. I realised then that it would never be used for another dance. Sitting alongside me Ashley asked if it was all over. I squeezed her hand gently and told her almost. Although I did cuddle or comfort her in a way that I would have Lucy, I felt her anguish, her pain and her sorrow. Moments later the phantasm began to fade away.

Before it disappeared completely, in one final act of defiance I saw Chancery look up and smile as he held aloft her underwear. The demented monster had claimed another victim and taken a trophy for himself. I could not be sure, but when he stood up he moved in closer as though looking directly at me. Then the image faded and disappeared.

'Has he gone?' she asked, daring not to look.

'He's gone Ashley, you're safe.' It was a ridiculous thing to say, but I couldn't think of anything else by which she would be released from her anguish. 'What happened to Adam?'

She looked up to where the stain was still evident.

'He regained consciousness soon after Chancery had left. When he saw me lying in a pool of blood with my throat cut and my body mutilated he panicked and freaked out. Adam grabbed his clothes and ran, only less than ten minutes later he was stopped by a foot patrol officer where he babbled out something about his girlfriend being murdered.' She looked at me. 'I can't blame Adam for the way he reacted, I would probably have done the same.'

I wondered what I would have done had I been in similar circumstances when Lucy had been attacked. Ashley suddenly got up and walked around the inside of the room.

'As women we beg, we plead and we promise to do anything that is necessary to stay alive and not be hurt, but despite all that we offer, none of what we say is ever enough. You see Mr Quinn the conscience of a madman hears and sees nothing, except the fear in a victim's voice, the control that he feels coursing through his veins and the blood that he watches leaving your body. Death means nothing to people like Jason

Chancery. Death is the final act, whereby there is nothing left upon which to feed.

'Do you know why he cuts his victim?'

She stopped pacing the floor, instead she turned her back to me and looked up at the moon outside.

'You might not believe that he lives in a state of permanent torment. His dreams become his nightmares. Jason Chancery sees his father assaulting, hurting and raping his mother. He beats her till she cannot move or speak any longer. Finally she dies alone and without Jason to protect her.

He believes that by cutting each his victims he will protect them from the evil of other men. You see who in their right mind would want to lay with a woman who has been mutilated. Before he cut me I asked him why and he told me that it was to save me from myself. Once cut I could not be immoral. Lust and temptation is what destroys the soul of men and women, not love. Just before he slit my throat, he told me that love was the cruellest emotion ever!'

She read my thoughts as I wondered if Lucy had suffered as much.

'We all suffer, albeit alive or dead. To answer that question she must tell you herself, I cannot answer for her pain. One day you will see her again, that I do know.'

I walked over to join her by the window and looked up at the moon.

'It's beautiful Ashley, really beautiful. I hope that there are moon's like this beyond the gateway.'

When I next looked to see her reaction she was no longer there and neither was I. The next time that I opened my eyes it was two twenty three according to the clock beside the bed. I reached over and took hold of the glass, consuming the rest of the whiskey. I needed it.

Somewhere in the void of space, in the equidistant, Mary Anne Chancery was looking down and affording her wayward son the protection that he so desperately needed. Whatever wrongs he performed, endorsed upon the living she would do she could as his mother. From each corner of his world the walls were closing in and soon it would be time to run and escape or be caught.

Chapter Twenty Six

When I told Jonathon about the demise of Phillip Chancery he showed little if any response, believing like so many others that justice had been at last served. We discussed the short conversation with Julianna Hesseltolph upon which he had more opinion.

'Maybe you caught her at an awkward moment?' he implied, knowing that it would get a reaction.

'Or perhaps she has been shielding Chancery all these years. She would have made a number of associations with various professional circles that would keep her updated on current police initiatives.'

Jonathon who was sitting opposite tweaked the sketch that he had been doodling on his note pad, he turned it around so that I could see, it was of a stag with huge antlers only dangling from the ends of each set of horns were questions. What was she hiding? Who did she know? What was her background? Did her work take her abroad and where? Questions that had been going around inside my head. It was pleasing to know that Jonathon was on my wavelength. As amazing was the fact that although he had not spoken to her, he also had created a visual image of how she looked.

'Do you think that she knows about Phillip Chancery?'

I shook my head. 'I doubt it. The police only found out themselves yesterday. If she is in contact with Jason Chancery and he does know, then it proves that the source must be coming from her end.

We discussed my meeting with Baines and Pearson in Windsor, although there wasn't much to tell. Jonathon had read most of what Lucy had collected as he copied it. He was silent as I told him about Ashley Jones although I did not tell all. What I had seen was for my eyes only, private and that Ashley had been beside me so that I understood the level of depravity to which Chancery worked, but also that I would have no doubts about how Lucy had suffered. Around nine thirty Jonathon hinted that we should prepare for court, I had to admit that I was looking forward to the session as it was something normal. Grabbing my gown and wig we left for the Strand.

The court room was almost empty for the hearing of Choy versus Everon Milchest which didn't surprise me, sitting a few stalls from the back a solitary reporter sat disinterested, absently spinning a pen between her fingers. I was proud of Suzi as she took the stand for the second day of legal grilling, she seemed calm and determined, whereas the representatives from the pharmaceutical company looked positively anxious. As the questions bounced between defence and prosecution Suzi answered each clearly and never once took her eyes off the men sat behind the prosecutor. Corporate espionage was a serious accusation, but Suzi adamantly denied the charge laid before her, stating that her immediate line manager had blackmailed her into having sex with him, If she denied him, it was made plainly obvious that her role within the company would become intolerable, her reputation would suffer, but more than anything her whole life would be turned upside down and not for the better. When the time came for the manager to stand in the witness box, I was completely pumped up and ready to go for his jugular.

Andrew Millicant was ill-prepared for my onslaught and within an hour of relentless questioning he conceded and admitted everything. Sex was a powerful, intimate and thrilling weapon, but when deployed or used upon for the wrong reasons the tables could so easily be turned.

Suzi Wang Choy punched the air with delight when the judge awarded her the case and filed for damages, substantial damages. Everon Milchest would later that day be looking for a new line manager and scientist because Suzi wisely decided to take her expertise elsewhere. In the end the pharmaceutical company had lost out in every conceivable way. When I walked out of the court building the air seemed a whole lot fresher and I felt more alive. Suzi had proved to me that there were still some things worth fighting for. Lucy and what we had for one, the determination to bring down Jason Chancery another and not least life itself.

Later that night as I prepared for bed I saw the impression on the note-pad that I always kept beside the bed in case I took a call during the night. Lightly rubbing across the page the words *'Bure-Upton'* started to appear.

Despite the lateness of the hour I called Bob Pearson and told him about the notepad, adding my experience with Ashley Jones. In return he told me that they had made contact with Adam Mottelson earlier that evening, opening up old wounds, not that it really mattered, because every stone however heavy had to be overturned if they were to catch Jason Chancery before he struck again.

Chapter Twenty Seven

The surroundings seemed unfamiliar, was dark, very dark and uninviting not that it worried Phillip Chancery, he'd been in worst places. Tentatively placing one foot before the other he edged forward his arms outstretched expecting any moment to touch something solid, only he never did. It was strange because everything had gone silent too, the machines in the workshop had been turned off and he could no longer hear the whispers or the shouts of the guards.

'About fucking time,' he said to himself *'all that noise was beginning to do my head in!'*

Somewhere ahead the glimmer of a light began to materialise, he made his way towards its source.

Flexing his biceps and shoulder muscles he got ready to strike out at the first thing that moved. Being in prison for so many years had taught him to always be on his guard, only you never knew when a blade was going to coming slashing through the air, or a sock filled with billiard balls was going to smash the side of your face. Blinking to clear his vison he got closer.

'Damn this dark, I can't see clearly,' he admonished, as his hands thrashed through seemingly nothing 'where the hell is everybody and why haven't the screws fixed the bloody lights they're forever blowing in the corridors. 'Poofters paradise' they call it' he scoffed *'more like fuckers alley.'*

The closer he got to the light the less unsuspecting and accustomed he grew to his surroundings, not realising that he had traded one prison for another, only this new facility was going to be his resting place for the rest of his miserable existence. Making the transition from life into death had been made without his knowing. Phillip Chancery saw somebody coming towards him, he clenched his fists into tight rock hard balls. When he saw that it was a woman, he licked his lips.

'About time, I could do with releasing some of my tension!'

It puzzled him why there were no cells, no bars or other inmates. Where was he going to screw her, where was there somewhere comfortable to lie down. There didn't seem to be anywhere. As she came closer he felt his body relax, sensing the hardening in his groin. It was a long time since he had tasted a woman, not that slut that had gone off with the bloke around the corner, but a real woman. And as for that useless, limp dick of a son, together he and she made a right pair. He scoffed as the light grew more intense. And why had he not visited lately, seen his old man and paid him more respect. The doctor had stamped schizophrenic across the front of his file, who were they to say that he was mad. When Phillip Chancery recognised the face, he smiled.

'You took your time coming woman,' he rebuked of his wife. 'Where have you been, a man can get very lonely in prison?'

Mary Anne Chancery took another step then stopped, dare not going within reach where he could grab her.

'I've been busy Phillip doing what you haven't, looking after our son!' Her voice was calm, unhurried, but strong.

Phillip Chancery pulled back his right hand meaning to strike her across the face for her insolence, but something powerful was forcing him back and holding fast his hand.

'What's this... let go of me,' he yelled, but the force keeping Mary Chancery safe maintained its grip. 'When I get hold of you woman, I'll show you how you should be respecting your husband, not acting like the whore that you are!'

His teeth were clenched tight as he hissed out the words, but to his surprise Mary only laughed at rage. The sudden mockery of his warning only made him all the more angry. He tried to move his feet, but couldn't.

'Hey, what gives...' he demanded *'Mary have the guards take these fucking clamps off my ankles or I will break every bone in your body when I get free!'*

Mary Chancery shook her head, nothing in him had changed. She wondered what it was that she had ever seen in him. Marrying Phillip Chancery had been her biggest mistake, sending her son for adoption the second.

'Get used to this place,' she advised 'only you will never leave it Phillip. For here eternity ends for you, but when the time comes that you realise why, it will probably be too late!'

Phillip Chancery looked around, but could see nothing beyond the gloom.

'I'll be good, honest I will, if you take off these bonds and release me. I'll never hurt you again Mary, I promise it!'

She smiled and shook her head.

'Nothing you say will help. Here you cannot abuse or maim. Here, nobody listens to your pleas or comes to help. The dark will be your world now.'

The flames of fury swept high in his eyes as he forced himself free to grab her and throttle her, but the force holding him back was more powerful than Billy Moffatt with whom he'd had the ruck in the machine workshop. When he did get free, he would deal with them all, first her, then Moffatt, a few others and if needs be some of the guards. They were all bastards and not worth the breath that he put inside his lungs. It was her smile once again that had the veins at the side of his forehead bugle out and pulse more rapid than normal. The doctors had been justified in stamping his file.

Mary Chancery knew that her time was running out, soon she could make her way to the gate where it would be opened and she could pass through. In the light the scars and bruises were no longer and the broken bones had all healed. Once again she had beautiful skin, smooth and richly tanned. In the light where she stood she looked almost reborn.

'Your life contaminated others in ways that only evil can penetrate and for that you have been judged Phillip. Jason has sadly become you and I cannot help him any longer. Take one last look if you wish, but here we part company, forever!'

Phillip Chancery however was in no mood for riddles or judgement. He was due parole in a couple of years and wanted nothing more than to be free. Suddenly the pain in his back, hurt and burnt like hell. He was still her husband and it was his right to have her body.

'*Come to me now woman,*' he demanded angrily, but Mary turned away and walked back the way that she had come.

'*That's it, go back to that fucking imbecile. It was like you to produce a useless piece of shit. I wanted a man for a son, a man who would grow up like me, not some freak of nature!*'

Without looking back she responded. 'Somewhere safe.' It was all that she was prepared to offer.

He continued to call out after her, making untold threats of what he would do to her when he got free, only freedom was never going to be given. Like a punch drunk fighter he flayed the air in front of him, but with each sweep of his arms the darkness closed in and surrounded the space where he stood. When he could see no longer, he screamed, but it was only he that heard the sound. Somewhere inside his head he heard the other prisoners laughing, the loudest being Billy Moffatt.

As the screaming went on and on, it would eventually turn to tears of frustration. A penitence had to be served for his wickedness, evil and crimes, but in his passing he had released his wife from her life of torment. Mary Chancery walked unhindered towards the open gate and passed through without peering behind her, at last she was free and ready to begin again.

She felt a pang of maternal guilt regarding her son, but there was nothing that she could do for him now and Jason's fate hinged on the path of his own destiny, probably going the same way as his father. Stepping tentatively through the equidistant she realised that there were, as she had experienced in life, no guarantees. Standing on the other side she absorbed the warmth of the sunlight ready to accept whatever would come next.

Chapter Twenty Eight

The Darker Side of Addiction on the big screen was an unsatisfying let down and the billboard image had not done justice to the film. The only scene that had excited him was when the woman had emerged from the shower naked before throwing a towel about her body, then looking out of the window not realising that a stranger brandishing a knife was standing, but a short distance behind her. Jason Chancery felt hugely disappointed.

A pair of teenage school girls playing hooky for the afternoon had screamed at the point that the killer moved forward and attacked the defenceless woman, slashing and cutting randomly without mercy. Jason had considered moving seats and sitting immediately behind where he could make their afternoon more interesting, but the usher was annoyingly keeping watch from the door. In the balcony above three young men insisted on making loud comments every time that the killer appeared. Their interruptions irritated Jason as much as the builder had earlier.

The moment that the film finished Jason left his chair and the auditorium, waiting in the foyer for when the trio came down the stairs. Tucked under his jacket he had ready his knife, it had been a disastrous afternoon, displeasing and he wanted something to show for it. When the audience from the balcony above emerged at the top of the stairs Jason identified the culprits that had helped spoil it, the loudest easily recognisable by his flame red hair. Cutting away in the foyer from the other two the lout went into the men's bathroom, Jason quickly followed.

Unlike Alex Machin the young man lived, but would never be able to take any stairs two at a time ever again. Standing at the urinal Jason Chancery had knocked him unconscious and cut the tendons at the back of his knees. He left the loud mouthed lout lying in a pool of urine before calmly walking back out and joining the last stragglers who had stayed behind to buy confectionery before going back out in the sunshine.

In some ways his annoyance had saved the teenage girls, although the unconscious stranger would never know it. Away in the distance Jason saw the girls meet with an older woman, undoubtedly a mother out on the hunt for her daughter and friend. With indifference he shrugged his shoulders, instantly turning his attention elsewhere looking about for something else to help pass the time. When he saw the darkened helmets bobbing above the crowd and heading his way he turned in the opposite direction and walked towards the bus station instead. Moments later the sirens of an approaching ambulance suggested that the injured man had been found by his friends. Some would say that the act was incomprehensible, violent a statement of today' society, but none new how Jason's father had moulded his son's future or mind.

Sticking out his hand he halted the bus and paid for a return fare back to Burtonmoor, where by chance he would be back in time to see the blonde that worked in the café before she closed up. Oxford could be revisited another day as it hadn't lost any of its appeal, today had just not been the right time to visit. Sitting at the back of the bus he heard other sirens rushing to the cinema.

Jason checked his mobile looking for any signs of a text or missed call, but there were none. It was so unlike Julianna not to call him or leave a message, he wondered why. Things inside his head hadn't felt right neither in the past twenty four hours. Suddenly the voices had ceased, that worried him as his mother had always been there when he needed her the most. He put the phone away concerned that she was still annoyed at him for having attracted so much attention in Brighton having visited the journalist and her sister. His saving grace had been when he had told her about Lucetta Tate and Richard Quinn.

On the edge of the village he passed the builders lorry which was still parked in the farm drive, surprisingly the young builder was again on the back of the tailboard only this time securing a set of ladders, this time Jason didn't wave when Gregory Steadman looked up. At the next stop Jason got off and walked towards the café only to find to it shut. It was a pity because he had a feeling that he and the waitress would have been fun together. Finding a seat in the shade he drew hard on a cigarette, contemplating what to do for the remainder of the day when out of nowhere a dark shadow momentarily obliterated the sun as a lorry passed by, he saw written down the sides *Blackwell & Son.* The lorry stopped just past the café where it dropped off the builder.

'Have a good evening and don't be late tomorrow.'

With that the driver engaged gear and pulled away. Gregory Steadman banged the side of the lorry with his fist then crossed the road. Jason smiled to himself, drew in one last inhalation from the end of his cigarette then tossed it to the ground. Oxford had been bitterly disappointing, but the day was not yet lost.

He followed the builder down the high street, holding back for a few minutes when the young man went into the convenience store to buy an evening paper. Maintaining a safe distance he continued to follow as the builder strutted his way home nodding at residents of the village that he knew and winking at any female that passed him by. Cutting through an alleyway he made it to the end before two young boys on bikes charged through preventing Jason from keeping up, he cursed them, then ran the remainder just managing to see Gregory Steadman turn and go down the back of the houses that lined either side of the small cul-de-sac. At the end of the street a wooden fence kept the cows from coming into the estate.

Jason Chancery followed his quarry turning various corners unseen and undetected. Gregory Steadman cockily strutting through the backstreets of the residential housing estate until they reached an alley that divided the road and went down to the field running at the back.

He waited till the builder disappeared into the gate of a rear garden before moving down the service alley hearing children playing on either side where they were protected by a ramshackle montage of wooden sheds, fencing and shrubs. Through a gap in the hedgerow Jason saw the builder and his wife in the back garden of their small terraced property. Brenda Steadman was not similar to Monica Moon. She was perhaps a couple of inches shorter, although equally as shapely and attractive.

Someway off the cows called in unison for the farmer, letting him know that it was way past milking time.

'Get off me...' admonished the woman as her husband's dirty hands fondled and groped her breasts 'you're as filthy as your mind, now piss off and go get showered!' She looked up at the next door neighbour's bedroom window to make sure that Josie or her husband Michael hadn't been watching. Gregory Steadman tried to kiss his wife, but she pushed him away adamant that she wasn't interested.

'You'll want me later Brend... you'll see!' whistling to himself Gregory Steadman stripped the tee-shirt from his back as he entered the kitchen door and moments later was on the floor above where the sound of a shower could be heard. When he leant out of the window Jason had to duck down quickly so as not to be seen.

'Get away from the window Greg, there are children playing in the back gardens. We've not been here long and I don't want to upset any of the residents.'

Laughing to himself as he imitated Tarzan, Gregory Steadman did as he was told stepping into the shower and adding shampoo to his dust laden hair. Down in the garden below as she reached up to hoist the last of her underwear onto the clothes line Brenda Steadman failed to hear the gate open or see the man come up behind her. With the water gushing down the inside of the drainage pipe Jason propelled the startled woman into the kitchen keeping the blade of the knife held under her chin. When he came back down towelling off his hair and clad only in a fresh pair of jeans Gregory Steadman found his wife stripped down to her underwear with a man's arm clamped across her midriff, the other containing a long vicious looking hunting knife.

'*What the fuck...*' but his voice trailed off, as Jason Chancery shook his head.

'Keeping a civil tongue in your head, will be better for everyone's health, least of all your wife's and if either of you make any unnecessary sudden movements or call out for help, I will end your lives quicker than you can blink. Do you comprehend?' They both nodded.

This was the moment that felt so good, the moment of control. Jason felt the surge of adrenalin power through his veins as he moved his hand up letting it rest on Brenda Steadman's left breast. He liked watching Gregory Steadman squirm.

'He wanted to do this to the blonde in the café earlier today. Did you know that your husband has a crush on her?' He sniffed her hair and ran his tongue down the side of her neck as Brenda Steadman digested what he had said. Venomously narrowing her eyes at her husband, she angrily announced.

'*You were making a pass at Monica Moon again. How many times do I have to tell you, that if you keep going there Greg, we're through?*'

Jason smiled, he had them both where he wanted them, she at his throat and Gregory Steadman belittled and helpless. There really was nothing to beat control. He whispered in her ear.

'*Not much of a catch was he?*' She swallowed the build-up of excess saliva in her throat when his free hand swept down over her abdomen and landed on the hem of her knickers. She was nice, tasted nice, had nice skin and was in the prime of her life.

'What do you mean?' she asked, as his hand moved sideways resting on her hip bone.

'Well, he obviously likes blondes and he's not entirely discreet about who he lets know, or that he's available for casual sex. Your man is very loud, flash and believes himself to be the original Don Juan. Gregory Steadman to a step forward, but Jason rearranged the knife and placed it under her right breast.

'This is as sharp as any that you'd find in a butchers shop. One more move and I take out her heart. It might have been promised to you, but right now it belongs to me!' Gregory Steadman stood perfectly still.

'You were the bloke in the café, sitting in the corner.'

Jason smiled back wryly.

'I don't like loud men, aggressive individuals who consider themselves better than anybody else. My father is like that and I hate him. Alex Machin used to be like it as well, until we met up one very dark night. Now he props up the daisies. I never did get the chance to ask if he liked gardening!'

'What do you want? We've not much money in the house and Brend's only got a small number of items of jewellery?

Jason laughed.

'His bargaining power is rather limited, wouldn't you say?' Brenda Steadman sensed where this was heading and her husband, being the thick dolt that he was, wasn't helping.

'Please, was it that you want of us?' she begged. He felt her body tense as she awaited the reply.

'To teach him a lesson of course, one that he will never forget. You see infidelity creates complications, which will gradually fester into much bigger problems. Betrayal breeds mistrust, hatred and ends in violence. Being disloyal will tear apart families, destroy the harmony within a household and take away the most important thing of all, love.

'My father was just like your husband, always chasing women, committing adultery, but when he accused my mother of being unfaithful, he beat her mercilessly, although he was never quite sure that she did ever cheat on him. After a lifetime of abuse, raping her, breaking her body and mind, he finally killed her.

'Coming here today was fate, a warning perhaps. I can see the same happening here, like an unseen cancer it would creep into your home and doubts would manifest into arguments before they turned into physical pain. As the cancer grew so would the rift in the marriage. Chasing blondes will never be enough Brenda. Men like Gregory only have one objective in life, their own pleasure.'

Contemptuously she looked into her husband's eyes, although it had only been a month the cracks were beginning to appear. Her mother had warned her about marrying Gregory Steadman stating that he had a reputation as long as the village green and back.

'*That ain't me Brend, you know it ain't!*' But Brenda Steadman shook her head in despair, her muscle-bound builder husband was a quivering idiot who was showing his true colours.

'Your wandering eye has brought this situation into my house Greg… don't you ever think beyond the end of your dick!'

'It's only ever harmless fun,' he implored, but Brenda Steadman wasn't laughing. As Jason told Gregory Steadman to turned around and head towards the front room he took his wife by the arm and told her to follow. Ordering Gregory Steadman down to the floor he handed over a pair of tights that he had snatched from the washing line and told Brenda Steadman to tie tight her husband's hands behind his back. When she announced that it was done Jason kicked the builder hard in the stomach taking the air from his lungs.

'That was for giving me indigestion this morning.'

He yanked down the builder's jeans to his knees making it impossible for him to right himself. Turning back round he slapped Brenda Steadman across the cheek, sending her toppling back onto the settee. With two swift cuts he sliced through her brassiere and knickers.

'It's a pity really that you should be the model to teach your husband his lesson, but that's what they mean when they say at the wedding ceremony *for better or worse.*'

Undoing the top of his jeans, he stabbed the knife into the arm of the settee near to the woman's head, but far enough out of her reach. When she opened her mouth to scream he hit her again, only this time sending her in semi-consciousness. As he forced himself upon her, Gregory Steadman could only watch and wait, knowing that he was next.

*****

A loud and intentional knocking on the back door interrupted the assault. Feeling his erection disappear Jason leapt to his feet did up his jeans and grabbed his knife, he was about to ask who could be calling when a woman's forced its way through the glass pane, followed by more accentuated knocking on the wooden frame.

'Come you two love birds... open up, there's plenty time enough for that later!'

Sensing that it was now or never Brenda Steadman screamed as loud as her pitch would take it. For the first time ever Jason Chancery had a dilemma. The kitchen door was already splintering under the force of the kicks being applied to the woodwork. Did he have time to slice the husband or the wife, after only a few seconds, he grabbed his tee-shirt and rucksack and made for the front door doing neither. Fumbling with the lock he managed to free it at the same time that the back door caved in. he ran as fast as his legs would go down the front path.

Josie Critcheon rushed in after her husband, only to come to a halt in the doorway of the front room where peering around his side she saw the naked Brenda Steadman sprawled along the settee and Greg bound on the floor. She rushed forward, grabbing a towel from the pile of laundry and promptly covered her neighbour telling her husband to avert his eyes. Taking Brenda Steadman upstairs she told Michael Critcheon to call for the police, before helping the builder.

Dialling the number Michael Critcheon told the operator that he needed the police and an ambulance. He told them to hurry before he put the phone down. Before going back into the front room Michael Critcheon took a few seconds to steady himself and reflect how close the attack had been to his own house. He knew that one day Gregory Steadman's philandering ways would bring trouble to the estate. At school he had been expelled for making suggestive connotations with a female member of staff. Becoming a builder had made him worse and even Josie was wary keeping Gregory at arm's length.

In the bedroom overhead Gregory Steadman heard his wife sobbing hard as she tried to come to terms with the intrusion into her life by a complete stranger and his abuse of her body. Lying helpless on the floor of his front room he looked up at his neighbour, knowing that life would never again be the same.

'I fucked up big time today Mick!'

Michael Critcheon shook his head in agreement. It was inevitable.

'A true man, a husband is supposed to be there for his wife at all times Greg.'

Chapter Twenty Nine

Jason Chancery careered into the two bicycles zig-zagging across one another as the boys played outside the gate, sending himself and the startled cyclists sprawling down onto the tarmac.

'Oi... wot's your bleedin' game!' The boy rubbed his knee vigorously where it had grazed the surface and torn his skin.

Chancery collected the rucksack from the gutter offered and apology then carried on running towards the fence at the end of the cul-de-sac.

Tommy Dodsworth checked out his bike, straightening the handle bars. He saw the scratches running down the front forks.

'My old man will kill me, he's only just had this resprayed.'

As they watched him climb over the fence and enter the field, another man, one they knew opened the front door and looked their way. They each pointed in the direction where the stranger had fled then looked at one another blankly when he nodded and closed it again. They had heard the screams, but there was nothing new in that, Woodcote Chase had its fair share of domestics the same as anywhere else.

On the far side of the field the cows stopped chewing the grass, looked up and saw somebody running towards them, some moved sensing that he was going to pass through as others stood their ground defiant that the field belonged to them.

The description that Michael Critcheon offered the police controller was relatively vague, but when he mentioned the hunting knife as being involved, the controller activated the button to open the channel so that she could relay the circumstances to all roving patrols. Moments later she passed the call across to another colleague so that she could dial the contact number for Bob Pearson.

Releasing his bonds, Michael Critcheon stood to one side as Gregory Steadman grabbed a tee-shirt from the pile of fresh laundry and made for the door to give chase, but was held back by his neighbour.

'If I was you Greg, I would let the police handle this only they'll be here very soon.'

'But... he raped my wife!' Steadman protested.

'Then best you stay here where you can offer her some comfort, rather than go and get yourself killed. I doubt that it would help the matter any.'

Gregory Steadman wasn't so sure, right now his wife didn't care if he was anywhere around. He nodded and felt Michael Critcheon let go of his arm.

Each step felt like a challenge as he ascended the stairs, knowing that the reception he would get when he arrived at the bedroom would not be over friendly. Knocking on the door he pushed it open and entered coming face to face with Josie Critcheon.

'I'd tread extremely carefully if I was you,' she warned 'Brenda's been hurt more than you could ever imagine!' Gregory Steadman thanked her, then closed the door as she left. Outside the first unit to attend arrived.

215

*****

Folding the nightdress over Brenda Steadman closed the suitcase and secured the catch. She was dressed and had next to the suitcase her handbag.

'Where are you going love?' Gregory Steadman asked, as if he needed to know.

'It's over between us Gregory,' she said, as she pulled the suitcase from the bed and let it swing down by her side.

Gregory Steadman felt the heavy blow of defeat on the back of his neck as his eyes pleaded for her to stay.

'He's gone... the police will pick him up soon and bang him away for life. Later on we'll get a good takeaway and start to put this behind us!'

But nothing would deter Brenda Steadman from leaving nor would anything convince her that Gregory Steadman was worth staying for. His actions, his lust for other women had brought a deranged stranger to their home, she had been raped and all that Gregory could worry about was having a takeaway later. She shook her head in utter dismay.

'You just don't get it Gregory... do you? To you love means getting your end away, having a romp when you feel like it. What do you and the other's down the pub describe it as, oh yes the three 'f's' a fumble, a fuck and then a fag after.

'Love is something that grows inside Gregory as a couple mould together. It means being loyal, attentive to one another's needs and

216

coming home at the end of the day because you really want to, not just because you have too or that you can have a feel of my tits in the back garden, or that they'll be a meal waiting for you on the table and that your dirty laundry will be washed and ironed or the bed made.

'Well... the rose coloured glass lens have finally shattered and are irreparable. I had been warned about you before I walked down the aisle. I should have listened. One thing that the stranger said that was true, was that you wasn't a good catch. You will never change, not even when what happened to us here sinks in. Eventually, it will just become a bad dream that you'll experience once in a while, but for me I will relive this horror forever and longer. He was right as well, men like you, do destroy a family.'

Brenda Steadman picked up her handbag and barged past her husband who stood speechless, unable to think of the right words with which to respond. She calmly walked down the stairs to be met by a police woman.

Standing alone in the bedroom Gregory Steadman looked at the framed photograph hanging over their bed. It depicted the day of their wedding and he had to admit to himself that they had looked so very happy as they posed for the camera. Brenda had looked resplendent in her dress and tiara and Gregory had on a permanent enigmatic smile plastered across his face. In the solitude of the bedroom he thought about the moment and realised that Brenda was right. The smile had been for the brunette guest standing by the photographer, he had always fancied her and knew that one day he would have her, whatever it took. In the street outside an ambulance came to a halt followed by an unmarked car.

Chapter Thirty

When Michael Critcheon shut the door of their kitchen he held his wife close letting her know that she was safe. The vicious attack and sexually motivated assault that had befallen their neighbours had been a stark reminder that society was changing and not for the better. Whatever that idiot Gregory Steadman was, there was no denying that over the years public opinions had changed, lost was the respect that fellow man gave another. Violence, depravity and disorder had crept in under the shadows and come to the fore. In the decay of wooden structures insects went about their daily business unaffected as nature had intended, watching and listening as mankind headed down the road of self-destruction. Evil itself stood back and waited for the inevitable.

'That could so easily have been me, or us!' Josie declared as she buried her face in her husband's chest.

'Well it wasn't Josie, so try not to dwell upon it. The police are swarming all over outside. I doubt the offender will ever think of coming back here, ever.'

She looked up in his eyes and managed a smile. Josie Critcheon squeezed him tight.

'I'm glad that you're not like Gregory Steadman. I'm glad that you're just plain Michael Critcheon because that's how I like you best.'

Although she would never tell, Josie Critcheon would never forget the moment that she saw her neighbour lying naked, having been brutally abused. Her dreams would occasionally be her nightmares as she saw the eyes of Brenda's attacker coming at her. When she took her husband to bed later that night she wanted him close to her and to have him look at her until she fell asleep, knowing that it was Michael with her and nobody else.

*****

Taking a moment to catch his breath Jason Chancery ducked low in the culvert as the sirens stopped wailing, the police had arrived much quicker than he had expected. When the dog jumped down from the back of the van barking frantically, wanting to be released from its lead he swore to himself, got up and continued running. Behind him the herd watched as he climbed the hill to the line of trees. From the ridge he looked back down lying low and out of sight. Way down below at the end of the cul-de-sac he saw two men scanning the field and outlying contour of the land, one pointed his way, but he doubted that they had seen him watching them. In the grass nearby the crickets beat their wings happy that the day had been both a little damp, yet ended warm.

Jason Chancery didn't like leaving behind loose ends, it was messy, unprofessional and frustrating. The blonde had been nice, struggled a bit which only added to the excitement, but it had annoyed him when the neighbour had banged on the back door. He didn't like interruptions. Taking stock of what lie below on the other side of the hill he wondered why he had not been forewarned. Normally the voices inside his head helped, told him of impending danger and what he should do, but suddenly, without warning they had gone silent, disappeared and not come back. Taking a look back at Woodcote Chase he saw the dog climb the fence with its handler. He slid away from the trees, got up and ran down through the meadow to the hedgerow on the far side.

If he went east the city would give him ample cover. Eight million people living, breathing and working in London could easily swallow him into their daily routines. Oxford was west, but after visiting the cinema, the police would be extra vigilant. Jason liked the south, always so exciting and vibrant, big open spaces and fresh sea salt air, but his last visit to Brighton had been cut short and like Oxford the efforts of the police would have been doubled. On the horizon he saw the faint outline of a helicopter, he ran faster and made the hedge watching it pass overhead. It didn't stop or turn around. North was the final option and would take him back to Julianna, but she had been angry with him the last time that they had spoken. He chose London where he could visit a friend.

Crouching low and peering through the gaps in the hawthorn he watched a policewoman kicking a pebble back and forth as she waited for her fellow partner, irritated that she couldn't be out on patrol by herself.

'Come on Kevin… for Pete's sake shake a leg. If the sergeant comes along and finds us idle, we'll be for the high jump. The helicopter has just passed overhead so it'll have recorded that we're static!'

Kevin Bates leant around the side of the tree careful not to splash himself down his trousers leg.

'Give it a rest Jules, when a man feels the urge to answer a call of nature, nothing can stop the want. I'm almost done!'

Julie Cotton had never been wrapped in wool nor expected anything as much and having been brought up with three older brothers was more than capable of looking after herself, but she had no desire to see Kevin's crown jewels. Hearing the last of his emission she turned away and faced opposite. Had she peered harder she would have seen the eyes that were watching her. When a wood pigeon took suddenly to flight further down the road, she positively screamed at her partner for the day to follow, running for all she was worth towards the spot where the bird had emerged. From behind the hawthorn Jason Chancery waited until they were both far enough away before leaping over the stye and crossing the lane into the copse opposite.

Amazed at how easy it was to evade their attention, he shook his head and passed through the trees entering the thicket where the light wasn't as penetrating as the field. He heard the car start up and pull away as the helicopter swept the field from where he had just come. Despite not being given any warning he had done well using his own initiative.

Chapter Thirty One

The closer that he got to the river the closer the evening sun drew him that way. In the meadow behind the dog handler pulled back his charge insisting that they try elsewhere. Although the dog had picked up the right scent the farmer had recently sprayed the meadow in readiness for the next season. Somewhere near the hawthorn his scent had become less intense.

Stepping onto the footpath Jason ambled along as though he was out enjoying the last of the evening sun before it disappeared, passing a concrete waste bin he reached in and withdrew a black rectangular carton that had contained the leftovers of a Chinese meal. Holding it in the grip of his palm it looked for all intense and purposes like a digital camera. Heading towards where the boats were moored he saw a man sat on the back of one enjoying the warmth of the sun before it disappeared.

'A nice evening to be out,' exclaimed the man as he spread wide his arms 'just right to be out taking some snaps. This is the best part of the river, this time of the year!'

Jason forced the carton down the side of his rucksack indicating that he had done with taking photographs. He smiled and approached the boat.

'I've taken enough for today and besides I'm losing the light. Sensitive things these modern camera's.'

'So I've been told.' Replied the mariner, although accepting that he knew little about photography, but could tell you everything connected to a twenty three foot long Freeman.

'Nice looking boat, is she yours?'

A broad smile beamed from ear to ear as the owner swept an imaginary paint brush from bow to stern.

'Every bit of the old gal. All paid for, ship shape and Bristol fashion, including the standard which the wife ironed earlier.'

Jason nodded as he looked up and down the boat, noticing the flag which was hanging limply atop of the cabin.

'It certainly looks in good shape. I've been looking at this model for myself, only I'm still not convinced that the cabin space is ample enough for my needs.'

Like a fish dangling on a raw hook, the bait was immediately taken as the man got up from his seat.

'Why not come aboard and see for yourself. I think that there's ample room for what we need on a boat. On a good weekend the wife, myself and the dog can get along just fine eating and sleeping taking in the occasional hike to the next shop where we can stock up with adequate supplies. Why don't you take a gander inside see what you think?'

Warily Jason stepped aboard looking out for the dog. The boat owner guessed his apprehension.

'Oh… don't worry about the wife and the dog, they're both at home. Evenings are my time for pottering about on the river. It'll be gone dark by the time I get home.'

Jason relaxed and gestured that the man should go first as it was his boat. Cecil Hawkins eagerly put aside his can of beer and passed through the cabin door. When the knife embedded itself in the right side of his back the tip of the blade punctured his lung, instantly taking him down onto the carpeted floor where he lay looking up at his attacker. Cecil Hawkins wanted to say something, but the blood was already filling his lungs and congealing in his throat. As his life ebbed away his thoughts turned to that of Margaret and the dog waiting for him at home. He would be much later than usual and they would worry.

Using a tea towel Jason cleaned the blade disposing of the cloth in a rubbish bag that he found under the sink. The boat was as Cecil Hawkins had described, well stock, had ample facilities for what was required and was well maintained. Testing the kettle to see that it had sufficient water he switched it on before rummaging through the cupboards for food. In the fridge he found a brown bag containing two rounds of tuna sandwiches, in another he located a packet of salt crisps, his favourite. Freemans were alright, cosy and easy to handle, he rubbed his palms together pleased with his latest find. Casting off the stern line he manoeuvred the boat out pulling left on the wheel taking the boat down river where it would be easy to find a suitable place to hide on the opposite bank. Wearing a brightly coloured cap and windcheater that had belonged to Cecil Hawkins, Jason looked every inch the part and would fool any passing helicopter crew. Down below in the galley the kettle

225

started to steam and whistle, announcing that it was time to find that mooring.

*****

'Any news yet?' Trevor Baines asked as he checked his watch, knowing that the longer the search prevailed, the longer Chancery had time to escape.

'None that I've heard come back on the radio,' replied Bob Pearson.

Overhead the helicopter continued to sweep back and forth, although it was becoming clear that they had not detected anything neither.

'I've told the crew up in the air to extend the search adding a five mile radius. It's been over an hour since the first unit arrived. Running continuously Chancery could make good ground and find a place to hide.'

Having already scanned the field they returned to where the cows were being rounded up by the farmer.

'The more I learn about this bastard the more I believe in what Richard Quinn told us. Maybe Chancery is getting help, here and elsewhere.'

'You mean up there! Said Bob Pearson as he pointed towards the sky.

'Maybe, although until he's caught I cannot rule out any theory.'

They heard footsteps coming up from behind.

'How's the wife holding up?' Baines asked.

Karen Appleton nodded. 'She's doing better than I thought she would, although there's something about her steely determination to get away from the house that concerns me. She won't have the husband anywhere near her and keeps repeating *'that it's over'* although I'm not quite sure to what she is referring too, whether she means the attack and the assault or her marriage!'

'I thought that they had only been married a month?'

'They have, but by all accounts, it's not been without its problems. The next door neighbours hinted at Gregory Steadman having a wandering eye for the ladies and several residents have confirmed that he's well known throughout the village. Many in the road were surprised when Brenda Steadman agreed to marry him.'

'Is it possible that Chancery knew of the Steadman's or was it more of a chance coming together?'

Karen Appleton shook her head. 'Chance. Brenda Steadman has never come across Jason Chancery before. The paramedics are almost finished inside. We're taking her to the hospital where I'll have her examined and see if I can get an on duty psychiatrist to pay her a visit. The sooner she gets help the more she'll be able to cope.'

'Have scenes of crime managed to collect any evidence.'

'All that was available, clothing, semen traces and fingerprints, although the description matches Chancery.'

Trevor Baines was happy that somebody was getting it right. Karen Appleton had been the latest detective to join his squad of officers, but she was fast proving her worth and noticeably showing some of the older one's up.

'Well done Karen. Keep Bob and myself posted when you get to the hospital. I'll have somebody talk to Gregory Steadman. He should have calmed down enough to obtain a statement. Wandering eye or not, I want to hear everything about his day, today.'

Turning their attention to the two boys who had been cycling outside of the house they wanted to hear what they had to say as well.

'And how are these two holding up?' Baines asked, directing his question to the detective that had been talking to the boys. Each had hold of a large ice-cream that had been purchased courtesy of the constabulary. Jon Franklin winked at Baines and Pearson before replying.

'They're holding up just fine as you can see guv'nor. So far we've established that the man that ran into the field was first seen hereabouts sometime around six perhaps quarter past. They ran into him in down one of the alleyways that cut across the back of the neighbouring streets and when he legged it out of the house he had in his hand a real big knife, they each say about seven to nine inches long, a hunting knife by the sounds of it. I've got a good description as well as he crashed into them before going over the fence.'

Tommy Dodsworth pointed to the scratches down his front wheel fork. 'Yeah, too right he bashed into us... look at my *fucking* bike mister. My old man's gonna tan my arse raw when he sees it!'

Ordinarily Trevor Baines would have reprimanded the boy for using such language, but society and moreover technological advancement had disruptively developed the modern day young boys and girls, seeing their street-wise education influenced largely by computers, iPhones, social

228

media sites and bad television. Using foul language was in some areas socially acceptable and part of everyday speech. Baines smiled and scratched the itch on his cheek.

'I'll tell you what. If that bike's serial number doesn't match anything lost or stolen, I'll book you in for a visit to our divisional garage, where the mechanics will fix you up with another respray.'

Seth Green wasn't going to be left out of any special arrangement, the man had knocked him over too. He quickly checked over his bike.

'Me as well guv'nor?'

Trevor Baines liked the boys, they had pluck and were not afraid of the police. That was just how he wanted it. He nodded, see both Pearson and Franklin smile.

'You too young man, although I warn you now, we've not got a wide variety of colours to choose from, so it might have to be yellow, blue or white on offer!'

*****

Finding a densely overgrown and unused bank Jason Chancery guided the boat in under the overhanging branches, tying off on a broken tree stump that had been cut in two by a lightning storm. Dragging Cecil Hawkins out from inside the cabin he hoisted the dead man over the side, managing to hold onto his leg before the weight took the cadaver deep under the boat. Lashing a line about the dead man's ankles Jason let go of the body and watched as it sunk to the bottom.

Come the next morning he would cast off the line and let the dead mariner float to whatever destination he so desired, but for now it was advisable to keep him hidden and out of sight. Making one final sweep of the river the police helicopter flew overhead ticking the water below as all clear on their search. Going back down into the galley Jason switched off the kettle, he was ready for that cup of coffee and Cecil's home-made tuna sandwiches.

Eight miles back up river in a moderate, but comfortable detached cottage Margaret and Charlie Hawkins checked the time on the mantel piece clock. It was well gone nine fifteen and Cecil should have been home the latest by eight forty five. Outside the dark clouds of the coming night crept up over the trees at the end of the garden, soon it would be too dark for him to drive home. Leaning forward Margaret affectionately stroked the little collie's head.

'Don't you go fretting yourself Charlie darling... daddy is much later than usual so we will just have to go to bed by ourselves and it's his own fault that his cocoa has gone cold. I swear that one day that damn boat will be the death of him!'

Chapter Thirty Two

Every so often we wake from a night and wonder why we dream at all. Seldom do we actually know the reason, who were the people we saw and where were the places that we went. Most of all what was it all about. More often than not we would rather not dream at all. When I woke and opened my eyes I felt guilty, it was ridiculous.

Sharon Rochester was a face form the past, a school boy crush, a moment that was sent to mould part of my destiny, not anything memorable or etched upon my heart, but there she was large as life and just as attractive, only not really my type.

When Lucy had to unexpectedly return to Sicily for an unknown family crisis and it was uncertain when she would return Sharon had seen her chance and like a limpet had latched onto me for all she was worth. Weeks turned to months and even I had begun to wonder if she was ever coming back, but becoming involved with another female whilst secretly loving another can be disastrous, whatever the age. Treading the path of adolescence was like walking through a minefield blindfolded.

During the four months from April to the end of July we had ourselves some fun, but it was only ever going to be fun. When Lucy returned to school Sharon's interest fell away faster than a stone falling to the bottom of a lake. We occasionally saw one another on school trips, friend's parties and in the pub as we got older, but Sharon always held up the shield of ice whenever I came anywhere close. That was until she entered my dream last night.

When she kissed me full on it was the moment that my eyes opened wide and I sat up on my elbows instantly realising that I wasn't alone. From out of the shadows emerged a man and a woman, much older than myself and wearing distinctive clothing although it wasn't instantly apparent from where. The man spoke first.

'Please do not fear us Richard Quinn because we mean you no harm. I am Thomas Hesseltolph and this is my wife Gabriele. We know that you know of our daughter Julianna because you spoke with her recently.'

I had expected to see Julianna Hesseltolph sitting somewhere in the room, but she wasn't there.

'Why come here, surely you've got the wrong address?'

Thomas Hesseltolph shook his head. 'No. I assure you that our visit was intended for you alone. We have been given permission to visit you, so that we can help you understand, whereby in turn you can possibly help us and perhaps when this is all over you will have served as guardian to Julianna's salvation, although regrettably not that of our son.'

I couldn't take my eyes away from Gabriele Hesseltolph, she was strikingly beautiful, her features chiselled like that of a statue that you find in a museum.

'I don't follow you?'

Thomas Hesseltolph smiled.

'I expected as much, but please hear me out then all will become clear. Time I must stress is of the importance as the end is coming near.'

232

'Your accent... German, maybe Austrian?' I asked.

'Austrian German. Now please remember that our coming is to help, not harm you in any way.'

I tried hard not to let Julianna Hesseltolph enter my thoughts knowing that they had the ability to read my mind. There was however something that I needed to know before allowing him to explain.

'You're both dead, that I can see, but am I connected?'

Gabriele Hesseltolph stepped forward and sat on the end of the bed. She was beautiful and yet she hid an awful secret inside of her that needed to be released.

'Connections appear in many various forms Mr Quinn. Our coming here tonight will help you prepare for yours. Before my husband begins, I must say beforehand that I am sorry, but we neither understood our son, nor realised how dangerous he had become. It is because of his evil ways that all this is happening.' She stayed sitting near to me as Thomas Hesseltolph unleashed his tale.

'Jakub Hesseltolph was our first born and we loved him dearly. As an infant he was a happy, carefree child, always giggling and laughing, content to play by himself and he gave us so much to be thankful for, however, things changed when he went to school. His time there was difficult and he would struggle with his lessons and rebel against the discipline of his teachers. Often we would be called before the school's governing board to explain our son's wayward behaviour where he would constantly disrupt classes, attack other pupils and deride the teaching

staff. It was not a surprise when his annual report marked him down as an average achiever, with little hope for the future. This was particularly hurtful because at home Jakub was always helpful, always doing things before being asked. Academically he seemed very bright for his age and when his younger sister was born he did much more than before. He idolised little Julianna, teaching her everything that he knew.

'As they grew so did their love, they were by each other's side constantly, playing together, going swimming together at the local river or helping one another with their studies, but whereas Julianna excelled academically, Jakub started to drown in the opposite direction. The older she got Julianna would help Jakub at night in his bedroom going over the school work that he needed to prepare for the next day. Sometimes we would hear them talking although we were never quite able to decipher what is was that they were confiding in one another, other times they would laugh and giggle like when they were younger. It was nice to see Jakub calm and not so withdrawn.

'Adolescence can be an extremely confusing period of a girl and a boy's life when certain changes come into effect. Not only does the mind need to differentiate between right and wrong, and gather as much information as it can before entering adulthood, physical attributes flourish and become prominent, especially in a girl. Jakub was forever getting into fights and protecting his sister from the ill-appropriate actions and remarks of the other boys in the village. As changes took place in Mary so too did Jakub develop, his sinews, arms, legs and chest growing in strength, he no longer looked a boy, but a young man.

'The problem was that some of the other boys did not work on the farm like Jakub whenever the school was on a holiday period. What they lacked in muscle they made up for in taunts. Over a length of time Jakub became sullen, moody and would lash out at anything that represented authority. The only person who could tame and calm him was Mary. But like the boys that taunted him, the teachers too had long memories, they remembered the difficulties that he had caused them. When it came to awarding the nominee's for the apprenticeships Jakub was ignored. That particular day changed his whole outlook and attitude towards life.

'Prior to leaving school Jakub's class participated in an educational outing for the day taking them to the local forest where having been split into groups they had to return that afternoon armed with things from the forest to evidence their understanding of environmental science and their homeland. When six boys failed to return to school later that day a search party was hastily organised and sent out to find them.'

I could not fail to notice the pain in Gabriele Hesseltolph's eyes.

'Two hours later they found the boys tied between the tall pines, their arms and ankles stretched as far as they could, leaving them just able to stand. Each boy had been stripped naked and cut with a knife, tortured by our son, or so they claimed. When I myself saw their injuries I felt ashamed, repulsed and sickened that a boy to whom I had given life could do such a thing. Jakub was arrested by the village constable and taken away for questioning.

'Sometime during the evening Jakub admitted the offences, he was released into my care to attend a special court the next morning. What *didn't help was that a local woman, a so-called sorceress, stated to the constable with whom she was a close friend that the cuts inflicted upon the boys had been the work of the devil and they represented black magic. With the help of the school governors the constable compiled his report for the court where it was deemed that our son had a serious mental problem. He was libelled a defective, destructive force that was beyond control.*

'When I collected my son from the constable's house, the journey home that evening was most difficult, charged with long periods of silence and painful confusion. How could my wife and I have created such a monster, when his sister took her brother to her room where they could talk we are ashamed to say that we both felt relieved. Do not judge us too harshly Mr Quinn. We loved our son, but what he had done that day had left us each numbed and mystified. We neither saw nor heard anything from our son that evening until it was time for us to retire to bed. As only a mother would she took her son a tray of food and something to quench his thirst.

'Climbing the stairs minutes later after having tended to the fire in the stove I saw from the landing Jakub's door wide open. Wishing to say goodnight to my first born I found my wife lying on the floor in a pool of blood. Her throat had been cut as she had delivered the tray. When Jakub stepped out from behind the door and plunged the knife through my heart I dropped like a stone, but I was dead before I hit the bedroom floor.

'When Jakub failed to attend the court the next morning the constable came to effect his arrest, only instead he had to force the door where he found the bodies of myself and my wife, but more distressing our daughter

tied to her bed. She had been raped and cut like the boys in the forest. When the authorities caught up with Jakub he was committed the nearest sanatorium for the mentally insane for an indefinite period. The magistrate signed the order, not wanting him in his court. Maybe the old woman did have a point, perhaps our son had been in league with the devil.'

I saw the thin dark line that swept from side of her neck to the other. 'Why did he choose to let his sister live?' I asked.

Thomas Hesseltolph shook his head like a madman would not believing the truth for all it merit.

'Because he loved her Mr Quinn, it was that simple. Jakub adored his sister, he always had from the moment that Julianna was conceived he pestered my wife until the moment the baby was born. He absolutely doted on her. They protected one another, always had.'

It had taken a courageous man to tell the story that he had reiterated to me, condemning his one and only son a madman, a monster. Suddenly a thought materialised in my head.

'Protecting as in the same, as protecting her from the evil of other men!'

He stared at me a defeated, broken man, his hands wrung together.

'So you know.' He looked at his wife.

'The others.' She said as she shook her head.

This time I couldn't help but think of Julianna. Gabriele Hesseltolph was closest, she picked up my thoughts. She put her hand over mine.

'She is not evil Mr Quinn, just misguided. Sometimes it is possible for a person to lose their ways in life, trade what values they hold dear and topple from the road of righteousness. Thomas has told you the truth as painful as it was for him and we came because we want you to understand. Jason Chancery took from you what you held most dear, we are afraid that he will do the same with our only daughter. You are the connection do you not see, if this killer is not stopped, he will eventually murder our beautiful Julianna. If he can be stopped his passing will release many others waiting in the equidistant.'

'You as well?' I asked. It was clinically cynical and I hadn't meant it to be so abrasive. She shook her head.

'No, not us. We can only be released when justice is served upon our son.'

Whether I wanted it or not, I had either stepped into or been cleverly tricked into a three sided equation with only one outcome. There were a good many more questions that I wanted to ask, but when I felt her hand slip away from mine, they started to fade from the bedroom, their time was over.

My mind went through a series of emotions, rage, pity, anger and a paradox of contradiction, but in the end none of what I concluded seemed to make any sense. I wished, wanted and begged for Lucy to appear and have her sit beside me on the bed, but the remainder of the night passed by without further incident. Even the vivacious Sharon Rochester wouldn't come back when I asked to see her again. Unable to sleep I showered early and waited for Giovanni to appear. I felt that I needed to be with somebody that I knew, somebody living and whose heart beat for all the right reasons.

Chapter Thirty Three

With my appointments blocked and Suzi Wang Choy out of the way, I could devote my time in unravelling the mystery surrounding Julianna Hesseltolph. Since the encounter with her parents the connection had grown stronger albeit that I sensed it rather than felt it. Jonathon although still involved had finally accepted that becoming a silent and unseen investigator was much safer for both he and Arabella, I had to say that I was relieved. Catching the eight fifty from Kings Cross I travelled north reaching Durham just before midday. The buffet car had served coffee and a day old sandwich, but it filled a space that would sustain my hunger till I got back to London.

My early morning call had been received with the expected annoyance and suspicion that I had anticipated, when I cancelled the call I imagined Julianna Hesseltolph hopping out of bed, hitting the shower and skipping breakfast to make contact with Jason Chancery. The mere suggestion that I knew something about her parents had secured my visit. Standing outside the station I hailed a taxi. The driver, an Asian gentlemen drew up alongside and beamed a welcoming smile happy to acquire a fare.

'She gets a regular flow of visitors to the clinic,' he advised as we made our way through the traffic.

'Do any look out of place?' I asked, probing to see if he mentioned anything that would relate to Jason Chancery.

'Many look like they need some sort of help. Some are sad, other's don't say much, but have much on their mind.' It wasn't what I meant, I probed again.

'Like they have a determined, maybe evil way about them?'

'Like they could kill.' He replied keeping one eye in the mirror, the other on the road ahead.

'Yes, just like they could kill.' I repeated.

'Maybe one. I picked him up many months back. He was liked a caged tiger sitting in the back, his eyes were everything as though waiting for the hunter to pounce. They were very dark, like the inside of his head had never seen the light of day. I know that when he climbed into my taxi I felt a cold shiver run down the length of my spine, as though death itself had wanted a ride. During the journey I tried to engage him in conversation, but I got the distinct impression that he didn't want to talk. He was scruffy, unshaven and smelt like he needed a good wash and not the kind that you'd consider would be visiting her posh clinic. You'll see what I mean when we arrive.'

It sounded like Chancery, it sounded very much like Julianna Hesseltolph was his bolt-hole, his secret place to hide up when things on the streets got that bit too much. What police force would even consider that a renowned psychologist and respected member of her profession would ever be harbouring a dangerous and wanted fugitive? It was beauty and the beast all over again, only this time it was unscripted, seriously unpredictable and I was heading into the middle of the tiger's lair.

241

I had what I wanted, we changed the subject and talked about the city instead, the recent developments, economic restraints and social changes. He was an educated man and wasted as a taxi driver, although pleasingly genial. I caught him checking me out several times to see if my eyes met or narrowed, wondering if I was a fruit-cake going to the clinic for a personal reason. I considered telling him about the first experience that I'd had with Pike only I was sure that it would have freaked him out.

On the outskirts of the city the housing changed, growing in size and style. Affluence positively jumped out from the long drives, well maintained hedgerows and white stoned buildings. It reminded me of the monopoly board, where you passed by the green houses, belonging to bankers, financial traders and successful professionals, medical and the like. Had I lived here, I would have been no different. The class structure was still very evident and yet when you met somebody like Jason Chancery in a darkened alley, on a boat or even in the rear garden of your house, class barriers would not keep you safe.

When the taxi swung right and crunched the gravel under the tyres I saw for the first time what he had implied. The house was grand, nothing like a mansion, but it exuded wealth and influence. The clinic was set to the side of the house. When the driver brought the vehicle to a halt he swivelled around holding a business card in his hand.

'Whatever the purpose for your visit, I hope you find the answer that you seek.' It was why I had come north. He handed me the card. 'When you call to go back to the station, you ask for Mattel, I do you special rate.' I put it where I could find it. The taxi driver waved then swung the vehicle around sending several stones beneath the recently cut hedge. Standing in the open doorway of an impressive entrance Julianna Hesseltolph was almost everything that I had imagined her to be. Tall, bespectacled, curvy in all the right places, well-groomed and her hair pulled back in a bun, she didn't' look overly happy to see me. With her arm crossed as though ready to do battle I ascended the short flight of steps.

'I cannot think what could be so important that you had to make a long journey north today Mr Quinn?'

I smiled, which I knew would irritate her more.

'Maybe you'll understand when we talk.' I wasn't about to discuss Chancery on her front doorstep. She stepped aside to let me in, closing the door behind.

'Follow me this way.' There was no polite offer of the hand or friendly tone in her invitation. We proceed through a small seated area to a reception area and down a very short corridor of which there were three doors and nobody manning the desk, her consulting room was the door immediately ahead. On the door a white engraved plate depicted her name and medical qualifications. Turning the handle she saw me looking back at the desk and read my thoughts.

'Andrea's out running errands for me. She will be back later not that her absence is of any consequence to our meeting!'

The consulting room was minimally furnished, a desk and chair, two leather settee's, no couch and a fireplace, set for the next time that it turned cold. On the table was a tray of fresh coffee, it surprised me as I had not expected any such courtesy. On either side of the mantel piece were two framed prints, I knew of both. The first by Winslow Homer was named *Snap the Whip*, which depicted a group of boys running across a field. I had always considered it an unusual painting which conjured up a number of various explanations, depending upon the mood of the day and whatever you took from the painting every time that you looked at it. Were the boys running away from something that was chasing them or innocently participating in a game? It was difficult to tell. I found it interesting that Julianna Hesseltolph should have a copy as the background could very well have represented the village and woodland from where she had originally hailed. The second was a better known picture by Edvard Munch, called *The Scream.* I wondered how many of her paying clients had held their head in their hands and screamed after meeting Julianna Hesseltolph. She poured two coffees without asking if I wanted one.

'You had a long journey, did you want to use the cloakroom, only it's the second door on the right, the first is a broom cupboard?'

'I'm fine thank you, although I might before I leave though, depending upon how long I'm here!' It was my turn to be reticent. Her eyes never left mine as I sipped the coffee. I wondered if it had been laced as she had not touched hers.

'Your persistence is very intriguing Mr Quinn I will give you that,' she started 'although I am cautiously suspicious as to why you needed to name members of my family to secure a personal meeting here?' the tone of her voice was controlled, yet loaded with hatred. I contemplated why and what she had against me that made her despise me.

'I'm here because they asked me to come.' It was a lie, but I could see the doubt going through her mind.

'And what was so important that they came to you, why not come directly here?'

I had been prepared for this and had the answer.

'Because they still feel the hostility that surrounds you Julianna, since the incarceration of your brother.' It was a long shot, but I detected a glimmer of light when I mentioned the brother's name.

'And what do you know of Jakub?' the tone had gone down a notch.

'That he meant a lot to you. That your mother and father still feel guilty that they had not helped more, when they had a duty to protect both of you.' Her eyes narrowed, she was interested to hear what I knew, but at the same time suspicious that I was grasping at straws.

'Protect us how?'

'They said that they should have understood Jakub's pain and suffering, his frustrations and just how much he had to endure throughout his schooling.' She raised her head, knowing that I did know, I went on as I now her full attention. 'Your mother is overwrought that she didn't protect you, when Jakub was hurting you, abusing you and cutting you!' I could tell that she knew that I hadn't uploaded such details from the internet.

'This still doesn't explain why you're here?' she said, intentionally putting the matter to one side.

'I'm here because they are concerned, worried in fact that you might be in more danger!'

Sarcastically she put her head back on her shoulders and laughed loudly.

'Danger, I hardly think so Mr Quinn. How could I possibly be in any danger, here in Durham, inside my own consulting room or this house?' She stopped laughing and sipped her coffee. I felt easier drinking mine Julianna Hesseltolph was clearly no fool.

'Putting aside their concerns what else did they have to say?'

'That Jakub had been wrongly understood when he attacked the boys on the school outing. That none suffered any retribution for what they had done to you!'

'You didn't say *accused* that was very clever Mr Quinn, you are however right. Jakub was only trying to protect me, instinctively reacting the same later that night when my parents died. Jakub knew that the boys in his class had been taunting me, touching me where they ought not and saying such horrible things trying to blackmail me into lying down with them in the hayfields. Jakub only acted because my father ignored my pleas for help. Thomas Hesseltolph was a fool, a pig-headed fool who proclaimed that such things were all part of growing up.' She looked up at the ceiling as if expecting to see a pair of faces looking down. 'If he's listening now, I hope he feels the shame of everything. Jakub might still be free if my father had been more protective and understanding of his children. I was a young woman Mr Quinn and the only one defending my honour was my brother.'

'But Jakub tied you to the bed and he raped you, cut you!'

She shook her head which surprised me. What she said next surprised me.

'Jakub should never have been locked away. The boys on the field trip and my parents deserved what was coming to them.'

I think she expected me to respond, but I didn't sensing that she wanted to tell me. With purpose she put her cup down on the saucer.

'I am concerned with what they do to poor Jakub every day. That bastard doctor keeps him constantly sedated believing that sleep will banish the demons that plague his mind. There are no demons Mr Quinn, only love.'

Professional opinion, judgement or diagnosis, I couldn't be sure. Was Julianna Hesseltolph as unhinged as her brother and Jason Chancery.

'The other boys were to blame. They were responsible for Jakub's anxiety. Down the years they had tormented and tried to belittle us both. What they did to me was unspeakable. They are the ones who should have been locked away.'

She stopped suddenly as though listening out for something or somebody. The receptionist, I wasn't sure, but I did hear a door catch click somewhere close by.

'Jakub was my senior and as such believed that it was his duty as my brother, my sibling to protect me at all times. All brothers and sisters have a bond that binds them together throughout life, but unlike other siblings our love was special. It was a love that our parents would not have understood. When Jakub came to my room that night, he didn't tie me to the bed to rape me, I let him do those things to me willingly.'

She smiled seeing the expression on my face alter.

'Our love wasn't just genealogically engineered, it was a gift of both physical and expressive deep meaning. We needed one another, but yearned for nothing or nobody else. Through their ignorance, not even our parents realised the depth of our love as it flowed through our veins. I waited patiently each night for Jakub to come to my room where I would put aside my books and let him take me. With our parents downstairs we would laugh in the face of their ignorance. Tying me up was all part of the game.

'The first time that Jakub took me was when we went to the river to swim. He suggested bathing naked, so we did, but soon our hands touched, explored and held fast. That afternoon we made love on the river bank under the sun. We went swimming a lot after that.

'The older I got the more I changed physically, breasts began to appear attracting the boys from Jakub's class my way. Either before or after school they would whisper what they would do to me if they ever got me alone. They would touch me, grope me and try to kiss me, but I once bit one of them on the lip. I never had any trouble from him ever again. At night I would cry and tell Jakub what they had done. He promised that he would make it right.

'Before the end of their last term the teacher arranged a field trip. Jakub seized the opportunity and waited until the boys that had caused me the most trouble became separated from the main party. In the woods a long way from Kurlor he made them suffer. Now other girls are safe from their loathsome, disgusting habits. I doubt none ever married or managed to hold down any long term relationships.'

I saw Julianna Hesseltolph in a different light, she wasn't far behind her brother.

'But to cut you too. That hardly sounds like he was protecting you!'

She smiled and offered more coffee, but I wisely refused.

'Jakub is the only man that has my love Mr Quinn. He was not repulsed by the scars that marked my flesh, not as others would be. So yes, he had protected me from the evil of others desire.'

'Did your mother never see them, surely when you took a shower, a bath or when you were in bed?'

She shook her head.

'They were descendants of the puritans. Sex and the presence of the naked human form was something that only ever happened in the dark. Their room was especially quiet, not like mine when Jakub was visiting. They were so disappointed when Jakub tortured the boys in the woods. Kurlor was their idyllic setting to raise a family.'

'Why did he kill them?'

'Because we overheard my father telling my mother that they were going to send me away the very next day. I was to live with my aunt on the Austrian, Germany boarder. I didn't want to leave my home nor Jakub. He needed me then more than ever. We talked it through for hours until my mother brought a tray of food and drink to his room. Jakub dealt with the problem the best way he thought and thus removed the equation to redress the balance.'

She was as mad as her brother. I checked my watch to see how long I had been in the house.

'When my father saw what Jakub had done, he only had time to turn and see the knife before it ended his life. Jakub is not wicked Mr Quinn, he is misunderstood. Had I been the eldest I might have been expected to deal with the problem!'

I glanced up at the picture beside the fireplace where the boys were running, I was convinced that something or somebody was chasing them.

'The other reason for my coming here today is that a former client of yours is running amok throughout England, leaving behind a trail of carnage and heartache. I thought that you might be able to shed some light on how he operates, what makes him tick and most importantly how he choose his victims.'

She straightened out her the wrinkles of her blouse, then adjusted her position in the seat, all time wasting to take a few extra moments to consider the question.

'And who precisely should we be talking about?'

'Jason Phillip Chancery.'

I watched as the underside of her tongue swept across the top line of teeth. It was a rue to make me think that she was trawling through the cells of her memory.

'Ah yes, now I remember. Mr Chancery, not quite what you would consider a client though Mr Quinn, more of passing episode in my life. If I recall correctly I performed an evaluation for the courts some years back. A troubled young man who'd suffered a violent and unenviable upbringing. I could have Andrea check the record, but I doubt that we even kept a file on him.'

I smiled. Julianna Hesseltolph would have made a first rate lawyer, she had the attributes to see through the lies, bend the truth and corner a witness. I would have believed her, if I hadn't seen her face in the photographs and security camera stills.

'I don't suppose that you believe in ghosts neither?'

'A strange question, but the answer to that is most definitely not. The imagination is a powerful tool that can produce hallucinatory fantasies or nightmares, depending upon the level of stress that one is suffering and for whatever purpose. Death often makes people look to the *other side* for comfort. Is that what you are suffering Mr Quinn, delusional anguish?'

It was her first mistake, being clever can sometimes make you falter and fall where you least expect. There was no way that she could associate Lucy with me, unless through Penny Schuchel and Jason

Chancery. In that moment the shift of power within the room crossed from her settee to mine.

'We've all got some ghosts in the cupboard Miss Hesseltolph, only some are still around to tell the tales!'

She didn't like my reply and it was evidently clear that she didn't like me. On the wall beside the fireplace, Edvard Munches *'the scream'* seemed to be yelling at me. I had touched on a raw nerve and it was clearly showing.

'As I advised Miss Hesseltolph at the beginning of this conversation, you yourself could be in danger. Chancery is an insane monster who will stop will stop at nothing until he himself is stopped. Maybe Andrea should check the files only I'm sure that the authorities will look favourably upon your assistance if he is caught through what you can tell them!'

Her eyes narrowed as she clenched her fingers into her palms.

'And if I have nothing to give...?'

'Then like Winslow's painting, the boy's never stopped running, only they didn't quite know why they were running in the first place. Evil has a way of catching up, whatever measures are put in place. Very often a caged tiger, will only ever consider one thing and that's its own survival. Of those that get in the way, death becomes an easy escape.'

Julianna Hesseltolph checked her watch and looked over at the door, we were almost done.

'I hear similar threats and stories every day in my profession Mr Quinn and I assure you that yours is nothing new. Clinical Psychology has long been considered dangerous as delving into the minds and lives of clients is a risky business. Meeting strangers that come bearing concerns should be heeded in similar fashion.'

With that she stood and went to the door.

'The cloakroom is second on the right if you wish to use it?'

I declined the invitation, I could hold it till I got back to the station. Passing through the short corridor I thought that I heard a sound inside the cloakroom, but Julianna Hesseltolph didn't seem at all surprised.

'Maybe it was best that you didn't use our facilities, Andrea must be back.'

Like a naughty schoolboy expelled from the school I was shown to the door, given no thanks for coming and had the door slammed shut in my face. I walked to the end of the drive where I called the number that Mattel had given me.

*****

Having heard the front door slam shut Jason Chancery emerged from the cloakroom with the hunting knife still in his hand.

'You should have let me deal with him,' he seemed annoyed, agitated 'only we could have resolved this matter here and now!'

Julianna Hesseltolph put a soothing hand on his chest and cooed at him to calm his anxiety.

253

'There'll be plenty of opportunities to silence Richard Quinn, Jason. For all we know he might have let the police know that he was coming here today. He might have been foolhardy to have not, but either way we should prepare ourselves.'

But Jason Chancery wasn't happy, loose ends needed dealing with quickly and effectively. Had he realised that Richard Quinn had been on the same train as himself, he would never have let him get anywhere near Julianna's door. She put her lips on his and pulled him in close.

'Stay focused Jason, everything will fall into place, as we planned. When Richard Quinn needs to be eliminated, gladly be the one to make it happen, only don't make it here in Durham and let some self-respecting psychiatric patients take the blame. Many have never forgiven the government for deinstitutionalised the hospitals.'

Jason Chancery nodded and smiled as he pulled apart the front of her blouse and gorged his eyes hungrily upon her breasts.

'That's much better, now let's go upstairs and find some way to help you release those pent up emotions.'

Casting aside his cloths he yanked down her trousers as she undid the band holding back her hair. When he stood back up she held her hand hard against his sternum.

'Before I let you take me, please shave and take a shower, you smell like you have been swimming in the river. Do this and I'll let you tie me to the bed.'

Jason Chancery followed her near naked body up the stairs. Later when he had done as she had asked, he slowly tied her ankles and wrists to the four corners of the bed. This was the moment that he liked most, the control. As he eagerly pumped away at her willing body Julianna Hesseltolph thought about her brother and the time that they had explored one another, ending with the consummation of their love, a bond that each vowed would never be broken.

Chapter Thirty Four

The return journey seemed much quicker, shorter than the one that I had taken earlier that morning, I put it down to knowing abundantly more than when I had arrived at Julianna Hesseltolph's private clinic. Although I couldn't put my finger on it, there was something very odd and peculiarly abnormal about the way that she showed me out, almost kicking me out. Professionals, irrespective of personal likes or dislikes of one another will still be courteous, albeit if only to show the other that they won't be dragged down to the same level of gutter interaction.

I also found her take on discounting ghosts out of hand somewhat puzzling. What I had described from the connexion with her parents had not convinced her that there was another dimension besides our own. I was still contemplating the possibility that she was either eccentrically insane or just plain mad. Her incest with her brother was way outside the bounds of normal activity. It wasn't until the train pulled into King's Cross that I realised that Andrea either had a weird taste in perfume or she liked swimming in stagnant water.

Later, back at home I double checked the doors and windows before picking up the hall phone. As I dialled the number I knew that before he answered that I was in for a bollocking. A teenage girl took the call, seemed instantly deflated that I was on the other end then asked me to hang on as she shouted to the floor above. It was annoying, but the audacity of my visit had suddenly deserted me and I felt vulnerable.

Trevor Baines picked up the receiver in his study, I apologised for the disruption to his evening.

'Don't let my daughter put you off calling,' he responded 'the kids should be used to my taking calls at home by now!'

All the same I felt sorry that I had not been the daughter's boyfriend calling. When I told where I had been his manner changed, he became authoritative and concerned in the same breath.

'You took one hell of a risk Richard and not one that I would have undertaken going in alone. There was no telling how Miss Hesseltolph might have reacted to seeing you on her doorstep.'

'She was expecting me.' I explained why.

'These experiences that you have, they ask a lot of you!'

'I know. What concerns me the most is when they stop or why they stop?'

'Is there a difference?'

'I suppose that depends on whether I live or die.'

He gave a short laugh. 'That'll do it.'

I started to reiterate the conversation between Julianna Hesseltolph and myself, Trevor Baines had not reached the rank of detective chief inspector without being a good listener.

'And did she heed the warning that she might be in danger?'

'Not entirely and that's because I think she's involved in some weird threesome involving Jason Chancery and her brother Jakub. When I told Trevor Baines about her incestuous relationship, he expressed the first thought that passed through his mind, momentarily forgetting that he was at home.

'Now that's a different *fuckin'* slant. I would never have added that into the reckoning, although it might help answer a few questions that I've had going around inside my head today.'

He had thawed al last, was less hostile regarding my visit. I heard the door of his study click shut.

'You've come back armed with some interesting information, probably more than if I or Bob Pearson had paid her a visit, but it was still very risky… what if Jason Chancery had been in the house?'

I told him about the stagnant water smell that I had detected in the reception area, it was annoying that I hadn't been thinking more clearly.

'I'll contact Durham and have their technical boys set up some surveillance equipment on the house and consulting room. It's surprising where they can hide their stuff these days. If Jason Chancery is around we'll initiate a joint task force and hit the house so hard that whoever's inside will spin.'

He asked me about Jakub Hesseltolph, when I had finished I could positively hear the cogs whirring inside his head.

'It might explain why Jason Chancery cuts his victims. If he is some kind of protégé for the brother then we have a connection. In a warped way

258

Julianna Hesseltolph is a sort of chrysalis, a larva, a cocoon where she hides Chancery sending him back out when the heat had died down. I can feel a trip to Austria might prove interesting.'

'Some butterfly.' I added.

'The deadly kind.'

'Julianna Hesseltolph believes that she is beyond reproach and yet she lights the litmus paper beneath a smouldering powder keg of immoral wickedness. I'd nicknamed her *'deadly nightshade.'* A toxic mix of beauty and destruction.'

'I like that... that's what we'll call the surveillance operation. *Deadly nightshade* will be an apt name. The star of poisonous plants and adeptly gifted to kill. We've stumbled one deadly trio Richard.' There was a brief pause for a few moments, the silence was deafening. 'You realise that now you've let the cat out of the bag, Jason Chancery will be hot on your heels and if I'm any judge of character, it will be soon!'

'I'm not afraid Trevor. By my reckoning our coming together is inevitable. How it pan's out is another discussion for another day, but I won't go down without a fight. I owe Lucy and the others that much!'

We finished the call much to the relief of Baines daughter. I replaced the receiver and looked at the mirror on the hall wall, the reflection that bounced back wasn't afraid. The eyes were steely set as was my jaw. Evil exudes a propagating wave of forewarned energy before it emerges as a physical form. The moment that Jason Chancery had hurt Lucy wad the moment that our destiny's crossed.

The next morning I was awoken to the sound of my mobile ringtone indicating that I had a text message. It was brief and to the point:

'No sign of deadly nightshade, everything set in place.'

Chapter Thirty Five

The day that I had been dreading finally arrived and wasn't it always the way, the weather was exceptionally good with clear blue skies and little breeze. Turning the wheel I drove slowly through the cemetery gates and entered a world of serenity, dark foreboding and mystery. Unless there was a specific reason that I had to attend a garden of remembrance I generally kept well away.

Cemeteries were haunting cities of the dead where weirdoes would come to take a video shoot or writers would come to get a *feel* for a current theme that they intended extending into a story. Somewhere in the grounds a hole had been dug in preparation to accept Lucy's coffin and yet ludicrously I knew that she was presently elsewhere. I pulled the car to allow those behind to pass on by, the faces of the occupants of whom I did not recognise. Taking in the short drive to the car park I located a space away from the other vehicles and got out near to where a generous gathering were swelling in numbers as additional mourners arrived to join those already milling about the entrance to a small chapel, uncertain of what to say or do. When the hearse came through the gate all heads turned and a minister took his cue to usher people inside.

Sitting at the front to the right I noticed that two spaces had been reserved for my parents, I was grateful that they would be attending as I felt embarrassingly outnumbered, most of the mourners filling the aisles either side were Italian with a few journalist colleagues and some of Lucy's closest friends. I looked at the two empty spaces to my other side, they would have been occupied by Penny and Sienna Schuchel, although by all accounts none of us should have had a reason to be here today. The only person that I wanted to see right now was Jason Chancery.

Thankful that I had not been asked to perform a eulogy I skipped much of what was being said during the service, placing my thoughts elsewhere. At one point I caught Mama Maria looking my way, I think she knew what I was doing and had similar distractions. When the pall bearers hoisted the coffin up on their shoulders I waited until last to leave the chapel. Lying amongst the other floral tributes I saw a wreath, small by comparison to some of the others, but neat and brightly coloured, I liked it more than most. Peering down I saw that it had been signed by two familiar names, Baines and Pearson. It was a thoughtful touch and I doubt that they did it for every victim that they investigated. Underneath those hard shells were a couple of honest, devoted family men just doing a job that many would have shied away from, they had my admiration. I watched the mourners follow the coffin, but had no real want to follow behind. I'd say my farewells when the others had left.

Finding a bench I parked myself down letting the warmth of the sun beat down on my face. On the far side of the cemetery a gardener was burning off some dead foliage, he stood for a moment with his head lowered out of respect as the coffin came close, but continued with his duties when the cortege took a turn in the opposite direction. Moments later he was joined by another man although I couldn't see the face as it was hidden under a cloth cowl. Out of the blue a voice suddenly came forward as though it had been waiting for the right moment to speak, I recognised it as belonging to Lucy. *'Be strong Quinn, only beware. Danger is close at hand!'* In the time that it had taken for her to say it, she had gone, disappeared. I looked around, knowing that she wouldn't be there, but I looked anyway. On the far side the two men continued to talk, but they were too far away to be heard. My thoughts were disturbed by a hand resting upon my shoulder, I looked up to see my father standing beside me, he sat himself down uninvited.

'Still bearing up son! I wish there was something that I could say or do that would help, only at times like this any words are irrelevant. Your mother is with Mama Maria and some big looking men, they remind me of nineteen thirties gangsters.' I smiled, he was right they were imposing. He was referring to Lucy's cousins.

'I'm alright, I just wanted to be alone whilst they lowered the coffin. It's not Lucy their putting in the ground, just a corpse without a soul. I'll say my goodbye's when everybody leaves.' Of course I wasn't really okay, I missed Lucy like mad. When my mother appeared I stood up and hugged her tight, something that I had not done for a long time.

It's funny in a way, but we take mothers for granted. Their always there, the backbone of the family, never sick, or they don't show it, always good for advice and yet the circles they move around in isn't entirely overflowing with a wealth of knowledge, but we rely upon them when times are bad. She responded by squeezing as tight and kissing my cheek.

'It's never easy Richard, but eventually the pain subsides and all that you're left with is memories of the good times you spent with one another. Hold onto them son because Lucetta has.'

I pulled away and stared her straight in the eye. It was a strange thing to say, but it implied that she knew. Long had she admired Lucy and so wanted her to be the daughter-in-law. Chancery had shattered her dreams. Shattered mine too.

'We're leaving soon, but you're welcome to come back home if you wish?'

I shook my head. I didn't want an afternoon taking a trip down memory lane. My mother understood. She pulled my father up from the bench and shook the conifer dust from the shoulder of his suit jacket.

'Come Ben let us say farewell to Mama Maria and her family.' She turned to face me. 'Visit when you want Richard, I am always there!' With that she kissed me and my father shook my hand as men do.

Taking myself over to the grave I stood beside the open pit looking down at the closed casket. I took a single rose from my wreath and dropped it down. Miraculously it landed just where her head would be lying and stayed her.

'I love you and one day soon, we will be together again!' They weren't just empty words, I inwardly felt that sometime soon Lucy and I would be reunited.

By the time that I returned to the car park a police officer was in attendance taking details from one of the mourners, it transpired that somebody had stolen his car during the service. I had just reached the gates and was about to turn back out onto the road when I took a call from Trevor Baines. He called to offer his condolences and to tell me that

Julianna Hesseltolph had been picked up at Holyhead where she had been trying to board a cross sea ferry to Dublin. It made me smile when he revealed that she'd been none too pleased at being detained, there was no mention of Chancery, so once again he had managed to evade capture. The call ended with Baines telling me that a boat owner, a Cecil Hawkins had been found drifting down river by another pleasure craft. What was left of his boat had been found burnt out near to the village of Burtonmoor. When Durham police raided the house belonging to Julianna Hesseltolph forensics obtained a number of biological samples that substantiated Chancery had been involved.

I thanked him for the wreath and promised to keep in touch. Putting the mobile on the passenger seat I was seized with a mixed emotion of anger and remorse for the boat owner. He was another innocent victim who had been living out his life peacefully and enjoying his boat, but he'd been in the wrong location at the wrong time. Jason Chancery was prepared to wreak havoc wherever he went and destroy whoever got in his way. I sensed too that he was close by.

Chapter Thirty Six

Jason Chancery left the stolen car in a side street then scaled the tall gate that should have secured the long drive to the impressive looking house. The gates shook as he jumped down, but the strong electro magnets held fast. Parked out front of the arched entrance was the blue coloured jaguar that he had followed from the cemetery. Using the shrubs for cover, he made his approach, the knife in his right hand and poised ready to deploy, not to maim, but to kill. He had come this far and had no intention of being impeded by man or beast.

The large white washed house was everything that he despised about the rich, their opulent lifestyle, the way that they flaunted their money and how it was all such a far cry from the streets where he had been raised. Expecting a gardener to be tending the flower beds or the lawns, or a maid to be hanging out laundry he cautiously ran across to the wall beside the kitchen window. Inside a man was mixing a cocktail of alcohol laced with fruit adding ice and a sprig of mint. He seemed pleased with his ratios as he put the jug of home-made pimm's on a tray along with two tall tumbler glasses. Calling from the kitchen doorway he informed the female on the floor above that the drinks were ready.

'Just give me a minute Horatio and I'll be right on down. These new shoes have been killing my feet!'

Chancery smiled then searched for a way in. Trying the kitchen door he found it locked, but it didn't matter as there was sure to be an opportunity somewhere else, there always was. Examining the padlock looped through the metal ring fortifying together a set of cellar doors he took himself off to the tool-shed returning with a good strong garden spade minutes later where with minimal resistance the padlock sprung apart and offered the way in, just as he had anticipated. He eased himself down into the darkness below glad that it had been sometime since the cellar had seen a delivery of coal. Crossing to the wooden staircase on the far side he kicked up pockets of dust, cursing his luck and the owner's lack of keeping the place clean. At the head of the staircase he slowly turned the handle of the door creating a small fissure with which to look through before pushing the door back wide.

The inside of the house was lavishly decorated, in pastel shades and cream coloured carpets, not musty floorboards and left over remnants of linoleum. On the walls expensive paintings enhanced the elaborate feature of the rooms as he passed on by. Looking behind he smiled to himself, like a piece of modern abstract art his footprints had left a dirty trail of soot laden tracks. Somewhere at the back of the house he heard the sound of a ladle stir the fruit around the inside of the glass jug.

Horatio Quinn filled the tumblers, placing one down beside his wife taking care that he didn't spill any of his own as he eased himself into the chair alongside Alison Quinn's. They chinked glasses and raised them in a toast and memory.

'To Lucetta, may she rest in peace, wherever she may be?'

Bathed in sunlight Jason Chancery smiled to himself, mocking their ignorance. With only the backs of their heads visible he stepped up behind Alison Quinn's chair and casually slipped the knife under her chin, causing her to release her grip on the glass tumbler as it fell to the floor and shattered into a thousand pieces. Horatio Quinn turned sideways, his mouth open to express his reproach until his eyes fell upon the man holding the knife.

'What the...' he didn't finish the sentence.

Jason Chancery moved the fingertips of his free hand up and down Alison Quinn's neck, he sensed her displeasure. 'I guess that this was one reunion which you never expected, eh Horatio?'

The high court judge looked hard at the face of the intruder, it was impossible to remember all the countless faces that he had seen down the years standing in the witness box. Vaguely he shook his head.

'Do I know you?' he asked.

Picking up the glass jug Jason raised it to his mouth and glugged down the cool refreshing cocktail quenching his thirst. He then poured some down the front of Alison Quinn's blouse instantly making the material see through exposing the pattern of her brassiere. Putting the jug back on the table he fondled her breast.

'For god's sake man, that's my wife!' Remonstrated Horatio Quinn, but it was the reaction that Jason had wanted. He kept his hand where it was.

'Think hard and long judge, we've got all afternoon in which to have some fun. In time you'll remember!'

Watching the intruder assault his wife Horatio Quinn searched deep, but nothing clear came forward. The eyes seemed distinctly familiar, but then he had seen many madmen pass through his court. He wasn't given to being bullied or coerced into any rash decisions, whereas his wife was unlike him. She liked things simple and uncomplicated. Having been married for almost forty years she had sat in the shadows in awe of the man whose meteoric rise to the bench had been unblemished by slander or tarnished by the changing world beyond the drive gates. Her only regret was the absence of grandchildren. Pleading with her eyes she begged her husband to find an answer to the intruders demand.

'I'm sorry,' he responded, 'but today has been rather tiring, hot and emotional, my memories not as good as it should be. What is it that you want of us... money, jewellery the car?'

The laugh was loud and raucous. What was on offer was materialistic goods, things that could be replaced by the insurance companies, what Jason Chancery wanted nobody could replace.

'What I would like is the years that you stole from me that would be a start, the other things we can negotiate as we go along.' Money above all else sounded good, it was always handy.

Horatio Quinn at last put down his glass tumbler.

'What was it that I stole from you?' he asked.

'Opportunities!' It was all that Chancery was prepared to offer. The tip of the knife slid down the front of the wet blouse slicing through the buttons until it rested upon the middle of the bra, with a single flick he cut through the thin material. Horatio Quinn's eyes opened wide with alarm as his wife shut hers, shutting out the inevitable. From out of the blue a name came forth.

'My god man, you're Jason Chancery!'

Tearing apart the blouse and bra Jason Chancery made Alison Quinn stand. He deftly cut the hem of her summer skirt and watched it drop to the floor, quickly followed by her briefs. With her hands covering her exposure he cradled her waist pulling her into him, so that she could feel where he was hard. He whispered in her ear and asked that she lower her arms so that her husband could suffer her indignity. Reluctantly she complied.

'You've seen enough accused and witnesses squirm judge, tell me how does it feel to see your own wife endure the same humiliation?'

Horatio Quinn could only shake his head. Chancery was a madman and the only way to appease his disgusting, deplorable demands was to play along.

'Whatever your sentence, the law dictates the length of the incarceration, not I. Surely you understand that?' It wasn't the answer that Alison Quinn had hoped for.

'Does it really matter Horatio, who dictates what... *for fucks sake* do whatever Mr Chancery asks.'

Jason kissed the side of her neck remembering how as a young child he would do the same to his mother as she read him a story.

'Now there's good advice Horatio. Had you approached my trial in the same manner, none of this might have been necessary. He took the time to look around the sunroom looking at the trimmings, the trappings of wealth in all of its elegance. Nothing was out of place. It was no wonder that the sunshine flooded in.

'You know this really is a lovely room, refreshingly light and airy. Every home should have a room like this where little children can play and feel safe. When I was little boy we had to keep moving from *shithole to shithole* never managing to find anything good enough that I could ever call home. Not once throughout my trial did you take into consideration anything that had moulded my life. To you Horatio Quinn I was already a lost cause.'

With his free hand he reached down into the rucksack and withdrew a length of blue twine, he handed it to Alison Quinn and ordered her to tie her husband's hands behind his back. When she stepped away from the chair, he checked her handiwork. The bond was good and tight which surprised him, was Alison Quinn sending a message to her husband, one that he had not considered.

Whatever Chancery wanted he was now in complete control and Horatio Quinn realised that he was powerless to intervene. The only thing that he could do was suffer the consequences and let the authorities deal with the madman later when they eventually caught up with him. Whatever the outcome, he would ensure that Chancery never ever walked free from prison again.

'This will all be over soon Alison,' he voiced unconvincingly trying to reassure his wife. She looked back at him in utter contempt. Was he really that incapable of showing any human emotion, love or compassion? She knew that there was another side to her husband, his professional side, but he was not the man that she had married forty years back. His hollow words ended any hope of his helping. Jason chancery raped Alison Quinn as her husband watched on bound to the chair and totally hopeless. When it was over, Chancery casually slid the knife across her throat and left her die on the summer room floor. Horatio Quinn sat silent, his mouth open wide in horror, his mind a jumbled conundrum of thoughts, feelings and anger.

'You're demented man. Alison played no part in your downfall, she did not deserve to die so horribly. I guarantee that the authorities will punish you accordingly for your crimes!'

Jason Chancery had expected the backlash, the anger. It was what he wanted, he intended for the judge to be beside himself, to feel hopelessly bereft and know that he caused his wife's death.

'Do you remember the girl from the trial?' he asked. 'The pretty brunette with the slightly turned up nose. That evening she had come to the end of the pier willingly knowing what was going to happen, only once we got down to the serious business she started screaming and protesting. Nowadays they don't have time to scream.' He looked down at the fixed staring eyes of Alison Quinn. She hadn't screamed.

'You cut her, scarred her body for life. You deserved your sentence!'

Jason Chancery shook his head as he took another swig from the jug.

'I saved her from the wicked atrocities that other men would inflict upon her in the future, only neither you nor the jury fully appreciated or understood my motives.'

Horatio Quinn felt the shame of his wife's death pass through his chest, he wanted to scream and break free from his bonds, but the more that he wriggled the tighter they became.

'You're nothing, but a sadistic psychopath Chancery. One day destiny will catch up with you and when it does, it will come swiftly yet be no less painful than what hell has to offer.'

Like a condemned man sitting on death row Horatio Quinn accepted his fate, he smiled at Jason Chancery having one final act of defiance up his sleeve.

'I heard rumours through the inner court that your father met with an untimely end in the prison workshop. I rejoiced when I heard how he had died, befitting of a man that like had a black heart for violence and destruction. Your upbringing had nothing to do with moulding your future. Others in similar position have dragged themselves from the gutter and bettered their existence, helping others or becoming a role model in society. You could have taken the same path, only you chose to go in the opposite direction. I pity you Jason Chancery, but at the same time despise every fibre in your body.'

Swiping the judge hard across the face with the back of his hand Jason Chancery clenched his teeth together. He gripped the handle of the knife and forced the blade into the other man's stomach not stopping till his own hand felt flesh. The judge fell forward and lay beside his wife. Chancery lent over and came close to the dying man's face.

'I didn't need no *fucking* jury to help me decide your fate your honour. You had already passed sentence on you and your family the day that you met me in court. Before the reaper comes to collect your soul, know that I enjoyed destroying your son's life. His girlfriend spent her last hours in this world entertaining me a lot longer than your wife did. Very soon I'll be paying your son a visit, one that he won't forget, but before that happens I've something else that I need to attend too. It's a pity that you won't be able to warn him, consider it justice served.'

The knife cut slowly through the thyroid cartilage spraying the floor about with blood as Horatio Quinn lowered his eyelids and joined his wife in the equidistant.

Jason Chancery checked the time on the summer room clock, Julianna should have crossed the Irish Sea and made her way to the hostel in Dublin. Soon he would join her, maybe in a couple of days if all went to plan. Wiping the blade on the back of the chair cushion he dropped it inside the rucksack then washed the blood from his hands and arms in the kitchen sink, checking out the cupboards and fridge for food before searching the house for the cash and jewellery that the judge had promised him earlier.

Taking the stairs to the landing above he removed clean clothing from the wardrobe in Richard Quinn's old room. Jason Chancery hated everything about the rich mainly because everything came so easy to them. They were ignorant of how others in society had to scrap by, beg, steal and borrow in order to survive. When he left with the jaguar keys in his hand he purposely left open the front door to the house shrewdly smiling that it would help the flies find the dead bodies inside. Horatio Quinn had been wrong about one detail, there were some things in life that Jason Chancery did like helping.

Chapter Thirty Seven

The early morning flight from Gatwick picked up a tail wind over and landed at Graz airport ahead of schedule. After breezing through customs Trevor Baines was picked up by a member of the Austrian detective division and driven directly to the village of Kurlor.

Ordinarily any establishment that housed the mentally disturbed would have been called an asylum, but the founding father of Ebenstatt, a Professor of Psychiatric Medicine and widely respected individual Gustav Von Hulst had wanted the inmates to be known as clients rather than patients. Growing vegetables in the allotment, tending the flowers in the gardens and assisting in the general maintenance, their problems had lessened and in places become controlled by being involved rather than ignored, but as always change is not always in the best interest of those closely enmeshed within the walls of such an environment. Change can alter the balance, destroy the myth set by others and challenge the harmony.

In and around Kurlor it was deemed wise by the locals, some of who worked within Ebenstatt, not to go mouthing off the practices of the current doctor in charge, Alexander Koskovsky. What measures he had introduced were meant to be seen as progress and measured in results, albeit that the patients were drugged up to the eyeballs and confined to their wards. If they ever went out into the grounds they did so escorted by at least two members of staff.

When Von Hulst had died quite suddenly with minimal information being recorded on the event of his passing and there was definitely no post-mortem performed to establish the true facts. Alexander Koskovsky an eminent, yet modern thinking man had mysteriously arrived the same night and elected himself doctor-in-charge with little opposition, of those that did speak up, they too disappeared without trace, allegedly resigning and taking work elsewhere. Presently the allotment, gardens and maintenance was contracted out, coming under Koskovsky's control.

The one true fact that didn't need to emerge from Ebenstatt or be discussed in the snook of some local beer Keller was that if you went into Ebenstatt, you rarely ever came back out, unless driven out in the back of a blacked out van, which the local residents described as deaf, dumb mutes without a heartbeat.

Leaving Bob Pearson behind to oversee the transfer of Julianna Hesseltolph from Anglesey to Berkshire, Trevor Baines sat in the passenger seat taking in the countryside as the car sped east towards Kurlor.

'It was an early flight chief inspector, did you want me to stop somewhere where you could have breakfast only I know of the ideal place?'

'No, I'm fine thanks, they served pastries with coffee on the plane. It'll be sufficient till I get back to Graz.'

The driver changed gear as the road narrowed and went into a series of steep winding bends flagged either side by green pines. Berkshire was softer, more rolling than Austria where the temperature was noticeably fresher. Sensing that the senior detective might be noticing the change, the driver pushed the heat exchange up another notch. Outside a light drizzle had started to form on the windscreen.

'It always seems to rain at this point of the journey. Residents hereabouts say it is the tears of the people who have been lost to the mountain forest, mainly tourists, climbers, walkers and thrill seeking backpackers. Me personally I think it's the bears or the wolves.' As they came out of the bends he pointed to a small graveyard at the side of the road. 'That is where Thomas and Gabriele Hesseltolph are laid to rest.'

'What do you know about Julianna Hesseltolph?' Baines asked.

Keeping his focus on the road ahead, the driver responded.

'I take it that you mean following the attack on her parents and her being found tied to the bed. She was taken directly to the local hospital where her injuries were treated. She remained there for a week before taking her own discharge, returning to the house against the advice of the district nurse, the village doctor, head teacher and constable. Julianna Hesseltolph is a strange kettle of fish chief inspector. If you ever come across her you'll remember my words. In my opinion, she borders on the intelligent, eccentric, wavering or maybe tottering on the brink of insanity. Although I am not married, she wouldn't be my first choice as a date out one evening!'

'Do you know what happened when she went back to the house?'

The driver smiled.

'She cleaned the place, top to bottom, including her brothers room. Ignoring help and offers from relatives to live elsewhere Julianna Hesseltolph remained in the house that she called home until she went to university. Qualifying as a clinical psychologist she vanished, disappeared completely off the radar for a while and it was almost two years later that we learnt she was in England. Through various sources we've added to the file that she has a reputation for taking on the more macabre, distinctively weird and unusual cases that others in her profession tend to steer away from.'

Trevor Baines imagined what it must have looked like the night of the murder.

'The missing two years, you've no idea where she went, who she saw, or what she was involved with?'

The driver shook his head, pulling away from the house and continuing with the journey.

'No. There were a number of theories, but none that were substantiated. It was surprising how she managed to travel around without the passport or custom agencies stamping her card.'

'Before she disappeared, did she see her brother at Ebenstatt?'

'No, or not that we know about. Alexander Koskovsky keeps the place under tight supervision and as far as I'm aware very few visitors are allowed there. Your enquiry must have pulled some important strings to gain access. Ebenstatt has a fierce reputation for privacy.'

'And what's your take on Koskovsky?'

This time the driver averted his eyes from the road ahead, this time Trevor Baines saw the look in his eyes.

'Good or bad?' he added.

'Perhaps a bit of both chief inspector. By all accounts the place hardly ever bops to the beat of a heart, but more sleeps to the sound of men and women snoring. Koskovsky is an ardent disciple of drugs, used medicinally of course. His approach is much different to that of his predecessor doctor Gustav Von Holst.'

'You didn't answer my question, good or bad?'

'Maybe a bit of both, depending upon how you view the circumstances. We've not had any reports of anybody escaping for some time now. Perhaps you could best answer your own question when you've completed your visit.' The detective took a sharp right and pushed the car down what looked like a dirt-track. It was bumpy and clearly not maintained.

'Your serial killer, Jason Phillip Chancery. Do you believe that he as a connection with your visit?'

'That's basically the objective of my coming here Anders. Why do you ask?'

'Because I saw the photograph that you released on the Interpol website. Sometime back I was part of an investigation team that was looking into a series of crimes not too dissimilar to your own. There's something unnerving about the eyes in the photograph, they look very much like Jakub Hesseltolph's. Do you have family Mr Baines?'

'Yes, two girls and you?'

'Twins, a boy and a girl aged twenty, soon to be twenty one. I want them to grow in a world where they don't have to fear what could around the next corner.'

'Then we best get to Ebenstatt soon only I've a feeling that Jakub Hesseltolph will tell me things that might help capture Jason Chancery.'

Countless trees flashed on by as they negotiated the uneven track, without the help of Anders Wimmer, Trevor Baines would have been hopelessly lost. Coming to a halt at a set of high wrought iron gates he switched off the engine.

'We're here, you press the intercom and speak to security.'

'You're not coming in?' asked Baines.

'No, my orders are to wait outside for you.' Anders Wimmer opened the glove compartment and produced a bar of chocolate, he offered Trevor Baines some, but the detective from England politely refused concerned about his cholesterol level. The Austrian watched the chief inspector approach the gate.

*****

Bob Pearson perused the details on the arrest sheet, then passed it across to the female standing by his side.

'Are you confident that we have everything that we need?' he asked.

Sandra Hallam flipped through the printed sheet. 'We're as ready as we are ever going to be with what we know. Hopefully at the end of the tape we'll know a lot more!'

'Right, let's go see what this bitch has got to say for herself.'

Julianna Hesseltolph sat bolt upright in the chair unaccompanied in the interview room wearing a white cotton suit where her outer garments had been sent to the forensics laboratory for analysis. When Pearson and Sandra Hallam entered the room she had one question.

'Where are my fucking clothes?'

Hallam looked at Pearson, this wasn't going to be an easy ride. They took the seat on the opposite side of the table, ignoring her outburst to the interview.

'You went to a lot of trouble to escape the Durham police.' Bob Pearson exclaimed before turning on the tape recorder.

'If you are referring to my travel arrangements to take a short holiday across to Ireland sergeant, then it was no trouble at all only I wasn't aware that the laws had changed regarding freedom of movement. I consider my detention in contravention of my civil rights.'

Sandra Hallam rubbed her chin thoughtfully. 'You took liberties with your civil rights the moment that you become involved with Jason Chancery!'

Bob Pearson was impressed, Hallam had gone straight for the jugular.

'My only involvement with that man was ten years ago when I conducted a professional assessment for the courts.' Julianna Hesseltolph looked confidently from one to the other expecting a moment of hesitation, but Hallam was prepared for the fight.

'Then who was it *fucking* Chancery in your bed in Durham, the tooth fairy? This time we've crossed all the *i's* and dotted the *t's*. A genome test puts you together.'

The confident arrogance had gone, Julia Hesseltolph ignored Sandra Hallam and prompted her response at Bob Pearson.

'If he broke into my private residence, then he did so without my knowledge. I am willing to press charges.'

Bob Pearson smiled back. She was cool under pressure, had well-rehearsed answers and yet Hallam had dented her armour.

'DNA analysis put you both there at the same time Miss Hesseltolph, now take some advice from one that seen most, heard most and been around the block more times than you've lied over the past ten years. Modern forensics is as advanced as the science can be, it doesn't need a reason to lie.'

'Do you want legal representation before we proceed?' Hallam asked, not offering a get out of jail card, but keeping within the legal parameters.

Julianna Hesseltolph shook her head, knowing when she was beat.

'No detective. I can manage my own affairs. I find lawyers irritating at the best of times and especially when they come snooping into your life.' The both knew that she was referring to Richard Quinn.

'So where is he?' Hallam asked.

'Jason Chancery, I don't know and it's the truth. I was arrested at the ferry terminal and if you check through my belongings you'll see that there was only one ticket, not two!'

There was an element of truth in what she had said. Anglesey police had reported no sightings when they had picked up Julianna Hesseltolph. Suddenly the clinical psychologist changed tact thinking of her brother Jakub.

'I want to enter a plea of rape on tape. Jason Chancery forced his way into my house and raped me in the bedroom and the shower. I wasn't running away from the police, but I did need to get away.' She looked at Sandra Hallam. 'Have you ever been molested, abused and forced to have sex Miss Hallam, I doubt it, you look too innocent, despite the ring on your finger.'

It was a clever ploy, but Sandra Hallam had also been around the block, not entirely taking the same route as Bob Pearson, but in a predominantly male orientated profession, the route to being a successful detective was no without its social barriers, professional obstacles and sexual references. The cat fight was beyond round one.

'Nice try Miss Hesseltolph, the only problem I have in believing you is that Jason Chancery was picked up on the outskirts of London this afternoon. He is being held in a secure unit when not even the devil could find him. Detectives from a special task force have already questioned him and he's given you up Julianna. He has admitted your involvement, how you've colluded together for years, become lovers and how you've aided and abetted his crimes by giving him shelter. Considering the nature of his crimes, I place your chances of getting off lightly as somewhat slim. Did I mention that forensics also made a match of river sediment in a downstairs cloakroom used by your clients? I hardly think Chancery forced his way into your house then decided to take a piss before assaulting you. What did you do, wait in the reception area whilst he used the cloakroom facilities. A man was murdered for no reason other than he was in the wrong place at the wrong time. For the sake of tape I going to add being an accomplice to your charge sheet. Now for all our sakes stop fucking around and come clean. Clear your conscience only you'll be surprised how invigorating it can be!'

Bob Pearson didn't interrupt, Sandra Hallam was on a roll. He watched and listened instead. Before Julianna Hesseltolph had time to answer Sandra Hallam continued laying the noose of guilt firmly at her feet.

'Chancery is a cockroach that should never have been born. He destroys everything that he touches and in time Julianna he will destroy you, not just professionally, but as a human being. You will serve his purpose until he tires of you. The list is growing daily with his crimes and to be honest it would be in your interest not to have your named added to that list. If you fail to see sense and continue with this pitiful charade then when they lock the cell door, it will be a very long time before they find the key again. That's the reality in a nutshell, the choice is yours!'

285

Julianna Hesseltolph adjusted herself on the seat and looked at Bob Pearson again.

'Where did you find her... it wasn't in some Tibetan nunnery was it, she has the claws of a mountain leopard.'

Bob Pearson smiled, Sandra Hallam had done well, exceptionally well.

'Police finishing school,' he replied.

Julianna Hesseltolph smiled for the first time, she nodded that she conceded.

'Alright, but I will need protection. If I tell you what you need to know, regardless of what Jason has already said I will need protection the like of which you've never experienced before. If for one moment he suspects that I have rolled over and talked to the police he will end my life as quick as you can blink. Somehow he will get to me, even in police custody.'

Sandra Hallam pulled a photograph from the envelope that had been on the table throughout the interview. She turned it around and placed it before Julianna Hesseltolph.

'Are you referring to something like this?' she asked. It was a photograph taken of Lucetta Tate's shoulder blades. They were badly cut and marked. What happened next took both detectives by surprise.

Julianna Hesseltolph calmly stood up and pushed her chair to one side. She turned her back on them then dropped the cotton suit down to her waist. When Sandra Hallam saw the scars that lined her body, she felt the saliva slip down her throat. Unashamed of her body she turned around where the scars were as evident. Moments later Julianna Hesseltolph covered herself once again. In that moment the fight had neither been won nor lost. She sat back down.

'I've suffered as much as any of the victims Mrs Hallam, maybe more. Death is a swift release, but my pain goes on and on.' Of course what they didn't realise was that she was referring to losing Jakub, not Jason Chancery.

Pearson decided that it was an appropriate moment to take a break. Perhaps he had not been around all the blocks and there were others yet to be conquered.

Standing by herself in the station kitchen using the plaster wall for support Sandra Hallam felt her hand caressing the skin beneath her blouse, feeling for any imaginary scars that she knew weren't there, but checking anyway. However many times she closed her eyes it didn't help. Jason Chancery was sitting astride her naked body, grinning as he cut her. A long way off, but present was her husband begging for the pain to stop. When it was over, she wondered how he would react seeing her alive, but disfigured. Sandra Hallam wanted to run home and be with her husband, she wanted him to take her to bed, to feel him close beside her and wanting her, needing her like never before.

Ignoring the whistle of the kettle she ran instead to the ladies cloakroom where she put her head down the pan. Julianna Hesseltolph had been right about one thing, the pain did indeed go on and on. Sometimes being a woman was a very poor excuse to be abused, despoiled, debased and insanely butchered.

Chapter Thirty Eight

Trevor Baines depressed the buzzer on the intercom for a second time, slightly agitated that he had been ignored the first time. In the distance high above the tree tops the snow-capped peak of a mountain commanded the view. It looked majestic, but he surmised that it was probably quite deadly come the night. With a high-pitched crackle the intercom answered, he gave his name and purpose of his visit, being allowed entry. Taking a walk around the field Anders Wimmer saw the gate shut again as Baines walked up the drive.

The front facia of the sanatorium was not as Trevor Baines had expected. It was designed in a baroque fashion with ornate carved stone, high windows and made all the more resplendent by a central staircase that swept up to the front door. Here and there pieces of stone had cracked or gone missing, but it only added to the charm and if you wasn't aware that it was an asylum it could well be mistaken for country retreat. Taking the renaissance staircase he ascended up to where a man was awaiting his arrival. Peering out of the windows, he saw several faces watching, their blank expressions needing no introduction as to why they were there.

Alexander Koskovsky, originally from Przybelcha in Poland beamed his smile wide across his face as Trevor Baines reached the top step. Engraved above the door was a Latin inscription *'fretus deo mederi vulnerbis.'* Baines reached out his hand to accept that offered by Koskovsky.

'Welcome to Ebenstatt chief inspector, I saw you looking up at our motto, it means *'to heal the wounds and trust in God'* a phrase that we use often within these walls, although there are times when even the good lord finds it difficult to offer any solace here. Some of our patients are too far gone to understand. You may well find Jakub Hesseltolph one such example.'

Baines watched as the faces at the windows disappeared. They seemed wary of Koskovsky's presence.

'The secure units that we have back in England has their fair share of similar disciples as well doctor. Satan's angels I call them!'

Koskovsky nodded his head up and down, agreeing as he stroked the beard on his chin.

'We do not allow the devil here Mr Baines, but I'm sure that he comes visiting in the night. The howls that penetrate these walls are not always from the wolves outside. With regards to Jakub I must warn you that he is on medication and that the side-effects can interfere with his dextral abilities.'

Walking through the entrance hall Trevor Baines noticed the framed pictures that adorned the walls.

'Past members of staff including the founder Gustav Von Hulst, a pioneer in his field. A man of great integrity, vision and wisdom. I am honoured to carry on his work. We honour them all by putting up their images. Sometimes it helps a patient when they can remember a friendly face.'

Trevor Baines looked at the doctor curiously, it was a strange phrase to use. Did he imply that the patients didn't see many friendly faces these days, or was it simply that their memories had been distorted by the drugs. Koskovsky continued walking down a long corridor, where the décor had suddenly changed quite dramatically, becoming spartan and badly in need of maintenance. Looking through the windows he noticed the overgrown areas where vegetables had once thrived.

'I understand that at one time the patients tended the gardens, growing vegetables and the like?'

Koskovsky stopped walking, he peered through.

'A noble programme with some experimental ideas, put into practice by Von Hulst until his untimely death. It was said that the good doctor died an agonising death possibly at the hands of a deranged patient, although no culprit has ever been accused of the crime. When Von Hulst was examined his oesophagus was full of soil from the vegetable garden. It was an extremely upsetting and disturbing end to the life of a dedicated and brilliant man. Of course in light of the unusual circumstances and as the elected head of the sanatorium I felt it best to withdraw the privileges afforded to those able to work outside. There were just too many tools around not to ignore the risk.'

Baines noticed the growth of several new trees.

'And yet new trees flourish where there are now weeds?' he prompted.

'Ah yes,' said Alexander Koskovsky 'acorns to saplings to demonstrate that life still goes on. In a way a fitting tribute to Gustav. We have a similar programme of tree growing in the wood at the rear of the sanatorium. During my time here I have grown to trust again and allowed one or two special patients the privilege of tending the trees. Ebenstatt has to give hope, where hope is still a belief.'

They continued with the brief tour, omitting the back wards where it was reputed the most violent and disturbed patients were housed.

'There is no point in showing you them chief inspector, you have the same in England, padded cells for special cases. Jakub Hesseltolph did occupy one at one time, but he had mellowed of recent. I take it that you are familiar with his family history. We ensure that no female is ever alone with him.'

'Doctor, are the walls where Jakub sleeps by any chance decorated in pictures that he has drawn?' he asked.

Alexander Koskovsky was plainly intrigued, although guarded and suspicious. 'That's either an educated guess Mr Baines, or a perceptive insight. The answer to your question is *yes*, but please tell me, had you been told prior to the visit about his paintings?'

'No, it was just a hunch. Prisoners and detainees in police cells, prison or secure wards nearly always express their anguish through doodling on the walls. I've been told that a specialist can red their thoughts merely by seeing the etchings. Perhaps before I leave I could see some of those done by Hesseltolph?'

'Why of course,' Koskovsky replied.

The tour seemed to end rather quickly after that. Koskovsky held open the door to a room leading off the corridor where the window was barred heavily from the inside. In the centre of the room was a table and two chairs, all bolted to the floor.

'It's for your safety Mr Baines,' Koskovsky implied, as he asked a member of staff to fetch Jakub Hesseltolph. 'Any items of furniture can be used at any time as a weapon. We find it better if it's all bolted to the floor. Please feel free to smoke if you wish.' With that the door was closed.

Beyond the grounds and the high fence he could see Anders Wimmer walking the field, he was about a third of the way around. Around the window reveal there were dark stains, splashes that looked like dried blood, the window was dirty and webbed so it was difficult to say whether a patient had tried to slash themselves by breaking the glass. The door behind opened and in walked a man badly in need of a shave, a shower and a fresh set of clothes. He immediately walked around the table and took the chair in front of the window.

'Not for the view,' said Jakub Hesseltolph, 'but, so that I can see those bastards outside in the corridor. You need to stay alert here, otherwise one wrong word out of place and they jab you full of sedative. You're lucky if you wake two days later!'

Baines put down a pack of new cigarettes on the table top and took one for himself, he offered the pack to Jakub then gave him a light.

'Do most of the windows have bars?' he asked.

'More or less. The rooms at the back, the padded cells don't have windows.' Jakub Hesseltolph drew hard and long on his cigarette sending up a thin trail of smoke. It had been a long time since he had last had a cigarette.

'Is the packet for me inspector, a bribe perhaps to have me open up my soul and bear all, or is it just an introductory gesture to loosen my tongue. Either way, you've come a long way on a whim?'

Trevor Baines liked people who were straight forward, didn't fanny around or take a single sentence and stretch it into a paragraph. He actually liked Jakub Hesseltolph.

'I've no jurisdiction here Jakub, that you must know already, but maybe you can help me to help somebody close to your own heart?'

Jakub smiled, 'And who might that be?' he asked.

'Your sister!'

Jakub Hesseltolph let the chair fall forward so that it righted itself. Baines had better not be pissing him about, Julianna was his only concern, albeit that he hadn't heard from her in a while. Jakub however was no fool. Long had he been playing Koskovsky at his own game.

'Is the packet mine?'

Baines nodded. 'Along with another if you co-operate Jakub.'

Jakub took the packet just to be sure.

'Has she been hurt inspector?'

'No, not yet, but there's every possibility that she could be.'

'By somebody she knows?'

Again Baines nodded, progress. Jakub stubbed out his cigarette and drew out another, Trevor Baines lit it for him.

'By a serial killer named Jason Phillip Chancery. Have you ever heard of him Jakub?'

'No inspector, but I know of him. I've seen him in my dreams. Is Julianna safe?'

'She's in protective custody where Chancery cannot get to her.' It was a part lie, although Baines had entrusted Bob Pearson to keep her safe. 'I hardly need tell you what he will do to her, should he find that she is helping the police.'

'So why have you come here, if you already know about him?'

'I came Jakub because there are some missing pieces to my puzzle!'

'And you expect me to fill in the blanks?'

'That's about the size of it.'

Jakub too liked Trevor Baines, he was wary of him because he was a policemen, but his eyes told the truth, not like that bastard that had arrested him, if the day came that he managed to escape, he would be the first to feel his wrath. For the sake of Julianna he was willing to co-operate. On the plane over Baines had read a recent dossier on Jakub

Hesseltolph. It stated that he liked to play chess, read as much as he could and paint whenever the materials became available. He shared a cell with another inmate called Victor.

From the top left hand frame of the window a spider swept down to catch a fly that had flown into the web. Jakub watched the spider spin its mummification around the struggling insect before retreating back to the corner. He offered Baines a cigarette, but placed the packet in his shirt pocket when the offer was politely refused. Seeing the cocoon stop moving he spoke.

'Death is the one surety that none of us can escape Mr Baines, but choosing when and how can sometimes be less painful. I know that you've been told about the equidistant and what happens when you go beyond; and that your opinions have changed recently to accept that there is another tomorrow beyond this lonely existence.

'Julianna and a farmer named Friedrich Hanson are the only two people I really care about. What I did to those boys in the woods they deserved. They had hurt Julianna and I could no longer stand by and see her humiliated, abused and tormented. I know that my actions changed my destiny and that of others, but I did it to save my sister. She means everything to me, she always will.'

'And your parents?'

'What happened to our parents was also necessary. They were going to send Julianna away, but I could not let that happen Mr Baines, only you see they just didn't understand the depth of our love. Sibling love is special, created from the same womb, we felt the same and wanted the same. We could only give each other love and nobody else. History has seen the power of love topple armies and win the battle without raising a single sword.

'I am aware that Julianna had recruited in England, but this serial killer was only supposed to carry on my work, not turn into a wild card. He selects and kills randomly, without reason, which is not how it is supposed to be.'

'But you cut Julianna the same night that you took your parents lives?'

'To protect, only protect. That was always a tangible reason. Beautiful women like my sister, Julianna suffer the humiliating ways of men, evil thoughts that permeate into sinful, lustful dishonour. Believe me chief inspector there are more monsters on the outside than inside the prisons and asylums. What I achieved in the woods that day was meant to be the start.

'The night our parents died Julianna agreed to take up the mantle that I had begun. She was only the Chrysalis responsible for recruiting men that she thought could take on this task, not to destroy women, but protect them. Jason Chancery is out of control Mr Baines and he needs stopping. He needs stopping before he seriously hurts my beautiful Julianna.'

Trevor Baines got up and walked over to the window, where he saw Anders Wimmer waiting beside the car. Behind him Jakub Hesseltolph got up and joined him, he too saw the policeman.

'I know that man, although he was a lot younger the last time that I saw him. You're now wondering Mr Baines... is this the rationale of an insane man or the ramblings of a drugged patient? I cannot read anybody's mind nor can I foresee the future, but I can see the beyond in my mind when I lay on my bunk at night and Victor is snoring.

'However, the one thing that I can read is people's expressions, their eyes and yours are no different chief inspector. I see the doubt in your face. Let me help! Chancery needs stopping, but whether it will be by your efforts or others, only fate can decide. Others will however die before this happens as long as one of them is not my Julianna.

'Did you know Mr Baines that she and I were lovers? Incest between siblings that was the extent of our love. We were not ashamed of our emotions and neither did we care about what our parents felt. That is why they were sending Julianna away because they could not live with the guilt that they had raised two children who only had love for one another. They had in effect planned how and when they died.'

Jakub nodded at the nurse standing outside the door.

'Our time together is almost over chief inspector, although I have enjoyed the visit. Before I go I must fill in one last blank for you. There are seven angels... Michael, Gabriel, Raphael, Uriel, Chamuel, Jophiel and Zadkiel. Each has a purpose which is to be performed on a particular day of the week. Gabriel, also known in the high order as 'the angel of death is the prince of fire and thunder. Elements that have meaning, elements with power!

'Throughout the centuries history has been written by the balance of power where battles were fought and kingdoms won and lost, not because the men doing the fighting understood the reason why, but because they had a sense of duty. Religion has always been at the forefront of a battle and it is no different today. Men fight their conscience, battling between good and evil.

'Read your bible Mr Baines and understand the sins that are mentioned within. One particular copy purports that Judas Iscariot was the saviour of mankind and not Jesus. Another bible permits the sin of adultery and yet again another spreads the word that 'thou shall kill and commit murder'. To the disciples of evil these copies are known as the *'testaments of the underworld'* where the sinners are allowed to roam free. I am not a sinner, but a disciple and I should not be incarcerated within these walls. I should be set free.

'Lucifer walks amongst us protecting not spreading evil as depicted by the pious who denounce and condemn the real scriptures. Our parents were ignorant Mr Baines, ignorant regarding the love that existed between Julianna and myself. It was not until I came here to Ebenstatt and I read many books that I fully appreciated the meaning of the name Gabriele, which is the Austrian feminine of Gabriel, the angel of death and destruction. By releasing my mother's soul I have absolved her of all sin and sent her onto a much better place.

'If you doubt all that I have said chief inspector, ask Richard Quinn for I am sure that he will verify everything I have said as the truth! It might benefit you also to obtain a copy of an astrology chart depicting the cycle of the lunar moons. Only when the moon is at its highest, werewolves leave their lair to strike fear amongst the people.

'And if you know anything of Egyptian history you will know that the plague that befell the people, the flood of Babylon and the eruption of Vesuvius all happened around a high moon. They were meant to destroy the tyranny and rid the earth of sin, but evil will always succeed where good fails.'

He held out his hand for the other packet, which Baines handed over.

'Good luck chief inspector. Be kind to my Julianna.'

Trevor Baines didn't visit Jakub's room nor see the paintings, Alexander Koskovsky promised to fax across copies so that they could be added to the police file. When he reached the gate Trevor Baines took one last look back at the entrance of the sanatorium, a man waved from the upper window and he recognised the face as belonging to Jakub Hesseltolph. Whatever Koskovsky and his dedicated team of professionals thought about Jakub, in his opinion the patient from Kurlor was still a delusional psychotic schizophrenic, but the one thing that could not be overlooked was the accuracy of his insight regarding Jason Chancery.

On the way back to the airport Trevor Baines asked Anders Wimmer if he had ever heard of the phrase *'fretus deo mederi vulnerbis'*. The Austrian detective responded without any hesitation *'to heal the wounds and trust in god'*.

Baines was still not sure about Alexander Koskovsky nor about his approach to his work, but what was clearly apparent was the lack of respect that the doctor afforded Jakub Hesseltolph. Mad he might be, but the affable inmate was highly intelligent and very dangerous, albeit confined to living out his life in the sanatorium.

Chapter Thirty Nine

Tediously I woke once again in the early hours only this time with the strangest feeling that somebody was trying to get in, not the apartment, but inside my head. It was a weird experience and not one that you could blame on a nightmare nor a dream, but moreover something that lived and breathed. At one point I remember Lucy's voice calling out, telling me to watch out. I tried to ask why, but she disappeared into the oblivion and didn't come through again. I turned my thoughts to Mama Maria, wondering if she could help. As if she had read my mind the phone rang. It was just shy of ten to three.

'Are you alright Mama?' I asked, only she sounded tired, very tired.

'Si... si, I am just finding it difficult to sleep, you are the same... No'?

'Me as well Mama.'

'You need to come see me Mr Quinn, the sooner the better!'

'In the morning, afternoon or the evening?'

'No... the sooner the better. I go now to get dressed so I see you soon.'

The call ended, typical of Mama Maria. I checked the time to make sure that I hadn't got it wrong, it was now ten to three. As I dressed I was in two minds to call the police believing that Jason Chancery had obtained her address, but it would take a battalion to get through Lucy's cousins. By five past three I was down in the car port and putting the key in the ignition.

Although London had the reputation that it never slept at least eighty five percent of the population did. Catching mostly green lights I passed through the metropolis and onto the A40 with moderate ease. Driving at night was comparatively relaxing and I was glad of an excuse to be out of the apartment as the reason that I been roused from my sleep was still haunting me and I was none the wiser. In the sky overhead a commercial jet cut a path through the dark blue heading west, America bound I guessed, its plume of spent fuel trailing behind like the long tail of the astrapia bird.

Before heading down to the cottage at the end of the lane I sat for a couple of minutes at the junction checking that all seemed undisturbed and as it should be. The only light on out of the six cottages on the left was Mama's. I rolled the car down the unmade road and parked behind the van outside the gate. Mama was waiting at the door for me. She seemed shorter than when I had seen her at the funeral, although it was the middle of the night. I kissed her on both cheeks before following her through to the small parlour.

'I had Lucetta come to me in my sleep, she was troubled and begged that I phone you.'

'I'm glad you did Mama, only she came to me to give me a warning, only she'd gone by the time I tried to ask why.'

'Coming through is a drain on her energy Richard. Lucetta is watching over you, that I do know!' She got up and walked over to a locked cabinet taking out a couple of glasses and a small brown bottle shaped like a

Sicilian monk. The gold label said it was brandy. She poured us a glass each and toasted Lucetta.

'She will always be beautiful.' I chinked the edge of her glass and agreed wholeheartedly, Lucy was the most beautiful woman that I had ever known.

'The nectar of the gods,' I embraced as I swallowed the brandy.

'It helps warm the soul, when all seems lost.' Like the dark horse Mama Maria was I got the distinct impression that what she had said, had another meaning attached. I apologised for not talking with her at the graveside, but explained my reasons for wanting to say goodbye in my own way. She smiled and offered more brandy, I politely refused as I was driving.

'Her death will be avenged before the lord calls for my tired and withered bones. My heart beats and yet I wish that it was Lucetta's instead of mine. That is how it should always be.'

I noticed that Lucy's photograph had pride of place alongside Papa Bernado. It seemed right that they were together.

'There is much evil in this world Richard and regrettably it is coming your way. I have tried to prevent it's coming, but the dark forces of the unseen world proved too strong for my fragile efforts.' She took down the remainder of her drink in one monumental gulp. I imagined the brandy warming her chest as it headed for her stomach.

'Are you talking about the serial killer that is causing terror throughout the country?' I didn't want to say his name in her home, it didn't seem right to besmirch her sanctuary.

She pursed her lips together and spat into her palm.

'The accursed bastard that took my beautiful Lucetta, yes him!'

'I'm not afraid Mama. I've a feeling that destiny has us heading down the same road.'

'Then you are a brave man Richard and you will be rewarded when you reach heaven.'

She filled my glass before I had time to refuse.

'Lucetta told me of her plans to have a family. She told me that the only man that she wanted to be the father of her children was you Richard. You made my Lucetta very happy and for that I am grateful. It is her smile that I miss the most.'

I was glad of the brandy, I'd take my chances back on the road and steer clear of the main roads where possible. What Mama told me next took my breath away and nearly crushed my heart.

'The child that she carried was yours and will still be yours when you are together again in the next life.'

'I have to stop him Mama before he hurts any others. He took something away from us both that meant so much.'

It had become all the more relevant having found out that Lucy bore my seed within her body and that we had been robbed of starting a family. Suddenly the quest for revenge had intensified, now I wanted to tear Chancery apart with my bare hands. Mama read my thoughts, she shook her head.

'You must stay focused at all times Richard. The dark forces are growing in power and not even the daylight can force them back.' She suddenly gripped both my hands and placed them in hers. I could see that she had a tear in her eye. 'Lucetta was not my reason for calling you in the middle of the night, there was another reason, but not one that I could tell over the phone.' She added more pressure and I was sure that I could feel her energy flowing through my body.

'The evil that I mention, it has been to your parent's house.' She lowered her head, as though she couldn't form the words on her tongue.

'Are they dead Mama?' When she looked up her eyes were awash with pain.

'When you go there Richard, remember them for who they were, not what they have become.'

I didn't need to ask why. I leant forward and kissed her forehead. We felt one another's hurt. Chancery had hurt the two women I loved more than anything else. She let go of my hands as I wiped the tear from my cheek. Inside my anger was beginning to boil over. To hell with the brandy, I finished my glass. I thanked Mama for asking me over to her cottage. It had taken a great deal of courage for her to tell me about my parents.

In the hallway I heard a noise in one of the other rooms. Mama placed her hand on my arm as I made to approach the bedroom door, her voice was calm and reassuring.

'Do not worry, it is only Frankie. He is staying here with me till this is all over.'

When he heard the mention of his name a colossal giant of an Italian filled the framework of the bedroom door. He nodded, but said nothing, knowing where I was heading. I kissed Mama then pulled open the front door.

'Destiny dictates our lives Richard, but do not be too eager to reach the end of the road, Lucetta will wait however it takes.' She pointed to the great expanse of sky outside. *'Il destino e il destino',* fate and destiny. Where the parallels meet one another. Be safe when you drive and take my love with you when you reach your parents' house.

Together they watched as I turned the car around and headed back up the unmade road. At the junction I dialled the number that Trevor Baines had given me. Overhead another passenger plane was travelling in the opposite direction on its way to Heathrow. Somewhere in the great void of the universe the powers that controlled fate and destiny were getting ready to witness the coming together of two men, each with an agenda to destroy the other. My reasons were stacking up fast, but I didn't give a shit what were Jason Chancery's. As far as I was concerned he was already dead.

Chapter Forty

The drive to Meldreth Wood was spontaneous, almost robotic as the lights on the central reservation flashed on by until I hit the back roads where the contours changed becoming overshadowed by the darkness, tall trees, dense hedgerows and rolling hills.

Trevor Baines sounded weary when he took my call, but he'd promised to meet me at the house, as soon as he and Bob Pearson could cover the distance between Berkshire and Hertfordshire. On the approach to the drive I was stopped at the gates by a lone policeman. He pointed to a convenient spot where I could park as the drive was relatively full of marked and unmarked units. Before switching off the engine I slipped a mint into my mouth masking any lingering aroma of Mama's Frangelico.

Standing in the doorway leading into the hall I was met by a giant of a man who looked like a prop forward. His shoulders dwarfed those around him and he was a good two inches taller than the tallest uniformed officer. As I walked towards him he said something to those nearby, they instantly sidestepped and let me through.

'You must be Richard Quinn, I was told that you were en route.' He held out his hand as a gentlemanly gesture. 'I'm Detective Superintendent David Meakin. I'm sorry that we meet under these circumstances.' His grip was strong, powerful. He would be my ideal choice to meet Jason Chancery down some dark alley.

'Can I go in?' I asked, peering around the wall of officers gathered all around.

'Forensics are doing their bit inside, but as long as you stick by my side, then yes, although we can only proceed as far as to the end of the hall.' I nodded indicating that I understood.

'I know who did this...' I said, causing a number of heads to turn my way.

This wasn't Meakin's first major crime scene, he was calm and studious as he contemplated my outburst.

'So I heard.' He got the nod from a white suited scenes of crime officer that it was safe to go into the kitchen.

'You've not exactly had an easy time of recent, are you sure that you're up for this Mr Quinn, only we can do this tomorrow, elsewhere?'

Looking at the fresh batch of cakes that my mother had made prior to attending the funeral I recalled the days when I had come home from school as a young boy and found a drink and a cake waiting for me. The icing had started to run down the cake stand. Where they had dripped onto the work surface they looked like tears.

'Richard, rather than anything formal please superintendent. No, I'm fine and I know what Chancery does to his victim's. Did Trevor Baines tell you anything else?'

'He brought me up to speed with the investigation. This bastard Chancery has a charmed life, although I've a feeling that it's nearing the end.' He sounded convincing. I could even see the alley in my mind, where they would meet.

'Destiny superintendent or because he'll make a mistake?'

David Meakin rubbed the underside of his nose with the back of his finger.

'Because the law of averages dictates as such Richard. Men like Chancery run the course, but sooner or later fate deals the wrong card and they end up somewhere, where they least expected to be.' He didn't elaborate although it wasn't necessary. David Meakin was a straight forward no-nonsense officer. It was obvious that he didn't believe in fantasy or chance.

'He's probably coming for me as well!' I threw in, but not a muscle flinched on Meakin's face.

'I'd considered that when I arrived. Your face is plastered hereabouts on the walls, tops of cabinets and even on the grand piano. It's not likely that Chancery could miss you, even if he passed you in the street.'

'I think that he knew what I looked like before he arrived at the house.' I didn't expand on how and Meakin already thought the same. Chancery was no fool. 'Is there any chance that I can see my parents?' I asked.

Meakin checked it with the lead forensic officer, then handed over a pair of sterile overshoes.

'Joanna's given us the go ahead, as long as we watch where we step and what we touch.'

Passing through the lounge to the sun room represented a slalom run on the Swiss piste, a trail had been marked out in numbered markers where Chancery had walked. The closer I got to the sun room the bigger my reflection grew in the windows ahead. Lying side by side, although shrouded from the feet up to the neck line in white cotton sheets my parents looked like they were sleeping. David Meakin ushered everyone from the room to give me the moment of dignity that I needed to say my goodbyes. All around smatterings of forensic dust powered the backs of the chairs, the furniture and the drinks tray. I saw the outline of a pair of lips on the rim of the glass jug. From behind where I was stood David Meakin spoke.

'Take as much time as you want, we can concentrate our efforts elsewhere until you've finished.' I thanked him as he left.

I couldn't get that close as the evidence was all around where they lay. I managed to make my way around to where I could kiss their foreheads. From the spray of fresh cut flowers on the windowsill I took a rose and placed one on each of their chests. My mother had been proud of her roses and it felt appropriate to let her take one into the next life. I had no inclination to raise either sheet, I only wanted to remember them as they were, not what they had become at the hands of a monster.

Before I got up I whispered to my mother and told her that Lucy was pregnant. The nursery had not been some foolish folly on her behalf and that one day we would all be together again. When I closed my eyes to choke back the tears I could have sworn that I saw her smile.

*****

Leaving the sunroom doors open I found Meakin talking to Baines and Pearson in the hall. We shook hands, I looked at Trevor Baines and though that he looked really tired, exhausted as though he'd been travelling all day and night.

'There's something upstairs that I think you should see Richard,' Meakin suggested. We went to the floor above avoiding the bannister rail where bloody hand prints were being lifted.

Standing on the landing I could see the room at the end which had been my parents' bedroom. Scattered over the quilt cover were various items of her personal effects, necklaces, earrings and bracelets. Of course I could not tell the value or appraise their sentimental value, but each had meant something to her. When David Meakin pushed open the door to my old room I noticed that Chancery had done pretty much the same. Scattered about were trophies that I had won at school and university, framed photographs and books. I put it down to envy. The only item missing was a photograph that had been removed from the frame.

'A picture of you?' Meakin asked.

I nodded. 'Of Lucy and me. I wonder why he took it.'

'A trophy or maybe to taunt you. Who knows the mind of a madman?' Meakin's voice was tinged with abhorrence.

I didn't think that the photograph was the reason that Meakin had asked me to accompany him upstairs. Standing behind me Bob Pearson pushed shut the bedroom door.

'You'd better take a look at Richard.'

312

When I turned I saw the lipstick wording scrawled across the gloss panels. In deep red the words said: *'YOUR NEXT PRETTY BOY'*.

I surprised them by not displaying any sign of emotion.

'Grammar clearly isn't his strongest argument!'

It attracted a snigger from all three.

'We could give you protection somewhere in the country?' Trevor Baines offered, but there was no way I was going to hide from Chancery. I shook my head.

'We're heading towards a collision whether I like it or not. I am not going to skulk around wondering who's come up on me from behind for the next week, month or even a year. I'm ready to meet this bastard, Trevor.'

Baines saw the determined look on my face. My eyes burned with revenge and nothing he could do or say would alter the future. The three policemen looked at one another. They could each have offered advice about my taking the law into my own hands, but not one of them were prepared to stop me. If I succeeded in stopping Chancery they'd each back me and sort out the legalities later. The crown prosecution service would never hear how or why, just that a serial killer had met with an untimely end. It saved public money, time and energy. I agreed to a panic alarm in the apartment, but not CCTV. What I omitted to tell was that I had a hunting rifle and pistol locked away in the apartment, both licenced and loaded ready. That was illegal, but I wasn't ready to admit that I would use both if it meant taking out Chancery. I could sort out the finer points later once he was stopped.

We stepped outside where the air was fresh as the first rays of the new day were creeping up over the hillside beyond the gated entrance.

'Was it likely that Chancery would have come across your father professionally?' asked Meakin.

'It's the only plausible reason why he should come after them.' I thought about Jonathon and Arabella, I needed to call Jonathon as soon as possible.

'Besides jewellery, was there anything else of value in the house that Chancery could use, like a passport?' Trevor Baines was ahead of David Meakin with that train of thought.

'Passports, yes they both had one, but I doubt Chancery found the safe unless he was told where it was.'

I took them to the cellar where the lingering smell of disturbed coal dust was still evident. At the back of the boiler I opened the safe and show them the two passports.

'That's good, at least he can't go travelling to distant shores without running into a wall of adversity.'

Heading over to the mobile command centre where we could continue talking I heard a voice inside my head. Without the others noticing I smiled when I recognised to whom it belonged.

'Horatio and Alison are here with me Quinn, they're safe!'

Chapter Forty One

Bob Pearson spread the documents and photographs across the table top which included a number of official records, medical and otherwise, from which an uninitiated investigator could rapidly draw their own conclusions regarding Jason Phillip Chancery.

'This is a lot for one man!' Meakin seemed in awe of what had been gathered in ten years.

'There's more back at the office,' Bob Pearson implied 'although this will give you a good appreciation of what we're up against.'

'So who's been hiding him, nobody can stay out of the limelight that long and not get caught?'

'A clinical psychologist, but we have her in custody so the opportunities are becoming limited for Chancery. It's just a matter of time.'

Trevor Baines interjected. 'In a way all police forces are to blame, we've become complacent and waited for something to happen rather than chasing down a potential threat. Everybody keeps crimes on their patch quiet because of government targets and finance. We should put politics to one side and concentrate on the real agenda and that's putting these bastards away for a long time.' Sitting beside him Bob Pearson nodded in agreement.

'And identity, does he ever change his appearance or the like?'

'No, not that we know about. Chancery is as brazen as the first time that he was apprehended, you've only got to see the smug expression in the photographs to see that.'

Meakin looked at the security shot outside the court, which I had found in Lucy's apartment.

'Either he's got a big ego or he's snubbing the law in general, either way it fucks me off that bastards like this think that they're invincible.'

Trevor Baines stifled a yawn then explained why he was so tired, he appraised us of his visit to Ebenstatt. David Meakin sat quietly absorbing every detail. When Baines had finished I took over with my time in equidistant all the time watching for signs of apathy in David Meakin, but saw none. When I was done he nodded very slowly considering everything that he had heard.

'If I didn't know any better I'd say you were slightly unhinged Richard and that recent events had affected the balance of your mind, but I'm not that naïve and strangely enough I believe everything that you've said. I have my own opinion of course on what happens, but my younger sister is into this sort of thing. She's always trying to convert me. Maybe now I'll be more attentive to what she has to say.'

'Believe me superintendent, a while back I would have been as cynical as you, but too much has happened for me not to be a convert.'

Meakin smiled, appreciating that I was holding up well.

'If the ball was in my court I would have a fire-arms unit take him out and save the tax-payer a lot of money, but a bullet would be too good for a psychotic madman like Chancery. What's happening with the sister?'

Bob Pearson answered. 'At present we've formally charged her with aiding and abetting, but we're digging deep to see what else we can make stick. We've also arranged for a psychiatric evaluation too, only I'm not convinced that she's not playing us for fools.'

'I promised her brother that we'd look after Julianna.' All eyes fell on Trevor Baines, he had black lines emerging under both eyes.

'Is she worth it?' Meakin asked.

Surprisingly Trevor Baines nodded.

'Call it a gut reaction, but I think that it's in our interest if we do. She's the chrysalis in this bizarre chain of events. We need to keep her safe so that we can explore all the avenues, only as chilling as it might sound Chancery might not be the serial killer operating at the moment!' Baines didn't reveal that he had promised Jakub Hesseltolph that he would do as much as he could to protect his sister.

'Will she end up in Ashworth?' Meakin asked.

'It's highly likely, Ashworth could accommodate her needs.'

David Meakin wasn't so sure. Ashworth was a secure unit for psychiatric detainees, but during the past five years mistakes had been made, whether through lack of manpower or genuine oversights, it was difficult to know and criticize.

'Has her passport been checked for movements?'

Bob Pearson delved into an envelope and handed it to David Meakin.

'She's well-travelled covering most of the European countries, East Asia, North and South America and Australia. That's a lot of territory to consider.'

'We'll keep probing, but she's clammed up. It's as though she knew I was in Kurlor and talking with her brother.'

Bob Pearson spread an astrological chart over the table and indicated the lunar cycles covering the past, present and future months.

'Adding dates, locations of attacks and full moons, we've managed to chart a pattern by which we think Chancery operates. There are a couple of anomalies outside of the lunar cycle, but I'd put that down to either opportunist hits or necessary kills to reduce witness identification.'

David Meakin studied the chart.

'Tough shit if you happen to be out strolling on a full moon. We already have plenty of loonies being influenced by the moon when it's big and bright, without adding Chancery into the equation.'

Whilst the three of them pondered over the chart I pulled a report that had caught my eye. Heavily embossed with an official looking stamp it belonged to Landerhaus Hospital in Austria and was dated around the time of Jakub Hesseltolph's incarceration.

Julianna Hesseltolph has an acute time-related psychiatric disorder. Her symptoms are described as having manifested from the primary condition of severe traumatic stress induced by long bouts of depression and disassociation. Clinical opinion is that she is border-line bipolar schizophrenia.

The unusual love that existed between brother and sister has undoubtedly resulted in her experiencing bouts of despondency as she languishes like a lost animal for a brother that she cannot hold or see. Considering the many sessions that we have engaged upon we have failed to unravel the full depth of this incestuous bond. Any future assessments should not underestimate the breadth of her intelligence, Julianna is indeed an extremely clever young woman, manipulative and totally engaging. A lesser being could easily be fooled by her charms.'

The name Jason Chancery sprang to mind.

Although Julianna has shown no outward tendency towards physical violence, we professionally and collectively believe that if cornered she would retaliate in such a manner, that the aggressor would come off worse. I was aware of some serious apprehension amongst the younger, less experienced colleagues who made comment that they felt threatened by her presence, although they were unable to explain their fears. One suggested that it was as though they had been taken in by the power of her mind.

Conclusively, Julianna revealed her intentions to attaining a professional degree, studying to become a doctor and making it quite clear that she had no desire to stay in Austria. Throughout our discussions, whilst unrelated, she often made reference to the Nuremberg investigation describing the Nazi war criminals that had sought refuge in

Salzburg after the war as the mistaken liberators of an oppressed world and not the evil extremists that the authorities labelled them to be. I conclusively agreed with my colleague's sentiments as I was never able to extract from her the reasons that would explain her theory. At times, I felt that it was I who was being examined and not Julianna.'

The report was endorsed by several members of the medical clinic in which she had received treatment and help following the horrific attack by her brother, although in reality none would believe her. Going over the last paragraph again I wondered if this was what Jakub Hesseltolph had referred too when he'd named Judas Iscariot, the saviour of mankind.'

Chapter Forty Two

The headlines of a double murder in a quiet leafy suburb of Hertfordshire involving a high court judge and his wife, immediately escalated Jason Chancery to the top of the most-wanted list. His image taken from the last time that he was arrested some fifteen years back was plastered over every police station wall, shouting out from the front page of every tabloid press and clipped to the counters at airports, ferry terminals and railway stations, anywhere where he was likely to be spotted.

Day and night detectives worked around the clock checking every possible place where he could hide away, hotels, halfway houses even turning over known haunts of the homeless. Throughout the cities the red light districts saw a sudden drop in business as police undercover operatives mingled with the punters. Wherever there was a river or a canal, the boats were checked thoroughly, but despite all efforts twenty four hours later he was still at large and posing a threat.

*****

When the train slowed the man wearing the military uniform seemingly woke from his slumber, he stretched out and raised the peak of his cap from his brow. He smiled at the passengers that cared to look his way, but didn't engage any in conversation. At some point in time the man from whom he had taken the uniform would be found, although what wouldn't be known was when he would come around and be able to answer any questions.

With barely a squeak of the brakes the train came to a gradual halt. Rasping down the length of the platform the voice over the tannoy announced the arrival of the eight ten from Kings Cross which was due to leave in an hour's time on the return journey.

Checking over the headrests Jason Chancery scanned both sides of the platform searching for signs of any police lurking about. The military uniform had worked well so far, but his khaki rucksack didn't really blend in. Taking advantage of a young family with three children he fell into step as they progressed down the platform. Several platforms away a group of noisy students were being observed by station personnel a two police officers. Jason kept pace with the family keeping an eye on the gate at the end of the platform.

Less than fifty yards away a pair of patrolling officers suddenly appeared at the gate to speak to the guard collecting the tickets. Jason kept walking to avoid being noticed, but when the driver opened his cab door he promptly pushed him back inside with the tip of the knife jabbing into the man's stomach.

'Call out or attract anybody's attention and I'll gut you faster than a fisher monger at Billingsgate.'

The driver edged back his lips sealed as Jason closed the door behind him. He ordered that he remove his uniform and minutes later emerged, cap, badge and all carrying a flask and shouldering a rucksack, ostensibly more appropriate for the occupation. He nodded at the guard at the gate and the two policeman casually walking through and heading towards the public conveniences on the far side without looking back. Who would stop or suspect a driver having travelled a couple of hundred miles and needing a welfare break.

When Ernest Stapleton came to the side of his head felt like a herd of elephants had trampled over him and gone around the block for a re-run. He tentatively touched the angry bump that was growing above his ear feeling a trickle of blood where the skin had been broken. Had he not been rendered unconscious, he probably would have been found dead in his cab. When Ernest opened the door in his underwear a woman commuter on the platform opposite screamed loud bringing every police officer and station official running her way. By the time that they got to Ernest, Jason Chancery had already dumped the uniform in the gent's toilets and left the station. It had been a huge risk coming back up north, but the thrill of the chase made it all worthwhile.

Passing by the taxi rank he kept his head down low as an ambulance went rushing on by coming to a halt at the entrance to the concourse. He scoffed to himself, the old boy would be seen as a hero and revel in the glory of all the attention, but by the time detectives got around to questioning him, he would probably forget the relevant details of his attackers face, in fact all that he would remember would be a soldier pushing him back into the cab and then nothing else till he regained consciousness and the woman screaming.

At the end of the narrow passageway he emerged out into the sunshine coming face to face with the market, its colourful array of roofs draping down over the stall tops like a Persian souk. He sniffed the air filling his lungs, it felt good to be back on turf where he had grown up.

Kirkgate had not seen his face for almost eleven going on twelve years. Jason wondered where the time had gone.

Using ready cash from the judge's wallet he purchased a large meat pie, a large bar of chocolate, a bag of mixed fruit and a bottled water. In a jewellers that he had used before, he sold the gold and diamond rings that he'd taken from Alison Quinn's dressing table. It surprised him how many of the shops were empty, their windows smeared heavily in whitewash. Kirkgate had gone with the times, but lacked the aggression to fight back, losing the battle to accept change.

Taking back alleys and side streets that he knew well he arrived at the corner of St' Luke's Church in Harbonworth where the scenery had long been forgotten. The two up and two down terraces looked like a painted Lego set only the paint was fading and peeling. Chimneys were still blackened by soot, but some had nests in the pot where central heating had replaced the log burners.

Further down the street and nestled between the builder's yard and the launderette was his old school, Brancaster Grove. It was still covered in grime from the nearby colliery and not a brick had been changed since he'd left. Watching from outside the church where the gateway offered some protection he thought about the cruel, perversion that had walked its corridors and manifested in the classrooms under the teachers guise. Men that had his schooldays a misery, men like that lecherous old bastard, Malcolm Robson and the headmaster Jeremiah Biggs. He hated them, despised them both, but the reason that he had come north was to say goodbye to his mum who was buried around the back of the school in the cemetery where she lay beneath the cherry tree. It was strange, but since avoiding capture at the builder's house, he'd not had any word from her. His gut told him that she had deserted him once again and yet his heart said different.

Taking a fresh bunch of flowers from another grave he placed them on his mother's plot. He knelt down and put his hand where her head would have been resting.

'Hello mum...' he said picking out the weeds that were strangling the base of the headstone 'I told you that I'd come back one day. You've gone quiet on me of late and I wondered why, was it something that I have done or said?' He shook his head believing that it wasn't his fault.

'You know that I miss you every day and think about you often, but other things sometimes get in the way, things that need my full attention. Julianna suggested that I should come and see you one more time because we're going travelling and in all likelihood we won't be coming back. We've not decided where exactly just yet, but maybe the Far East, America or Australia, but somewhere warm and where the opportunities are more richly rewarding.

'I tried to make contact with the old man the other day, but somebody told me that he'd been hurt in a scuffle in the prison and died as a result of his injuries. Serves the old bastard right really because he hurt you bad, real bad.

'I've been searching for a way in which I can communicate with you mum, but it's proving more difficult than I had imagined. Lucetta Tate wouldn't give up the 'gift' despite my threats, but I think I know a way that

I can succeed before I take off. Maybe then we can catch up like we did when the old man wasn't around. Perhaps one day we'll be together again mum. I really do miss you!'

Lowering his head he kissed the earth of the mound.

'I love you mum.'

He asked that she didn't watch him in the next couple of days as there was something that he had to do before leaving England for good. Looking up at the second floor window he thought he saw the ghostly face of Malcolm Robson looking back down, but it only the sun playing tricks with his eyes.

That bastard Robson, queer fucker that he was. Always out to show Jason up whenever he could, belittling his abilities in the classroom and watching him in the shower after sports. More often than not he sent Jason to see Jeremiah Biggs for no particular reason other than to inflict pain and suffering on the weak, sickly boy. In class he would torment Jason and make the other boys and girls laugh, only when it failed to raise a titter, Robson would hit the back of his head with a wooden ruler or the palm of his hand. Jason vowed the day that he left that he would get Robson and Biggs alone one day and show them the error of their ways. Taking one last look at the grave he said goodbye, then looked up at the second floor window.

'One day you bastards, we'll meet again. You see we don't!'

Like a haunting memory, a voice appeared in his mind, not his mother's, but one belonging to Malcolm Robson. It annoyed Jason that it should come to remind him, but he listened all the same.

'You are a complete imbecile Chancery. A cloying child like you should not be allowed to have good Yorkshire blood run through your veins. Simpletons such as you could not find your way out of a rice pudding lad, let alone across the moor!'

Somewhere in the cemetery Jeremiah Biggs was buried his body ravaged by cancer. Jason of course didn't know that, not that it mattered, but had he known he would have danced over his grave. He was about to head over to the gate when a young dog foraging between the headstones came up to sniff his leg, he stroked the dogs head and would have played some more, but the owner called the dog back. When Jason looked at the man's face he couldn't believe his eyes, sitting not too far away under the shelter of an elm tree was Malcolm Robson, decidedly older, but irrefutably it was him alright. Jason felt his hand grip the hilt of the knife, but he dropped it back into the rucksack not wishing to blight his mother's resting place, instead, he waited till Robson looped a lead over the dog's head then followed a short distance behind.

Selecting the over grown path of a property that looked deserted he observed the old geography come physical education teacher enter the front garden of the house at the end. It was a passable street, lined with a few trees, but the houses had seen better days. Walking towards Robsons house he noticed several curtains twitching before they fell back into place when he stared their way, unable to see the occupants, but knowing that they were watching. When he had been a teenager it was rumoured that many a boy or young man would be seen entering the house at the very end and not coming back out until the lights in the rooms upstairs had been extinguished or the residents were asleep in their beds.

Casually walking down the short path beyond the tall conifer hedge he heard music coming from inside of the bay window. To the right hand side of the house a badly fitting gate was secured by a loop of string, Jason flipped the loop and heard the patter of enthusiastic paws coming from around the back. He took the bar of chocolate from his pocket and pulled back the wrapper.

Chapter Forty Three

The dog arrived its tongue lolling happily down from its jaw, silent with its tail wagging frantically left and right. Jason knelt, snapped of a section of chocolate which he gave to the dog, then calmly slit its throat. What came next could now be done that much quicker and without the interruption or annoyance of a barking dog. To the rear of the property he found the kitchen door propped open wide. It was all so easy.

Listening to the sound coming from the old radiogram Malcolm Robson was unaware that he had a visitor. Standing in the doorway Jason looked about the small room, it was a mess, a disgraceful dive and in the air, the plasterwork, the musty stale odour of urine and dog lingered heavily about. Jason thought that some of the places that he had stayed in had been bad, but Malcolm Robson's home was a hovel.

The furniture was old and stained, the carpet threadbare and torn in places by the dog. On either side of the fireplace the paper had long peeled away from the wall tainted brown by the smoke form the fire and in the grate were the remnants of an old chicken. Positioned under the bay window was a wicker basket that had been used by the dog. All around the edge the strands had been chewed bare.

Jason was astonished by what he saw. For all the years that he had been a teacher the profession had done little to compensate his lifestyle. Lying beside the chair where Robson was resting his head lay a pile of well-thumbed foreign magazines. The top copy portrayed a group of naked teenage boy's leap-frogging over one another in a shallow stream.

Feeling the tension clenching the sinews of his fingers he stepped forward the knife thrust out ready.

'You loathsome, lecherous and corrupt old bastard. I always knew the rumours about you were true!'

Malcolm Robson tried to rise from the chair, but the hand that pressed down hard on his left shoulder was like a vice crushing down on his clavicle. The blade of the knife rested on the bridge of his nose. In the reflection Malcolm Robson watched the man come around front of his chair.

'Remember me, you fucking pervert!' Jason asked.

Like a fly hovering over a hot pie Malcolm Robson's eyes blinked fast as he tried hard to put a name to the face. When he recognised the eyes, he felt the saliva escape the back of his throat. The trickle of urine spread wide staining the inside of his trousers and groin.

'Oh Jesus no,' he exclaimed, his voice croaky and tinged with fear 'you're Jason Chancery!' Malcolm Robson realised why the dog had not come into the room.

Jason grinned. 'Not so cocky now are you, you old fuck!'

Stuttering to find the right words Robson was thinking fast, trying to find a way out of the predicament.

'Wha... what do you want, only I've no money in the house!'

Jason laughed loud and long as he prowled back and forth like a caged panther, occasionally stopping to pick the dirt from under his fingernail.

'I'm not interested in money you daft old fool. If I had not been in the cemetery saying my goodbyes to someone special I might have missed you. It was your misfortune that you were there the same time. Why?' he asked.

'I had been visiting Jeremiah Biggs grave. I promised that I'd tend to it now and again, only his wife can't. She's not in good health so I do it out of respect for an old colleague.'

Jason rubbed the bristles on his chin.

'That's touching. It's a pity that the pious old git is six feet under. I would have enjoyed having him here as well.' He dragged a chair across so that he could sit directly in front of Malcolm Robson. 'Never mind perhaps we can go down memory lane together and remember old Biggsy as we touch on certain subjects!'

The odour of urine was strong coming up from the carpet where Robson had wet himself. Jason bounced the tip of the knife on the curve of Robsons' patella.

'That's often the problem with old people, they just can't control their bladders. Do you recall when you took the piss out of me Robson?' How in the showers you'd ask the other boys to look at the size of my penis. Then later in class with the girls present you'd draw a shrinking grub on the blackboard and say *'here look, it's Chancery, it must be cold outside!'*

'It was just harmless fun.' Robson excused, but Jason wasn't laughing.

Taking half a dozen plastic ties from the rucksack he secured Robson's wrists to the wooden arms of the chair and did the same with his ankles.

Removing one of the old man's socks he rolled it and pushed it into Robsons mouth. Standing up he admired his handiwork.

'Like a hog at a banquet.'

He went over to the radiogram and adjusted the volume slightly.

'That's much better, now we can have our little chat without you slapping me around the back of the head or kicking me in the shins like you used to do. Do you remember doing that?'

Before Malcolm Robson had the chance to respond Jason slapped the side of the man's head hard with his open palm. The old teacher reeled sideways struggling to hold onto his senses.

'Hurts... doesn't it, you bastard.'

He kicked his shin. The retired teacher winced with pain as the arthritis attacked the spot where he had been kicked. He tried to say something, but nothing was coming out of his mouth except a muffled groan.

Taking the top copy from the pile of magazines Jason flicked through the pages.

'You like little boys, young men don't you Robson. I bet you masturbate yourself senseless over these pictures don't you?' Jason threw the magazine into the hearth. 'Everybody in school knew about you and your trips to the stationery cupboard. You'd come back to class all hot and sweaty, and your eyes were be blood shot. Did you ever wonder why you were removed from the scout troupe so quick? The police got wind of your perverted ways.'

Malcolm Robson looked at the magazine on the floor, he recalled that they had been the good old days, when he could order a boy into the stationery cupboard and make the young lad do things to him, good things. Or the times that he had spent at summer camp where he would go bathing with the boys in the local river, laughing, touching and masturbating under the water.

When Jason suddenly grabbed hold of the top of Robson's trousers and cut through the thin material his eyes almost popped out of his sockets. Slicing long and across Jason shredded the material until Robson sat naked with the remnants of his trousers limply gathered about his ankles.

'Fuck... I don't know what to do Robson, laugh or cry. Have you looked at yourself in the mirror lately... it's not a grub down there man, more of a fucking maggot!'

Malcolm Robson closed his eyes and willed his penis to shrink as Chancery paced back and forth, then without warning the ex-pupil knelt and pulled hard on the end of the penis. When it was a good three inches and the teacher's eyes were open as wide as they could go Jason sliced through the soft membrane throwing it across the room and into the dog's basket.

'It's a pity that the mutt had to die, otherwise it could have chewed on that for an hour or so.'

The tears were streaming down his cheeks stinging the sores on his chest, but Jason wasn't about to let up. The years of torment and torture had affected him badly, left scars and at times made him vulnerable. Robson had to suffer and hurt for both he and Jeremiah Biggs.

'Have you nothing to say, you bent bastard?' He removed the sock.

'I'm sorry... I'm sorry...I'm sorry!'

The apology trailed away as the tears turned into racking sobs. The years of abuse and perversion had at last caught up with him. He had always checked over his shoulder knowing that one day Jason Chancery would come for him. Jeremiah had been lucky, he had only had to suffer the agony of cancer, Chancery was worse, much worse. His eyes pleaded to be set free from his torment. Jason replaced the sock and slapped the side of Robson's head for good measure.

'It wasn't my fault that I was starved of oxygen at birth. All my life I've had to prove that I was no different from other men. If you could ask the women that I have been with lately, they would tell you just how good I can be. But of course you wouldn't know what a women felt like, would you. How many poor souls have you infected down the years Robson? Fifty, a hundred, two, five, maybe a thousand or more. The papers describe me as a monster, only they don't understand that I am a saviour of mankind, a healer you could say. I rid the world of evil and spread a harmony across the land, where women feel safe to walk the streets alone not fearing the threat of man. In your case men need fear you!'

Jason Chancery took each finger one by one slicing through flesh and bone until both hands were nothing, but bloody stumps.

'Where you're going you won't need to hold anything warm and soft!'

Taking the knife he cut deep into the man's chest, arms, legs and buttocks. With the blood running freely down over the vanquished school master, he placed the knife across the throat.

'One last thing Robson before you die. Do you remember calling me a complete imbecile? A cloying child that should not have been privileged the honour of having good Yorkshire blood run through his veins and that I would find it difficult clawing my way out of a rice pudding let alone across the moor... well it so happens that I have travelled all over this island of ours and sometimes beyond. I found my way back here today as you well know, so I wasn't quite the imbecile you thought me to be.'

Jason Chancery used the knife once more and ended the retired teacher's life. He wiped clean the blade with the dead man's shirt then left side stepping around the dead dog. It was pity that the dog had to die, but whether it was man, woman or beast you could never leave loose ends behind.

Passing back down the tree lined avenue he saw the curtains twitch once again only in a short while they'd be twitching incessantly in blue lights and curiosity. Never again would they see any young men go visiting the house at the end of the street.

At a convenience store he purchased a packet of cigarettes, they weren't his favourite brand, but soon he'd know where to buy some. Kirkgate had changed, but change was always inevitable and the outcome could go both ways, either disappointing some or pleasing others. It was like meeting old friends, it was always good to catch up with the past.

Amidst the dirt, blood and grime Malcolm Robson lay with his eyes fixed on the doorway as the last moments of his life ebbed from his broken body. This was not how he had wanted to end his life, but then like the last years of his teaching, it had not stimulated his interests any longer. The sores on his chest were the first signs that he had the human immunodeficiency virus or more commonly known as aids. Death would have been only months from his door. In the background the radiogram continued to play on as the presenter introduced the next record bringing in the first bars of the memorable pop tune *'these are the days of our lives'*.

Chapter Forty Four

Responding to the call the marked unit arrived in less than three minutes and drew up outside twenty seven Park Lane, Harbonworth where the informant, a teenage boy was waiting under the street light. He pointed to the open gate, but refused to go down the path once again, he'd already seen all he wanted and had no inclination to revisit the dead dog.

Denise Jordan with only one year on patrol hesitantly pushed the gate back wide. She instantly felt the bile sting the back of her throat as she called her colleague over.

'Who would do such a thing Neil?'

The older and more experienced officer by five years went first stepping around the dog, he drew his baton and flicked it out to it full extent.

'Stick close to me Denise and if anybody jumps out, we hit out then ask questions later. I am not pissing about here!'

Denise Jordan extended her baton and did as she was asked. When they emerged a few minutes later they emptied the contents of their stomach on the back lawn. Neil Hislop recovered first, he depressed the button on his radio and asked control for the immediate attendance of CID and a supervisory officer.

'Is there anything bad inside?' asked the teenager who'd abandoned delivering leaflets for the night.

'Bad enough mate,' replied Hislop 'did you only go as far as the gate?'

The young man nodded, seeing the dead dog wasn't what he had expected to find. He guessed that the occupant was dead going by the ashen faces of the two officers. It was a pity because the retired schoolteacher had always been good for the loan of a dirty magazine.

Seeing other residents coming down their front paths and kids arriving on bikes Jordan and Hislop set up a perimeter around the property. Other than getting a first-hand account from the teenager their job was more or less done until the sergeant arrived. Keeping the speculative circus at bay would earn them both extra brownie points.

As always with comparable incidents where the bystanders watch and listen, hungry for a titbit of information theories pass back and forth mainly from the older women present. The most putative of opinions being that the homosexual had been involved with auto erotic sexual stimulation. Some even mentioned seeing a man leave the house before the teenager dropped the leaflet through the door, others hinted at him hanging himself from the roof rafters with a plastic bag slung over his head.

'Whatever... the dirty old bastard won't be fiddling with any young boys ever again!' the old woman spat contemptuously at the ground next to where she stood. *'The filthy old goat got all that he deserved. Do you know our Johnny had him for sports when he was at school and he said*

back then that the lecherous bastard was always watching the boys when they were showering!'

Whether they told the police what they had seen or not was down to the interest of the detectives arriving on scene and whether they could be bothered to ask. Social practices and differences had not improved and often as not the women went back indoors and kept the information to themselves discussing the details over coffee with a next door neighbour of somebody serving behind the counter at the corner shop. Down the years it had served Jason Chancery well and kept him safe.

*****

Having been dragged from his bed just before midnight Shaun Templeton, the current head teacher at Brancaster Academy, begrudgingly flicked through the metal cabinet in the archive cupboard, finding the file that the detectives had sought he pulled it from the drawer and handed it over.

'Did you know Malcom Robson?'

'Not personally, he had taken retirement before I arrived at Brancaster.' He hesitated for a moment, then considered that it didn't matter one way or the other whether he mentioned why the ex-teacher's had been forced to retire. 'Eventually, the rumours caught up with him!'

'Meaning what exactly?'

'That Malcom Robson had been expressively asked by the school management to take retirement as opposed to being sacked and losing his pension rights.' He tapped the cover of the file held by the detective.

'You'll see for yourselves that he was similarly forced out of the scout movement a way back for allegedly interfering with young boys. When I took over after the death of Jeremiah Biggs, several of my colleagues expressed their concerns about working with him. I was only marginally involved as the board of governors already had the matter in hand.'

Shaun Templeton was asked to pull anything he had on Jason Phillip Chancery.

'I've heard of that name recently,' he said, only he couldn't think where.

'In the papers and on the news perhaps? He's being investigated regarding a double homicide and three others prior to that.'

Templeton nodded, now he remembered. He checked his secretary's desk.

'Everything that we had on Chancery was handed over to a courier only last week. A motorcycle messenger all the way from Berkshire came here and collected the lot. You would have to call a Chief Inspector Baines at Reading Central about him now.'

Back at Park Lane, Harbonworth forensic officers were busy scanning the entire place with a video camera, taking photographs and bagging, tagging everything that they considered relevant. The RSPCA took the dog away to be cremated as the home office pathologist gave her permission for the body of Malcolm Robson to be transferred to her mortuary. Later that morning she would carry out a full examination.

*****

I declined the invitation from Baines and Pearson to drop me off back at my apartment, wanting the time to myself to clear the thoughts in my head. We had finished off as the moon was disappearing over the horizon and giving way to the new day. I'd hardly slept in the past forty eight hours and my head was beginning to spin not that Mama's special late night tonic helped. As I pulled into the car port beneath the apartment block I did check around before getting out, although I wasn't really in the right frame of mind to consider Jason Chancery. If he was there waiting, I was ready for him.

Taking a glass and the brandy out onto the balcony I watched the sun coming up. It hit my face in a blaze of warmth and uplifting morality, although inside I felt that I was anything, but good. My integrity had been challenged and the test was now whether I could win the fight ahead.

I don't know why, but something instinctively made me turn around. I saw a face looking at me from inside the lounge. I smiled and walked towards it. I wanted to take Lucy in my arms and never let go, but she put out a hand to halt my advance.

'Please Quinn, hear me out as I don't have much time. You are in great danger and Jason Chancery is heading your way soon. What you see before you is not really me, but more a spiritual cohesion sent to deliver a message, a molecular hologram from the equidistant.'

She looked real to me, although I could not see the injuries where she'd been cut.

342

'Be careful what you think or do and get some rest. I will watch over you as best I can, but I cannot intervene. Rest now and sleep. I love you Quinn.'

Lucy or whatever she was disappeared. I held my head in my hands and shook it hoping that when I let go, I'd realise that it had just been something that I had imagined, but the voice in my head told me different. I could hear her still as she re-joined my parents. Rather than mess up the bed I slept on the settee with the patio doors open wide letting the sunshine flow through.

Later that morning I called Jonathon then took myself off to Giovanni's, when he laid his hand on my shoulder, it felt heavy and full of burden.

'You look like shit my friend, eat and drink!' He crossed himself then left me to watch the river.

The hourly news on the radio inside the delicatessen reported on the vicious murder of a retired teacher from Leeds. The report heralded scant details, but police were widening their search for the suspect and co-operating with surrounding forces in their inquiry. I knew intuitively that they were looking for Jason Chancery. When the newscaster ended with a story concerning rival fans fighting at a local derby between two Yorkshire championship teams I felt sorry for the police because like me they'd had a bad night.

Chapter Forty Five

Certain aspects of a gruesome crime fascinates the imagination, conjuring up a mixed bag of emotions ranging from intrigue through to fear and yet the mind will somehow overcome the latter to hear out the truth, or feast your eyes on something so horrific, however macabre. Like watching a scary movie from behind the cushions, the human instinct to be acquainted with fact not fiction will push the boundaries of our courage that bit extra. In court I had always found the witness as bloodthirsty as the assailant. The public were a funny lot, safe behind their front door where they could read about the victim who had been abhorrently cut up and left for dead, the reality however when experienced first-hand was immeasurably different.

When the true facts emerged about the victim in Park Lane, Harbonworth the shock of how the retired teacher had been tortured and butchered met with a diverse response. Some felt sympathy where others looked beyond the horror and felt that Malcom Robson's death was long overdue. The only concern that any had was that the killer could still be lurking in the area.

Trying several times throughout the night Jason was becoming concerned that Julianna wasn't picking up his messages. It made him edgy. From the corner seat he had a good view of the driver in the all night café. When the driver left so did Jason, slipping through the gap in the rear tarpaulin he'd assumed the lorry was heading south as it was sign written with a London telephone number.

Just outside of Peterborough the driver stopped to unload a crate before continuing his journey. Pulling shut the tarpaulin he thought that he had heard a movement from the back of the lorry, but when a fox appeared from under the rear axle he dismissed the notion that somebody was hiding inside. At the junction with Hendon Broadway Jason jumped down narrowly avoiding a vehicle coming to a halt at the traffic lights. The startled driver gestured angrily at Jason, but selected a lower gear when the lights changed to green.

Walking down the Broadway he avoided mingling with the crowds keeping instead to the walls and shop fronts, where the open doors beckoned should trouble be unavoidable. Taking the first bus that arrived at the stop he paid his fare and went to the upper deck where he could see any approaching police units. He was close to West Hampstead where he intended visiting his favourite tobacconists and an old friend when he put in a final call to Julianna. When a man answered he cut the call dead knowing that in all probability she had been arrested.

Asking an Asian youth who was busy on his iPad the direction of Tower Bridge he saw the architecture of the buildings change as the bus headed down the hill and took the bend into West Hampstead. Ringing the bell for the bus to stop at the next junction he saw the firemen washing down the engine out front of the station. They looked relaxed and happy as they went about their business. Bringing the bus to a halt a passing driver honked loudly in frustration at being made to stop. London was like no other place that Jason knew. It was full of colour, noise and dust, but he liked it. With almost nine million inhabitants it was hard to be seen.

The tobacconists was tucked away down an alley where the thoroughfare ran between the shops and residential properties at the back. It was an inconspicuous small half shop, but well stocked and visited by those discerning customers willing to pay that little extra for quality and speciality products. Jason knew that they stocked his favourite brand.

'It's good to see you again. Is two enough?' asked the large lady behind the counter, the smile creasing the loose fat around the jowls of her cheeks.

'No you had better make it three.' Jason replied 'only I'm taking a long journey soon and I won't know where I can get this brand again, until I arrive!' Checking the wallet for ready cash, he changed his mind and ordered four packets. He handed over two twenty pound notes and took his change, dropping the loose coins in the charity box for abandoned children.

'They probably need it much more than I do.' He said as he headed to the door. The lady wished him a safe journey and promised to have sufficient stock the next time he came visiting.

Turning left he went to the end of the alley then took the road west towards Cricklewood and the artist. Pushing open the metal gate he descended the short flight of steps down to the basement flat below. Depressing the bell he heard her footfalls coming down the short hallway. When the petite brunette opened the door her face glowed with surprise.

'Hello stranger, I was only thinking about you the other day, come on through to the studio. I've something that I want you to see!'

Jason closed the door behind him and dropped the rucksack down by the door. He noticed that she had painted streaks in her hair, red, blues and yellow where she had been working. Like Jason, Melanie Osbourne liked her paintings full of colour, full of expressive emotion. He especially liked her portraits of children. They always looked so young and innocent, untarnished by the harsh realities of the world.

For two weeks the last summer he had stayed at the flat with Melanie when things had become too dangerous to be seen out on the streets. She put no restrictions on his movements, made no demands and he liked her, almost as much as Julianna, although in some ways more. When she pulled back the cover hiding the canvas beneath, he smiled.

'It's really good Mel, I like it… in fact I like it a lot.'

Melanie had painted her impression of the story that he had told her on his last visit about the repressed Red Indians of South Dakota. She looped her arms through his and came in very close, putting her head on his chest. She liked to hear his heart beat.

'You see I do listen. If you look close you'll see a likeness where I've put you sitting next to the Sioux chief.'

Jason checked out the painting and studied the faces seeing his own exactly where she had it would be. He started to undo the buttons of her blouse as his mouth found hers. She dropped the brushes that she'd been holding letting them fall to the wooden floor, right now all she wanted was his body next to hers.

'How long can you stay?' she asked, her breaths coming in quick succession as his lips found the nipples tilting up her breasts.

'All afternoon, although I must be somewhere important later!'

I spent the morning with a funeral director making the necessary arrangements for my parents, then telephoning a friend who was an estate agent. When the house had been professionally cleaned throughout I would have it put on the market and hopefully sold to a young family who would enjoy many years there, overlooking its recent history.

Come the afternoon with all the calls done I decided that I needed a complete break from work and tradition. Appraising Jonathon of my intentions he agreed to deal with anything current assignments and future cases. He mentioned the murder of the retired schoolteacher before I did. The good bit of news that he had to tell was that Michael Cattigan had rubber stamped the petitions for Reginald Benjamin Pike and Mary Jane Garman giving both an official pardon. I was pleased that their good names and dignity had finally been restored. Naturally, it would be seen as a feather in Cattigan's cap and help his political career, but that was the nature of the game. Behind the scenes I wished him every success.

That afternoon with time to kill I took myself off to the national gallery where I sat for ages admiring the many framed pieces of art, some to my taste, others invoking a longer appreciation of my time. I strolled both sides of the Mall passing through horse guard's parade, nodding respectfully at the cenotaph, before checking the time with Big Ben ending my afternoon with tea at a corner shop which had once been visited by the famous and the rich.

In Covent Garden I mingled with the crowds although I had the strangest sensation that I was being watched, but I put it down to nervous exhaustion. In a way I envied the street entertainers, the bohemian artists and talented musicians. They each had an a determination to their life, struggling to make ends meet, but forever smiling in the face of adversity. Suddenly, my life had lost it purpose.

Around nine I took a call from Trevor Baines who asked where I was. It was one of those calls where you that he was checking on my welfare, I wondered what it was that he knew, although he wouldn't say. He stated the obvious, informing me that Chancery had slipped through the net once again and neither of us mentioned luck as the reason.

Ordering a drink I sat at a courtyard table where I had a good view of the quartet below in the lower gallery. I felt unimaginably very alone as couples held hands and watched the violinists below leaning over the metal balustrade. I raised my glass and prayed that none came into contact with Jason Chancery.

Sometime around a quarter to eleven I left Covent Garden and headed down past the Royal Opera House towards the Tower. As I meandered with the contours of the streets the shadows grew long and impenetrable, several times I stopped and checked behind to see who was following as I was convinced that somebody was hot on my trail. The closer that I got to the apartment the less the streets were occupied by pedestrians or cars.

I cannot explain why but I thought about Julianna Hesseltolph sitting all alone in her cell at Ashworth High Security Hospital for the Mentally Insane, I wondered how she was coping with her first night. The door of a public house opened and a young couple appeared from within arm-in-arm, their infectious laughter welcome in the silence. The man waved and I returned the gesture before turning down towards the river. I wanted to warn them, only it sounded ridiculous to me, so goodness knows what they would have thought had I made the approach.

Following the river east I became mesmerised by the murky soup of swirling water which like unwashed suds moved in and out of the currents forever summoning that I jump in and join Lucy in the hereafter. I shook myself from the trance and virtually ran the rest of the way. It was not how I was to end my days and Lucy would never have forgiven me. From the shower I heard the phone in the hall ring a couple of times, but ignored it, letting the water drained down over my body. The water felt good, warm and invigorating. If the call was important they could leave a message.

When I took the towel from my face the next sound that I heard was much different, like breaking glass. I remembered leaving the half empty wine bottle on the balcony table, but the air outside was still almost non-existent. Putting the towel to one side I slipped back into my jeans and went through to investigate. When the shadow in the hall moved I barely had time to shield my face with my forearm, before everything went very dark. I heard myself cry out *'Chancery'* only the word never materialised.

Rolling my chin on my chest I came too finding myself pinned to the arms and legs of a chair by plastic ties. My intruder was prowling the apartment looking at photographs and picking up, putting down various ornaments before he realised that I was awake.

'Welcome back, I thought that you'd never come round!' It wasn't so much that he was surprised, more concerned that I might have suffered more than a bump on the head.

'It would take more than that to stop me Chancery.' It sounded venomous, full of hate.

Jason Chancery tutted and shook his head.

'I'm sorry about the wine, it's stained the stonework outside when I jumped down from the flat roof.' I knew that he wasn't really apologising, but revealing to me how he had got in. I thought about my neighbours asleep next door and hoped that they were still alive. He flashed a small torch into my eyes and examined the side of my head for signs of permanent injury then turned off the beam.

'You'll live.' He exclaimed.

'Do you care?' I asked. The throbbing ache intensifying as I spoke. 'I thought hurting people was your style!'

Jason Chancery came in close and lifted my chin.

'That's no way for adversaries to start off a friendly chat, is it? Here am I paying you an unexpected visit and you sit full of aggression and loathing for me. If we get off to a bad start, things can only turn ugly, it's the nature of the beast Richard.'

I shook my head disbelievingly, Chancery was completely insane. His mind was split between two worlds, one of fantasy, the other violence.

Playing him at his own game, I asked. 'Why the restraints, surely if we're going to be courteous, then you could at least undo the ties. You have already demonstrated that you're more powerful than me, so I would not be so foolhardy to believe that I could overpower you.'

He prowled back and forth like a caged tiger, checking the sky outside. I wondered if he was looking up at the moon for inspiration.

'Interesting suggestion although for the meantime it's best that we leave them on.' He came back over from the balcony doors. 'First there's something that I need from you before I let you go.'

He pulled up a chair and sat directly opposite me. Our knees almost touched.

'Let's start with Lucetta Tate. She toyed with me, made me angry. I didn't want to hurt her, but she refused to give me what I needed most.'

I struggled with the plastic ties, but the more I moved the more they cut into my skin. Chancery gripped my wrists and held on fast, he was indeed powerful. He slapped the side of my head hard, I reeled back the determination in my eyes telling him that if I could break free I would kill him.

'That's better, now I have your undivided attention. Your girlfriend refused to give me the *gift* and that's why she had to die. All I want is the power to talk to the other side, to speak to my mother again!'

'You're more deranged than what Julianna Hesseltolph told the police.'

The second slap was more a punch, this time it took several seconds to clear my head. This time I came back up smiling.

'Yes Jason, the police have her and she's told them everything. You've nowhere to hide now, you're on your own!'

He went to hit me again, but decided against it, he was totally unpredictable.

'Tell me how you can pass over the gift, or I'll start cutting where it will cause the most pain.'

I shook my head, not out of defiance, but scorn. Chancery was a fool.

'I cannot give you the gift, it's not something that is handed down or passed over. You are born with the ability to talk and hear those on the other side. Lucetta Tate didn't refuse because it was you, she couldn't give what you asked. Don't you understand and why has your mother stopped talking to you, helping you?'

Jason Chancery gripped Richard Quinn's chin.

'Why?'

'Because with the death of your father she's been able to move on, go on to a better life. She's gone Jason, left you again, only this time she will not be coming back.'

In a fit of rage he slashed the blade from my left shoulder across my chest coming to a halt somewhere down my side. The blood started to flow from the wound and stain the carpet.

'Don't fuck with me!' He came in very close to my face. 'Your father once fucked with my life, stealing valuable years that were meant to be mine. He died because he altered the course of my destiny. Had I not been sent to prison I might have become a different person.'

'Your destiny was set the day that you were born, the day that the cord nearly strangled you!'

He took a pair of black lace knickers from his pocket and stuffed them under my nose.

'Recognise these. She wore them the day that she came looking for me. Dear sweet, sexy Lucetta. We fucked one another all afternoon before I got down to the real reason why I tricked her into coming to the river.'

I could smell tobacco on his breathe, it was foul, like decaying camel dung.

'By the time that I had finished with her, she was willing to do anything so long as it didn't hurt anymore.' He grabbed my chin once again. 'We got in some real fun that afternoon before I fed what was left of her to the fish.'

Somewhere in my head a voice kept repeating over and over that she loved me.

The madman was trying to goad me and make me angry, he wanted to revel in my hurt and feel my pain, but I fought hard and resisted the temptation to react. With no emotion in my voice I unnerved him.

'It was you looking up at me in the cricket pavilion. You knew that I was watching.'

He released the hold on my chin, got up and walked around. He laughed.

'I hope you enjoyed the show. Ashley Jones was also a willing partner. By the time I had cut her, she would have endured any amount of displeasure to have pleased me. Unlike the two women in Brighton, they gave in far too easily,' he came back over fast and slapped my face 'they were all like my mother, whores who would sell their sex rather than show any loyalty. When it comes to love and sex, they cannot tell the difference.'

He put his hand on my injured shoulder and squeezed, I bit my upper lip to reject the immense pain passing through the sides of my head.

'Lucetta Tate would have been alive today had she not hounded me all those years ago. At the time it was fun, like a mouse chasing the cat, but after a while it became boring, almost intrusive. Although that day in Uxbridge I knew that at one time I would take her body and have her worship me. It was my choosing that I let her live so long, so you should thank me Richard.' He pressed down harder and this time I had to relent, I squirmed as the pain shot through my body and head like sharp knives.

'You perverted bastard that was her job,' he let go of my shoulder 'whatever she collected over the years, the police have it all now!'

His laughter mocked the air in the room.

'Those fools couldn't catch Jack the Ripper, so I doubt they will ever catch me. They've always been two, possibly three paces behind me over the past ten years. When this is over I'm going to disappear and never come back. I'll be the one that got away. It will haunt Trevor Baines for the rest of his life.'

I wasn't sure how he knew of the detective chief inspector, but at present there was nothing I could do to warn him.

'They caught up with Julianna Hesseltolph and they've also talked to Jakub, her brother. Your times almost up Jason, you're cornered.'

For the first time I saw the doubt in his eyes. The not knowing was starting to gnaw away at his resolve. He looked confused. Despite the pain I laughed which confused him even more.

'You've been chasing a dream, chasing a phenomenon that doesn't exist except in the minds of those to whom it's given. God chooses who has the gift, not man. You've abused, hurt and killed all for nothing. The Hesseltolph's are a spent force Jason and soon you'll join them. Did you know that there's a place in the hereafter where there is nothing, a black hole without sound or light. I expect that your father is there already and soon, you'll join him. Your mother on the other hand has gone onto somewhere, where the sun suns constantly, where it's peaceful and where she can be free. When the time comes, she'll not even be a memory!'

The knife swept downward and went through my rectos femoral muscle, it near cut my leg in half. My teeth came together and I felt one crack at the side, but I was determined not to cry out, I didn't want to be rescued, I didn't want to put others in jeopardy. Through the pain I smiled. Chancery yanked my head back.

'*What's so fucking funny?*' he asked.

'You...' I replied. 'Your whole life has been a sham Jason. You have been chasing shadows since the day that you were born. You've been used by the Hesseltolph's and been blinded by what will never be yours. In the end Jason your victims are the victors, not you, they won because they had the control.'

'Why... how?'

'Because they were in the right destiny, only the location changed. You played out your part, but failed where they have succeeded. You won't believe anything that I say because madmen never do accept the truth. When the darkness descends sends you to a place worse than hell then you'll have an eternity to remember my words.'

Like all psychotic schizophrenics he suddenly felt cornered, trapped and wanted a way out.

'Then help me...' he begged, but I wasn't about to help the man who had destroyed the people that I loved most.

'Even if I could, I wouldn't. This lunacy has to end and maybe it does tonight. The legacy of your bloodlust was borne from that of your father, not your mother. Perhaps at your birth God had an insight into your future and tried to prevent your living. Who knows, if he had succeeded you might have stood a chance to be with your mother, but you have forfeited that right Jason. Destiny is unforgiving and so are the dead.'

Desperate, seeing his life for what it was, he clutched at straws. 'Then I will find Julianna and help her escape. She loves me and together we will go somewhere safe where I will prove you wrong Richard Quinn!'

Again I shook my head, the end wasn't far away. I had lost a lot of blood.

'I doubt that, but even if you did find a way to help her escape the clutches of the authorities, Julianna Hesseltolph has only ever loved one person and that's her brother Jakub. Did you not know that they were incestuous, inseparable lovers?'

His eyes blazed with anger seeing how he had deceived for so long. I was determined to have my say, now that I had him cornered and doubting his existence.

'The first time that she took you to her bed, did you not wonder about how she came to be scarred. Did you not wonder at why she would let you tie her down? These are things that she let Jakub do with her. *You've been used Jason, you've been used!*'

I could see from the expression that his brain going into overdrive. Distracted, hopelessly embittered he felt that everybody around him had abandoned him, his mother, father and now Julianna. Like a teenager after the first rush of love, he was confused, hurt and mystified by the emotions that he didn't know how to handle.

'The fucking bitch…'

He wiped the blood from the knife on the jeans of my good leg.

'When I do catch up with her, I'll do more than tie her down and cut her, I'll slice her apart until she begs for mercy. Why is it that men cannot trust women?' he mused, 'they use, abuse and lie. Does love mean nothing to them?'

He walked about the room punching into his palm, thinking.

'That explains why when she climaxed she would call out Jakub's name and not mine. When I asked why she did it, she told me later that it was so he could hear and know that we were thinking about him. I was so naive.'

He suddenly focused his attention on me.

'One last time… are you going to give me the gift or not?'

I shook my head and closed my eyes. I could see the image of Lucy waiting and smiling. She looked so beautiful. I felt the cold steel cut through my throat, but felt no pain. When I looked down at the carpet it was stained dark and wide, which was a pity because I had always liked it. From the corner of the room I sensed another presence, not malevolent, but comforting. I turned my eyes that way to see Lucy standing in the corner with her hands outstretched.

'Be brave Quinn, the end is coming soon.'

I tried to warn her that Chancery was in the room, but however hard I struggled my mouth wouldn't open wide enough to put together the words. With one last defiant effort I raised my head and looked directly at my killer. With a stupid grin masking my final moments my head dropped hard onto my chest then I died. Lucy came forward, took my hand then together we went somewhere better, far away from London.

Jason Chancery cleaned the knife on the towel that he found in the bathroom then grabbed his rucksack and left taking he lift down to the ground floor. Stepping away from the apartment block he filled his lungs with air. Once again he had failed. He took a cigarette from the packet and lit the end. It was a long way across the city to Rickmansworth, but the old woman was his last hope.

Chapter Forty Seven

Walking away from the private apartments he failed to notice the blue van tucked in the corner near the delicatessen, deliveries started early in the city so it wasn't something that concerned him. With a purpose in his stride he looked back once, then forged ahead. With every step he saw Julianna laughing at him, deriding him. Had what Richard Quinn said, been right, had she used him and was she in the hands of the police, there was no way of knowing. It might prove why she hadn't answered any of his calls.

The two men in the van flexed their muscles and got ready to leave, they had been there for over an hour wondering why the lawyer had not gone to bed. Every so often the apartment had been illuminated then plunged back into darkness, like a man unable to relax, going from room to room searching for something to give him peace. When they saw the face of the stranger appear in the lobby they looked at one another, troubled and anxious.

'Are you sure that's him?' asked the big man in the passenger seat.

The driver nodded. 'He matches the description that we were given Frankie. You know Mama, she is never wrong.' He depressed the message on his mobile and watched as it headed off into the airwaves.

The big man cracked together the knuckles of his hands, this was the moment that he had been patiently waiting for and this was the moment that he would avenge his cousin's death. Frankie didn't like sitting around doing nothing, his idea of a good night was eating and drinking, watching some sport until late then sorting out business when the situation demanded his particular talent and attention. Sitting in the driving seat his brother noticed the big man's restless agitation.

'Easy Frankie, he won't get far!'

'You think we should go upstairs first and check on Mr Quinn?'

Marcello Brassicatus shook his head, he turned the key in the ignition and fired up the engine.

'No, we can't afford to lose this one. We'll come back later and make sure that he's alright.' He moved the van forward at an even speed following the figure walking ahead. 'Get ready Frankie, when I say *'take him'* hit him like he's never been hit before!' Frankie Brassicatus grinned, this was going to be worth the long wait.

In the cottage sitting by the fireplace Mama Maria picked up the telephone and dialled the number. When the call was answered she told the recipient to go open up the yard. She said that there was no need to rush, but that he was to make sure everything was in place.

Jason Chancery sensed that everything wasn't right as he quickened the pace, some distance behind the van had started rolling his way only it was going on past. On the pavement opposite he saw a street cleaner gathering up a batch of discarded papers. The man looked up and nodded, but didn't smile. Jason expected him to speak into his shoulder and others to suddenly jump out from the shadows, he expected the police. Looking back at the van he felt his palms becoming moist and his rate quicken.

Inside the van Frankie's stomach grumbled, it made his brother look sideways.

Frankie apologised. 'It's been a long wait Marcello and I'm hungry. After this is done, can we go get something to eat?'

Marcello kept his eyes on the road and the quarry ahead, he scoffed.

'Frankie... you're always hungry, it's in your blood to be hungry!'

Marcello glanced sideways momentarily and looked at his brother, he was a giant amongst other men, all brute muscle and full of Italian testosterone, but food had always come before women. When he wasn't crushing rock or skulls, he was a gentle giant, easily amused unless provoked.

'Once this is done Frankie, Mama has promised that we will all eat.'

Frankie patted his stomach like it was a pet. He nodded.

'That is good Marcello, let's go to work only the sooner this is done I can eat. Is the yard open?'

'Mama has it arranged with Louis and Santino. You just concern yourself with grabbing this bastard and conveying him back west.' Out of the corner of his eye he saw his brother slip the metal knuckle duster over his right hand, not that it was needed because Frankie had a punch that would rival any heavy weight contender. As a boy he would easily beat his older brother and cousins, besides any others that fancied their chances in the village.

Marcello suddenly increased the vans speed as the man on the pavement started to run.

'Now.' Marcello called out. *'Now Frankie.'*

As Jason took the corner he scanned the buildings on either side looking for an alleyway, a glass door, anything by which he could smash or enter and escape, but London was built solid, granite rock carved smooth lined the pavement and ascended high on either side. He continued running knowing that the driver had changed gear and increased the revolutions of the vans engine. It was coming fast in his direction.

When the passenger door slammed into his back it sent him sprawling across the pavement, he lost his grip on the rucksack as he went rolling on down the sharp incline towards the river. Jason tried to reach for the knife that had landed nearby, but something very heavy and metal like a sledgehammer smashed down on the side of his face. He heard the sound of breaking bones and his jaw gave way. Several kicks broke ribs and took the wind from his lungs. Jason looked out for the street cleaner, but he was nowhere in sight. By the time Marcello had got around the other side of the van Jason Chancery was limp and unconscious. He placed a hand on Frankie's shoulder.

'Not yet, remember Mama wants him alive for when he arrives at the yard!'

Frankie stopped kicking the unmoving body, 'But... Lucetta?'

Marcello Brassicatus nodded his head, he appreciated the hatred felt for the man lying on the pavement, but the punishment had only just begun.

'The devil will have his day Frankie, I promise you.'

Together they threw Jason Chancery into the back of the van and covered him with empty sacks used for collecting horse manure. Frankie got in the back too and pulled shut the sliding door. A short while later the street cleaner picked up the rucksack and knife. He put both on his trolley taking them home when he finished his shift, where he'd sift through the contents, women's underwear and all.

In the back of the van Frankie pushed aside the sacks as they got close to home and stripped the unconscious man of his clothes, he tied his wrists behind his back with twine then moved up front to sit beside his brother. Marcello looked over and smiled.

'Is it done?'

Frankie smiled back. 'Just like when we we're boys, we'd chase the rabbit till h tripped and fell down our trap. He's not going anywhere fast!'

Jason Chancery came too momentarily felt a great weight pressing down on his chest and found that he couldn't move his hands, he lost consciousness again calling out for his mother.

When the van rolled over the cattle grid it shook the shock absorbers violently waking him once again. He could hear the men talking up front, but had the sense not to attract their attention. His left eye was partially closed and his jaw hung limply on one side. When the van stopped moving the side door was pulled back allowing the light from the arc lamps to flood in. Shapes moved forward and rough, strong hands yanked him clear of the van floor. Jason Chancery landed on the ground where the small stones cut into his flesh.

'So this is the filthy scum that hurt Lucetta!' A swift vicious kick landed in Chancery's gut, doubling him up as the men standing beside the attacker did their best to calm him.

'Easy Louis, it won't be long before Mama arrives!'

The man nodded, showing that he understood. Through the dust thrown up by the kick Jason caught sight of an old woman hobbling towards him. Mama Maria held up her hand implying that she didn't need their offer to help. One of her boy's called over.

'Hey mama... your pigs have got a bigger dick than this swine of a bastard!'

The old woman smiled back at her grandson then peered down at the man on the ground. She spat at him, watching the spittle streak his cheek.

'My pigs have souls Frankie, but not this man.' The point of her shoe hit Jason Chancery on the shoulder almost sending herself toppling backwards with the effort. Her grandson's caught her before she did fall.

From the dust Chancery chortled.

'Is that the best you've got you old witch, at least your grand-daughter put up a good fight as I fucked her!'

It was some minutes before the beating ceased. Chancery groaned insensibly as the night sky rolled around in the heavens above. When they stepped back Mama Maria stepped between his spread legs and delivered her retribution kicking him hard in the groin. The pain shot through his body like a hot branding iron. He dropped his head onto his chest.

'Know this Jason Chancery...' she said, supported on either side by her boys 'before this night ends you will meet the devil in a place worse than hell where you will spend an eternity contemplating your actions!'

Gathering the phlegm from the back of her throat she spat contemptuously down at his chest. She looked at the faces of each of Lucetta's cousins. 'You took from us somebody so beautiful, a woman who was an angel on earth and a guiding light elsewhere. A filthy pig such as you didn't have the right to look upon such beauty, let alone spoil it. What we have planned will make you believe that hell really does exist.' She turned to face Santiago. 'Is the pit ready?' she asked.

The man nodded then turned and walked away, moments later the dragon roared loud as the engine to a mechanical digger cut through the still of the night. As Santiago brought the digger over Mama Maria walked back to the car, her grandsons knew what to do. Easing her frail frame into the front seat she watched.

Grabbing his limbs they hoisted Chancery high then threw him into the pit making sure that he landed on his back. It was essential that he was facing the sky overhead, essential that he saw what was coming. The pit was deep, at least ten feet below the surface, not quite hell, but good enough for what they had planned.

Facing the stars overhead Jason wondered which belonged to his mother. He remembered her telling him as a young boy that when people died they went straight to heaven and became a shining star to light the world below. He tried to call out to her, but he was too busted up to put any words together, the end was near.

With a roar the huge bucket appeared eclipsing the light overhead. When the first batch of rock salt came tumbling down Jason felt the scream rise in his throat, but nothing emerged. When the heavy particles landed they immediately invaded his many cuts, tortured the broken bones and scorched out both his eyes.

When Louis gave the signal that the ground was level one again Santiago cut the engine and jumped down to join his brother and cousins.

'Not even the devil himself could climb out of there!' he said.

They went over to where Mama was waiting in the car. She smiled at her boys, they had done well.

'Let's pay Giovanni a visit,' she suggested 'we can take care of Mr Quinn later.'

Marcello looked across at Frankie and winked, it was just as he had promised. Frankie patted his stomach knowing that Giovanni, a friend from his old school would feed him well.

Way, way above where the darkness met the stars and galaxies beyond a gateway opened and allowed many to pass through. They were free at last. Lucy smiled at the man holding her hand, she pulled it closer so that he could feel her abdomen.

'I love you Quinn.' They followed the others accompanied by his parents. At last Alison Quinn had her wish.

Making sure that the padlock was secure Marcello the car pulled away from the quarry. East of their location Giovanni was arriving at the delicatessen. For a short while the world was at peace.

Chapter Forty Eight

The air was much fresher than it had been of late, bringing with it the expected changes of autumn. Alexander Koskovsky stood at the head of the stone steps and waved at the two nurses escorting the elderly patient around the garden. He saw the patient turn his head.

'It is good to see you back outside Victor.' Koskovsky called over, but he received no response.

He smiled before descending the steps taking a route in the opposite direction. Clasping his hands behind his back he nodded to himself, satisfied that at last the patients appreciated the value of his drug programme. They were less hostile, seemingly quieter and at last Ebenstatt had found a peace that had long been missing. Even Jakub Hesseltolph had calmed.

Following the path around the impressive building where the wards above had barred windows he continued walking towards the woods. Koskovsky liked the woods, where alone he could think. When the figure stepped out from the tall shrub he only had time to unlock his hands before the tip of the kitchen knife jabbed his ribcage. Jakub Hesseltolph smiled wide as his eyes blazed full of purpose, taking hold of the doctor's arm he guided him up the path.

'It's a good day to take a walk Alexander, it beats being cooped up in a stuffy ward!'

Alexander Koskovsky felt the fear grip his heart. Jakub Hesseltolph didn't have the glazed look that he had expected. Jakub saw him looking.

'Oh come, come doctor! Surely even you would have realised that I had stopped taking the pills sometime back. Did it not occur to you why Victor had suddenly become more complacent, less troubled. I am not a medical man, but even I could see that poor Victor needed his rest more than I ever did.'

The tip of the blade dug deeper causing a small stain of blood to appear on the doctor's shirt.

'Now let's head for the woods. Julianna and I always felt as one when we were lying together under the trees.'

From the windows on the first and second floor the patients watched the two men walking away from the gardens. Alexander Koskovsky wanted to call out and ask that they help, but he saw only blank faces watching. One by one they drew away then disappeared.

When the trees closed in on one another the shadows grew tall making the breeze whistle inharmoniously and all about you could smell the pine. A short time later only one man would walk away from the wood alive. Jakub Hesseltolph had served his time in Ebenstatt, but it was time to leave.

*****

Watching the events below unfold the souls belonging to Gabriele and Thomas Hesseltolph waited, knowing that this was not yet their time. One day it would be, but not today. Standing alongside one another they wondered where they had gone wrong and how fate could be so cruel.

As one of their children took flight the other languished in a cell rocking back and forth. Gabriele looked at her husband.

'Thomas will be lost without his sister!'